Praise for *A Different Kind of Brave*

"*A Different Kind of Brave* is **a thrilling adventure and romance** that gripped me from the first page with a daring escape. Nico and Sam's story is one of courage and self-discovery that Lee Wind has masterfully told while also paying tribute to James Bond. **Readers are going to love this tale of rebellion, standing up for what's right, the struggle for identity, and young love.** I already need the next installment!"

—**JEFF ADAMS**, author of the Codename: Winger series

"**Be prepared to fall in love with Nico and Sam** in Lee Wind's fast-paced super fun romance adventure. Masterfully told through dual points of view, the story **keeps you on the edge of your seat as the teen heroes discover themselves and each other.**"

—**ALEX SANCHEZ**, author of *Rainbow Boys* and *You Brought Me the Ocean*

"Lee Wind is a longtime booster of gay YA, and boy, has he learned a lot. *A Different Kind of Brave* is **bold, breezy, and fun.**"

—**BRENT HARTINGER**, author of *Geography Club*

WITHDRAWN

A DIFFERENT KIND OF BRAVE

LEE WIND

duet

interlude **press**

CHICAGO

Published by Duet of Interlude Press
An imprint of Chicago Review Press Incorporated
814 North Franklin Street
Chicago, Illinois 60610
ISBN 978-1-64160-950-0

Library of Congress Control Number: 2023950239

Cover design: CB Messer
Interior design: Jonathan Hahn

Printed in the United States of America

For my husband, Mark, for making
my life the best kind of adventure!

"Your joy is part of the revolution, too."

—Robin Arzón

CLASSIFIED

LIST OF ALIASES

SUBJECT 1: NICOLAS HALL
        "NICO"
        NO OBSTACLES
        PETER JOSEFS
        JACQUES MONTAGNE
        WARREN BENNETT

SUBJECT 2: SAMUEL JONAS SOLOMON
        "SAM"
        JAMES

1

NICO

FOR THE THIRTY-FIFTH TIME THAT morning the buzzer sounded, and the light on Nico's cell doorway finally switched to green.

Go! Bec mouthed from the cell opposite him, unhooking her zipper from the metal necklace they all wore and pulling the top of her jumpsuit off her shoulders so it was more club and less prison. Her blonde buzzcut glowed green from her own doorway's light as she strut-hopped down the stone hallway of cells on her good foot like it was a red-lit dance floor, kicking the air with the medical boot in time to some electronic music no one else could hear.

Hoping all eyes were on Bec's performance, Nico flung his mattress under the security camera mounted to the wall just above his doorway, and grabbed it as he ran around the corner.

She's crazy. Awesome. Crazy-awesome!

Counting down from 360, Nico raced past the two bathrooms where he and Bec were supposed to be, to the cafeteria. It was empty—they weren't serving food for hours yet. Inside, the frame of the glass door to the courtyard glowed red, threatening to zap anyone with a metal necklace who dared get too close. But first he had a guard to deal with.

3

Nico left the mattress in the entryway and stayed low against the north wall. He avoided the guardroom's big window looking onto the cafeteria and instead made his way to the smaller window of the guardroom's side door. He peeked in.

Empty.

Maybe they didn't have a second guard here this early?

He tried the door. *Unlocked.* Because they knew they could zap the prisoners at any time.

Nico silently let himself in, searching the two flat-screen computer monitors for a way to override the whole system. One screen showed the security camera views: the courtyard outside with its glowing red columns, inside/outside views of the garage doorway where he'd been brought in a week ago, the two red-lit stone corridors where all their cells were, and the cafeteria right out that guardroom window. The other monitor had all their photos in a grid. Seventy teen prisoners on a color-coded control panel.

His own photo was last, but Nico almost didn't recognize himself with the buzzcut, face all weird and slack from having just been zapped by the metal collar. Like he was drugged or something. All the photos were terrible, and this wave of compassion hit Nico hard. Each photo had obviously been taken right after they'd been shocked for the first time too. No one had their guard up or any walls to protect them. They were all lying on the floor of the intake room, where they'd been brought down by the electroshock collar newly around their neck. Just like him. Reduced to this most basic, humiliating moment of being in pain, not able to control anything, gasping for breath... And that's how Gold Wheels Preacher saw them. As biblical "lumps of clay." That *he'd* reshape.

Nico's hands trembled with rage. He fought the urge to pull off the metal at his neck—he wasn't going to trigger the tamper when he was finally escaping. The security camera on the upper corridor showed Bec, still dancing, the other guard approaching her with a raised tablet. His mouth was moving, but the monitors didn't have sound. Anxiety for his friend flared inside him, but Nico knew if he just stood there watching and got caught, her distraction would be for nothing. And he'd made Bec a promise: he'd get out, and come back to free her.

He shifted focus to the keyboard. How could he power down the system? Was there some master switch he was missing? Was there a combination of keys that might do it?

Suddenly a toilet flushed behind him.

Nico's eyes snapped to a door in the back. The guard was in the bathroom! The bathroom door had a thick metal handle, like a bar designed for disabled people to push open. Metal door frame.

He could hear water running inside. If there was something he could shove in between the bar and the door frame, Nico could trap him in there.

But there was nothing...

Nico scanned the room in a quick catalog: mini fridge, leather office chair on wheels, metal garbage can, desk with two computer monitors on it... the monitor! It was just thin and solid enough. He didn't want to zap himself—or anyone else—by mistake, so he yanked the cords out of the back of the one with the security camera views and rushed the bathroom door, shoving the monitor through the bar. Six inches of it overlapped the doorjamb. He wedged the monitor base in tight.

The door rattled from inside. The guard's voice: "Very funny, Brian. Let me the hell out!" A pause. "Brian!"

A fist banged the door, but it held.

The guy would probably lose his job over this, but Nico didn't care. At all. The garbage can under the desk had a few crumpled McDonald's bags inside—every day, this jerk made a big show of eating fast food while all they got was lukewarm gluey oatmeal. Or, for those willing to rat someone out for talking, pizza. Today was day seven for Nico, and he hadn't snitched. Neither had Bec, and she'd been here sixty-two days more than him.

Ignoring the guard's shouts of *Hey! Let me out!* Nico emptied the bags, raining oily napkins and other fast food trash on the desk. He just needed one... There! He grabbed an unused ketchup packet and tore it open, then climbed on the desk to smear it across the camera lens aimed at the cafeteria. Hopefully it would be enough to hide where he was going... For a second, he wished he'd used the other monitor so he could check on Bec. Was she already zapped? Was the other guard on his way, or would he be busy getting her unconscious body back into her cell?

Nico shut the guardroom door behind him as he entered the cafeteria. It was harder to hear the guard yelling through both doors. He headed right to the sign above the counter:

GOD SAYS HOMOSEXUALITY IS SIN.

He could totally reach it.

Next, Nico pushed the closest ten-foot table toward the door to the courtyard. Metal legs screeched against the linoleum, but he didn't have time to worry about it.

He had 198 seconds before the other guard would expect him back in his cell. Before they tried to zap him. Nico pushed again, figuring eight feet would be enough to not feel any shock. Like one of those squirrels jumping from wire to wire in the neighborhood below his cell window. As long as he didn't touch the ground there would be no way for the electricity to close the circuit back to earth. The door's push-bar was too high, so he had to tilt the tabletop. He slammed it—*BAM!* The door opened an inch.

Nico shoved the table with force, levering the door all the way open, and then pushed past it. The collar at his neck started to tingle and he stopped. Three feet of table poked through to the outside, on an angle. He ran and grabbed his mattress and tossed it along the tabletop, hoping it would stop on the far side so he could grab it as he sailed through. But he threw too hard, and it flopped over onto the concrete pavers, one end sticking up a half foot against the table edge.

Nico told himself he could grab that end as he passed.

He lined up three other tables as fast as he could, end to end with the first one, making a runway.

Seventy seconds.

Nico vaulted onto the table nearest the counter, took a breath, and set his path. He didn't need to stay in the air for long—ten feet without touching, and hopefully grab the mattress to cushion his landing. Nico flashed on the image of long jumpers in the Olympics, traveling all that distance without touching the ground. But there was only five feet of clearance between the top of the doorway and the table. He'd have to dive, sideways.

No obstacles.

He ran at the doorway, speeding up to a full-out sprint. Just as Nico's feet reached the angled table holding the door open, he lunged into a dive. Squirrel jumping off an electric wire.

Nico passed through the door frame, snagging the mattress with his left hand but not getting it under him in time. About to hit the ground, he twisted, and the impact scraped the hell out of his right shoulder and back as he skidded to a messy stop.

The mattress flopped on top of him, bread on a blood-and-paving-stone sandwich. He lay there, struggling for air.

He'd made it to the courtyard. And he hadn't gotten zapped.

It was cold outside. No moon, just stars in the darkness above. Still another hour till sunrise… An hour… Time! *Get up!*

Staggering to his feet, Nico realized he'd lost count. *Fifty-five? Forty?* How many seconds before they knew he was gone? Before they tried to zap him? How long would that monitor jammed in the bathroom door hold?

Courtyard camera. Above the cafeteria door. It was next on the plan. Nico grabbed the table edge. He gritted his teeth as the metal at his neck hummed with the beginning of a zap for being too close to a red light. He pulled the table toward him, all the way outside. Once it was free, the door swung shut. If they were watching, they'd be able to see him. Nico propped the table on its end, letting it lean back into the window frame above the door. Ten-foot-long table—seven-foot-tall door.

Camera: Blocked.

Whew.

Nico swiveled on his bare feet, checking out the thirty-foot slope that led to the street, which was covered in crushed glass and guarded by glowing red columns that threatened to zap anyone who tried to escape. So close, but with no shoes and the electroshock collar on his neck, completely out of reach. *Stick to the plan.*

He hustled to the elevator, dragging the mattress with him. He punched the call button. *Come on!* The overhead light showed it was on level minus one. Machinery whirred. Nico tried to hide in the predawn shadow of the elevator doorway, hoping no one could see him from the cells facing the courtyard.

Bec's cell faced in, but Nico wouldn't let himself look. There was nothing he could do for her now, except make sure this worked.

He tried to ignore the pain and the blood seeping through the fabric at his shoulder, as he worked the mattress spring bracelet off his bicep and used the point he'd sharpened to rip at the stitches holding the zipper to his jumpsuit. He'd gotten it mostly freed when the elevator doors opened, car empty.

Twenty-five seconds, maybe. Nico got in with the mattress as the doors closed behind him. He was inside the concrete elevator shaft, but if the doors opened, there would be nothing to block the transmission from the guards' tablets and he'd get zapped by the necklace. He needed to be surrounded by cement. Nico hit the button for minus two and ripped out the rest of the zipper. The neon yellow jumpsuit flopped open down to the pockets.

Eighteen seconds. He stood on the elevator car's handrail so he could reach the roof hatch. Bracing himself with one hand and using the zipper pull like a screwdriver in the other, he got to work on the three screws.

Fourteen seconds. The first screw fell past his hand, clattering to the elevator car floor. He didn't have time to grab it.

Nine seconds. He caught the second one as it came loose and pocketed it.

Five seconds. The third came free, and he grabbed it as well. He pushed and the service hatch flipped open. Nico hoisted himself up.

One.

Zero.

The elevator arrived on level minus two. Nico reached down and yanked the thin mattress up out of sight a moment before the doors opened to an empty hallway, then closed again.

Nico carefully lowered the service hatch. Now it was dark, with only three pinholes of light coming from the screw holes under him.

He didn't feel any tingling or heat at his neck. Were they trying to bring him down?

He'd made it this far. But Nico was still in the "Institute." He tied the zipper around his waist like a belt to keep the jumpsuit together and sat on the mattress, telling himself to be patient. They would sound the alarm soon enough.

0551

Nico guessed it was a half hour later when the elevator started moving up. The doors slid open and a shaft of light cut into the darkness around him. He got a narrow view of Gold Wheels Preacher getting in on level minus one. Furious. Unshaved. And his shoulder-length silver-streaked hair wasn't its usual slicked-back helmet.

"How in the name of all that's holy did this happen?" Gold Wheels Preacher barked into his cell phone. "Hello? Hello?" He slapped at the screen on his phone and shoved it in his pinstripe blazer as the doors closed.

Nico worried that Gold Wheels Preacher would see the screw on the floor. Glance up and catch Nico staring down at him through one of the open screw holes. Zap the hell out of him with the tablet in his hands. Nico took shallow, silent breaths as Gold Wheels Preacher seethed.

The instant the doors opened on the courtyard level, Gold Wheels Preacher was shouting, "Search it again! Every inch of the compound! And check the construction area!"

Nico watched Gold Wheels Preacher stalk off, and then the doors closed again, protecting him. It got quiet. And dark. Nico's shoulder throbbed.

10:14

Nico startled when the elevator moved. He wasn't sure how much time had passed, but if they'd been trying to zap him—and he was sure they had—the thick concrete of the elevator shaft was working.

The elevator stopped, and the doors slid open. Nico watched the slice of minus one corridor and saw the pizza delivery guy ride in on his bike with the hot box in back. The bribe to get them all to turn on each other. But Nico was focused on the three bike wheels—rubber wheels with rubber inner tubes. They were his ticket out, down the crushed glass to the street. He'd have three flat tires, but he'd be on the street outside.

As the elevator rose to the courtyard, Pizza Guy made a multipoint turn to get the bike facing the doors. When they opened, he wheeled his bike partway out, then stopped. "Hey, Dr. H." Pizza Guy said. The doors started to close on his bike, but he held them open with his palm. "What's going on? Ken said you had a problem?"

Nico couldn't see Gold Wheels Preacher, but he could hear him. Frustrated. Impatient. Personally affronted. "It's like when you can't find your car keys, except you know they're here because you drove here."

Nico had a quick fantasy of finding Gold Wheels Preacher's matte black electric BMW with its flashy gold wheels unlocked in its garage spot, key fob in the cupholder, so he could just drive away from the Institute in style… But even if he could get the car, he didn't have a way to open the garage door. The guards did that from watching the video monitors. *Stick to the plan—you just have to get the bike.*

Meanwhile, Gold Wheels Preacher was all charm. "No pizza today."

"But you ordered…" Pizza Guy trailed off. "I don't have change for this."

"It's to make up for canceling. Keep today's order. I'll call when I want our regular deliveries resumed."

Oh crap. Everyone's going to hate me now.

But as Nico thought about it, it made sense. This was Gold Wheels Preacher's strategy to make sure no one helped him. Take away the stab-each-other-in-the-back bribe of pizza, and what was left for them to look forward to?

"You should come on out so they can see you're here." Gold Wheels Preacher said. "And also see you go."

"All right." Pizza Guy pulled the red stop toggle to freeze the elevator, and wheeled out. Nico could imagine how sixty-nine pairs of eyes were tracking him through the glass walls of the cafeteria. If Bec was there. Sixty-eight if she was still too messed up… *Stay focused.*

A minute later Pizza Guy was back, walking his bike in. He pressed the button and the doors shut. They rode down, and once again Pizza

Guy did a couple-of-inches-forward, couple-of-inches-back turning pattern to face the door.

Nico studied the bike, noticing the metal chain and padlock wound around the seat post and the quick-release latch on the front tire. He didn't want to fight Pizza Guy for it—*he* hadn't done anything to Nico. But how else was he going to get out of there? And Pizza Guy was the only one with a way out who didn't have a tablet to zap him. He needed the guy's bike or sneakers... preferably both. The mattress was to muffle the guy's screams until Nico could knock him out. His fingers wrapped the edge of the service hatch. This was the part of the plan Nico hated most.

Pizza Guy hopped on the seat as the elevator doors started to open, and Nico told himself he had to move, drop down on the guy, kick him in the head, do *something*, or his one chance of escape would be gone. But Pizza Guy didn't pedal out. Instead, he was searching the floor of the elevator.

Nico listened carefully... there! A low *hissss*.

"You've got to be kidding me." Pizza Guy said, climbing down from the seat to poke at the front tire.

Nico could see it was flat. He wouldn't be able to ride it now. Without the rubber wheels insulating him he'd get zapped as soon as he was close to the columns. He'd have to get the guy's sneakers.

But he couldn't make himself move. It just felt wrong.

Pizza Guy dug his fingers into the front tire, pulling out a screw. *The screw!*

"Fucking construction." Pizza Guy dropped the screw into the slot between the elevator floor and the hallway, then pulled the collapsing-forward bike out. Nico hunched down to watch. Instead of dealing with the tire, Pizza Guy wiped his hands on his shirt and opened the hot box on the back. He grabbed a slice, shoving it in his mouth. Nico could smell the pineapple and ham.

Pizza Guy pulled out his phone and walked down the hall. "Keysh, you're not going to believe this. Can you hear me? Hold on."

The bike was right there in the hallway. Maybe Nico wouldn't need his sneakers after all...

Nico raised the hatch and stuck his foot down between the closing doors so they opened again. Quietly, he lowered himself into the elevator car. He snuck a fast glance down the corridor. No sign of Pizza Guy. Maybe he'd gone into the garage. Nico pulled the red stop toggle so the elevator doors stayed open.

He darted to the bike and pulled the quick release latch. The flat front tire came off in his hand and he silently lowered the frame to the ground. Then he was back in the elevator.

Nico closed the doors and pushed the button for the courtyard. When the car was between floors he pulled the toggle to freeze it in place. He had to work fast. Pizza Guy would be back soon, notice the missing wheel, and they would all know Nico took it.

He jammed the heel of his hand against the side of the wheel, pulling the tire up and away from the metal circle. His scraped-up shoulder burned with the impact, but he rotated the tire five inches and hit it again. And again. Three more pushes and he managed to pull the tire free. Inside the tread, the floppy rubber inner tube was a large circle. He pulled the spring bracelet off and used the sharp point again, this time to slice through the whole tube. Now he had a rubber hose. He used the point on the inside to slice it lengthwise, cutting against the floor. When a foot and a half was curling in on itself but open, he cut it off the rest of the tube. Nico's hands were streaked with grease as he fed the rubber between his neck and the metal collar, working it around, taking extra care to not touch the tamper box in the back when he slid the rubber past it. In about a minute, he couldn't feel the cold metal on his skin at all.

Nico pulled the mattress down from the cab roof, took a deep breath, and pushed the stop toggle. The elevator resumed its way up, and in a moment the doors slid open to the courtyard. He set his path.

No obstacles.

Holding the mattress like a sled, Nico raced directly across the courtyard, for the slope of crushed glass.

"There he is!" Someone yelled.

Nico ran like he was on fire.

The columns glowed red with menace as Nico got close, but he was counting on the rubber insulation. And momentum. And gravity.

Nico hurled himself, mattress under him this time, to sled down the hill of glass.

"Correct him!" Gold Wheels Preacher shouted.

"I'm trying!" one of the others yelled back.

The rubber at Nico's neck was working—it was a fast, rough ride down the hill, all the way to the low stone wall edging the road. He swung around and got his bare feet on asphalt without getting cut and ran.

Gold Wheels Preacher screamed the order, "Call the police, now!"

Their shouts continued as Nico raced across the street, into a backyard, and out of view.

1027

Nico cut across two more streets, staying on lawns and watching every step before he spotted a pair of green rubber gardening clogs by the side door of 1613 Bradford Way. They were too tight, but at least he wasn't barefoot anymore. Five more blocks until he saw an open garage.

He walked cautiously down the driveway of 911 Jacaranda Street, staying low as he passed the kitchen window. A mountain bike was newly washed and propped against the side of the house. Muddy sneakers sat drying in a patch of sun. Inside the garage, clothes sloshed in a washing machine. Rubber gloves hung over the edge of a utility sink. A workshop along the back wall displayed well-used tools on a pegboard.

The gloves were tight too, but Nico worked them on. He remembered Nelson, the first "graduate" of the Institute, coming back like a trained pet to tell them about his job at Target in Lost Hills, and his girlfriend Sarah who he'd met at Bible study. But when Nico asked, "If everything's so great, how come you still have one of the zap-you collars on?" Nelson's eyes darted to Gold Wheels Preacher, whose face turned murderous at the challenge.

"They didn't... I..." Nelson struggled to pull his words together. "It's not on." He reached behind his neck, unlatched it somehow, and pulled it off. It left behind a tan line, like Nelson's head wasn't quite attached to his body. Gold Wheels Preacher put a hand on Nelson's shoulder and explained that the necklace was "a way for Nelson to feel connected to the safety of the Institute outside these walls. An outward symbol of his inner devotion." Such bullshit. But Nico had learned that taking the metal collar off wasn't hard to do. Only thing that had stopped him trying before was the tamper trigger. But now he was in rubber clogs. Wearing rubber gloves. A careful check of the inner tube confirmed that rubber was still protecting his neck.

Twisting in opposite directions, Nico yanked the box and collar apart as hard as he could—there was a *snap!*

WhooP WhooP WhooP!

The alarm shrieked from the box as the collar spilt into two half circles in his hands. Nico dropped it to the floor.

WhooP! WhooP!

He grabbed a hammer. *SMASH! SMASH!*

It went silent.

SMASH!

Nico was panting.

Someone had to have heard that.

Hoping his luck held out, he checked the dryer. *Jackpot!*

Two minutes later, Nico was riding the bike south, away from the Institute. He was wearing clean cotton boxers under too-baggy jeans, a large T-shirt of a band he'd never heard of before, a purple sweatshirt, warm socks, and muddy sneakers that were only one size too big. He'd taken the silver bike helmet too. If the police were searching for him, it would hide his buzzcut and make it harder to see his face.

He left behind a note, using a drafting pencil and writing on the cement driveway where the bike had been parked:

I will pay you back. I promise.

1948
BAKERSFIELD CA

"I'll give you eighty." The guy's face was hidden in the shade of his baseball cap. A three-quarter moon and the buzzing amber lights of the Bakersfield bus station made the shadows they were in even deeper.

"Come on. It's worth at least eight hundred," Nico said, brushing his hand along the crossbar. *Truth.* But they both knew the same two things: the bike was stolen, and Nico was in no position to haggle.

"You want to sell it, or not? Final offer."

Nico reached for the four twenties. "Helmet for your hat?"

They made that swap too, and Nico settled the red baseball cap low on his head.

In the bus station's bathroom, Nico used soap and paper towels to clean up his scraped shoulder and back as best as he could, turning the T-shirt inside out so it was cleaner against his raw skin. He grabbed a greasy burrito that tasted way better than it should have after only a week of prison food, and hopped on the 10:05 PM for San Diego. The police wouldn't be searching for him that far away—he hoped. He wasn't going back to Janice, the foster "mom" who sold him out. Or the system. Or tenth grade, for that matter.

Settling in an empty row toward the back of the bus, Nico told himself running was the only thing to do. If he hung around and got caught, that wasn't going to help anyone—and it wouldn't get Bec free.

I'm helping myself, so later I can help her.

Help all of them?

Bec was the only one who'd ever been kind to Nico. Squirrel Boy too—sort of. Ratting Nico out for pizza that first day but then giving him Squirrel Boy's own bowl of goop. Was that kindness?

The kid was maybe twelve. Probably not fair to judge him.

Nico sighed. It was all so unfair. None of them were locked up for anything other than being Queer, and tossed away by a system, or families, that wanted them to be someone other than who they were.

But Bec was the only one Nico had promised. The only one who helped him actually escape.

For now, all Nico could do was run. Stay free. Come up with a plan.

At least... he'd left them all a surprise.

Nico pulled the plastic letter he'd swiped from the cafeteria sign out of the jeans pocket. A rectangle the size of his palm, it had a clear plastic background around a large black capital *S*.

They'd have seen it by now. Bec, and the others.

He remembered how the sign read without the letter in his hands:

GOD SAYS HOMOSEXUALITY IS IN.

Nico's eyes caught a reflection in the window as the bus pulled out of the station. It was him—smirking.

2

SAM

SAM KNEW IT WAS SOMETHING James Bond—even if he were Gay like him—would never do in the afterglow, but he did it anyway.

He turned to Kevin on the pillow next to him and said what he'd been thinking for the last ten days. "Hey, I love you."

Sam could feel the smile on his face slowly harden like drying cement as Kevin didn't say anything. For a really long time. Like count-to-sixty long time. He wasn't asleep. Sam could see his eyes searching the ceiling, like the right words were up there somewhere. Sam didn't understand the delay. He *could* just say it back... Maybe he was too overcome with emotion?

Finally, Kevin spoke. "Uhh, I was gonna tell you. I think we should start seeing other people."

Sam shook his head, thinking Kevin hadn't heard what he just said. Or maybe he'd heard Kevin wrong. Like some kind of bliss-induced misfire between his ears and brain. Like his subconscious sabotaging something that was going so good in real life. So he said it again to make sure: "Kevin, I love you. I'm *in* love with you."

Kevin turned away, and Sam watched his back, thinking, *Maybe he's got a card by his clothes.* Something Kevin wrote earlier and was

18

just waiting for the perfect time to give him. One of those cards that are blank on the inside but the perfect place to say "I love you" for the first time. The kind with a black-and-white photo of some buff gym guy on the cover. The kind Kevin could have totally posed for—enough people told him he could be a model, trying to get into his pants.

It wasn't anything Sam had to say. Kevin made the first move. And since school started, it had been like a dance. "What's ups" on the way into Latin II to questions about homework Sam knew Kevin already had the answers to. Homework to flirting. Flirting to hanging out. Hanging out to hanging out without clothes… Sam wanted to enjoy the memory, but he couldn't because the damn seconds ticked by and he realized Kevin wasn't turning back around.

Which meant there was no card.

"Kevin?"

The color on Kevin's back was perfect—booth tanned—even though he'd spent most of the summer at his family's villa in Cannes. Sam reached out to touch him, just over the shoulder blade, but stopped himself. What if Kevin scooted away? What if he *had* heard him right, and Kevin didn't even want Sam to touch him?

"Kevin?" Sam said it again, hating how needy he sounded but not able to take back how it squeaked out.

And then Kevin said, voice all casual, "I kind of already have."

It took Sam a second, but then it connected: He was talking about *other people.*

Other people, when Kevin had told him he was the only one. That they didn't have to be safe because he was safe. *Thank God you didn't do anything you would have needed a condom for. What if you had?*

Other people.

He thought they were both—

He thought—

And then Sam was gasping, like the air in his bedroom was suddenly too thin to hold any oxygen in it. Like he was suddenly Jill Masterson, the Bond Girl murdered once she slept with James Bond—Goldfinger painted her entire body with gold and she died of skin suffocation, whatever the hell that was. But Sam wasn't supposed to be some disposable Bond Girl, or Bond Boy. He wasn't the one supposed to be painted gold!

Kevin still wouldn't turn around. "Hey, we had some fun, right?"

It felt like a physical punch, but inside, where the bruising wouldn't show. *Had* some fun. Not *having* fun. Had.

Had.

The past tense felt violent. And Bond's world of *Mr. Right Now* rather than *Mr. Right* was suddenly real, with Sam on the losing side of the equation.

Sam got up too fast, stumbling into his ukulele—it jangled and echoed as it hit the heated hardwood floor. Why had he left it propped against the wall unit where Kevin could see it? It ruined his whole Bond bedroom mode! It probably looked like some kid's toy, rather than the cool Jake Shimabukuro musician thing Sam was going for. He was even learning the Bond theme song on it, which his tutor said was going to be a "tour de force" once he got it. But Kevin hadn't heard him play anything. Because he'd kind of been hiding it. Until now, when he'd been stupid enough to leave it out in plain sight. Was this why Kevin was dumping him? Nerdy hobby too much to even be around?

Oh shit. He was getting dumped.

Had been dumped.

Sam fled to his bathroom off the hallway, shutting the door behind him. He slid down, forehead against the solid mahogany. *Bond wouldn't care!* Sam told himself. But it was just words.

Face hot, breaths shallow, Sam fought every second to stay in control, to be silent—desperate to avoid humiliating himself any more.

There was nothing at first. Then, finally, the rustle of keys in Burberry plaid pants. The whoosh of leather driving shoes against the silk hallway carpet. The apartment door deadbolt being thrown open, and then the thud of the door closing behind the guy Sam realized wasn't *his* guy. Not anymore.

Maybe he never was, and this whole "maybe we're boyfriends" thing was all in your head…

Sam didn't move, huddled there on the cold mosaic, naked except for the Omega Seamaster 300M Chronometer 2531.80.00 stainless steel watch with a sapphire blue face like Pierce Brosnan wore as Bond in *The World Is Not Enough*. And this sound came out of his throat, released like some crazed animal, and he heard it roar and squeak and rage and he grabbed a towel to scream into because even his own ears couldn't take it and he cried.

Cried.

Cried.

Dr. Sanchez told him not to be embarrassed about crying—that it was the body's natural stress reliever and would help him feel better. But when Sam calmed down enough to face the mirror, all he could see were endless reasons Kevin had just dumped him. Red eyes. Big nose. Snotty mess. Not like any of the Bonds at all.

Idiot. Idiot. Idiot. Bond never says "I love you." You can be cool, and save the world, or you can try for some fantasy "happily ever after" while the world crumbles and takes you down anyway. Bond doesn't get both. Why would you?

And Sam started to cry all over again, even though he knew it wouldn't make him feel any better. He messaged Ari and Frida. It was past ten on a Wednesday night, but hey, this was an emergency.

2238

"It's all because of that stupid ukulele," Sam complained to Frida, who had draped herself over the living room couch, checking out comments on her latest performance post. He'd managed to throw on sweatpants and a T-shirt, but Sam still felt like roadkill plastered on the Eames lounge chair. Each photo-filter-perfect image of Kevin on his phone made him feel run over—all over again.

"He's an ass!" Ari shouted like a protest-march slogan as they let themselves in the unlocked apartment door. Ari came into view, today's Smurfette rhinestone tiny hat just-so askew on their polished shaved head. Their mouth puckered in concern. "Your parents hear that?"

Sam waved it off. "They're working late, and even if they were here, they've heard the word *ass* before."

"Well, he is. An ass." Ari blinked at Sam in sympathy. "I mean… you're too good for him."

Sam snorted at how untrue that was. Kevin really did have perfect abs, even in real life. An eight-pack, dammit.

Frida picked her words like she was trying to be delicate. She— and especially her drag king persona, Crank Shaft—wasn't known for "delicate." "You weren't… totally honest with Kevin about who *you* were. So maybe he was feeding off that."

"Like a slutty Gay shark hanging out with a Gay dolphin," Ari offered, taking one of the bar stools by the floor-to-ceiling windows. "He was always going to go off to another shark."

Sam wondered why he could never convince anyone he was a shark.

"We love you for who you are—ukulele and all." Frida glanced up from her phone. "Isn't that the whole point? To be our full selves without pretending? And find someone who'll love us *and* our quirks?" She paused to consider. "Maybe even *for* our quirks."

It sounded good for a slam poem, and maybe it worked for friends, but Sam had figured out back in eighth grade he wasn't going to get lucky with any hot guys by being *quirky* Samuel Jonas Solomon, living the most boring un-action-movie life ever. But in those moments he could channel James Bond he *could* be adventurous, daring, sexy... He flipped to the pic from his last sports car training session. Zoltan had snapped it from the passenger seat—Sam driving a sleek gunmetal Aston Martin DBS Superleggera Volante, red leather interior. His mouth was open, caught mid-*whoop!* as he passed the last orange cone and opened it up on the old airport runway just north of Jersey City. The top was down, and even though his hair was flying in every direction like some clown wig in a blender instead of the swoop he worked so hard on, with his Vuarnet Legend 06 smoky brown sunglasses and the power of the V12 under him, Sam had *felt* just like Craig-Bond in *No Time to Die*.

Bond car. Bond sunglasses. Bond life... If Sam could drive a hot car he could get a hot guy. Wasn't Kevin proof of that?

Except Kevin just dumped him. And now he was just Sam again. And anyway, he only got two hours a week driving hot cars full out on crazy obstacle courses. The small window of time where he could imagine he was hot, too, was just rented.

Fake.

Like him and Kevin.

He scrolled back to Kevin's shots from the last swim meet. *God, he's hot in that tiny Speedo...* The stupid tears and snot kept coming.

"Frida..." Ari scolded.

"What?"

Ari jutted their chin at her phone. "Crank Shaft's fans can't wait?"

"*He's* regret scrolling!"

"I'm not." Sam defended himself. *Regret* would be images of him leaving that stupid ukulele out and not stashing it before Kevin got here so he wouldn't have broken the "Bond guy" spell. Kevin's stream was all shots of himself: his pecs, biceps, swimmer's V... Maybe Sam *was* regret scrolling. It for sure wasn't helping. He switched the phone off as Ari and Frida bantered for "best friend in a supporting role"...

"Anyway, I got here before you did!" Frida said.

"You can walk here!" Ari pointed out the obvious. "At least *I'm* present and being supportive... Not multitasking on a huge security risk and being rude."

"Fine. Airplane mode. Happy?" Frida dropped her phone on the cushion next to her and gave Sam her full attention. "The problem with St. Bacchus is it's this tiny little pond that's completely overfished. Everyone's dated everyone by tenth grade, especially on the rainbow side of the pond."

"One of the benefits of leaving the pond early," Ari chimed in, "is you avoid all those inbred fish."

"Listen to the wisdom of the one that got away," Frida said.

"Oh, so now it's wisdom." Ari looked pleased.

"*Annoying* wisdom, but yes." Frida pushed Sam's foot with her own, gently. "You need to swim out into the world, little fish."

"Wasn't I a dolphin a minute ago?" Sam asked. "How did I get demoted?"

"Fine, little dolphin." Frida allowed. "Find another Gay little dolphin, someone who's not a dick."

"Hold on." Sam was out of tissues. He pulled himself up and headed to the hallway. "Why are all the names for horrible guys sex things? Dick? Ass? Jerk?"

"Jerk-off!" Ari added.

"Point!" Sam called back as he entered his bathroom. They could hear him blow his nose.

Ari sighed. "Poor guy. Just giving his heart away."

"To all the wrong people." Frida shot Ari a look as she picked up her phone.

"Don't you dare." Ari narrowed their eyes at her, not talking about the phone at all. They zipped two manicured fingernails in front of their own lips.

Frida kept her voice low. "I'm just saying… This could be your chance."

They could both hear Sam running water in the sink.

"You know what happens to the friend who doesn't say anything about wanting more?" Ari whispered. "They *stay* a friend."

"But isn't love worth any risk?" Frida sounded like she was composing her next *Dear Mx. Crank Shaft* piece.

"You've seen Kevin… And Ryan… Oh, and Michael! He doesn't want *this*," Ari swooped a hand from their flowing white and turquoise pinstripe pants with a paper-bag waist, past a bedazzled Papa Smurf sweatshirt, to their tiny hat.

"*You* are fabulous." Frida told them.

"No argument," Ari said. "But he wants butch, not bitch."

"That sounds like an excuse to not put your heart out there," Frida said. "And maybe you're underestimating him."

"Maybe I'm being realistic."

"Is that another word for coward?"

Ari rolled their eyes. "It must be *ex-hausting* always knowing what everyone *else* should do."

"Oh, honey." Frida matched their eye roll and tone. "The *ex-hausting* part is when you all don't do it."

Face wet and hair newly slicked down, Sam came back in carrying a tissue box. "What did I miss?"

Ari and Frida shifted gears, as if they hadn't been saying anything important at all.

"Actually…" Frida's eyes were friendly daggers. "Ari has something they want to tell you."

Sam fell back into the chair, missing Ari mouthing *Evil* at Frida. Sam looked at Ari expectantly.

"I can hack into his school account, if you want. Kevin's."

"Revenge?" Sam shook his head, which made his massive headache even worse. That didn't feel very Bond.

"We could make him flunk everything." Ari managed to sound like a generous hacker version of Santa Claus as they threw their arms wide and shouted, "Schadenfreude for everyone!"

"Forget revenge," Frida said. "There's a whole world of Gay dolphins out there. You try again, but next time with someone you can be yourself with." She looked at Ari, who glared at her in warning.

"I feel so stupid." Sam could feel the tears starting up again.

Frida pulled Sam to his feet, then jerked her head for Ari to join them. "Group hug." It was an order, not a request.

The three of them held each other for a long moment as the lights of the city and East River sparkled outside.

Sam managed to take a shaky breath. Ari and Frida shared a pained look for him.

"It's okay," Ari said into Sam's hair.

But Sam knew it wasn't okay. *He* wasn't okay. Not at all.

<u>One Good Thing</u>

Dr. Sanchez said to end every day that "poses challenges" with one good thing in this journal. Even if it's just a lesson learned. That it "resets your unconscious to focus on the positive." And she promised it was <u>For Your Eyes Only</u>, not even knowing that was a Bond movie! Roger Moore.

Bullshit therapy homework.

But you promised Dad and Mom you'd try.

So fine. Get to it, Solomon.

On this shittiest day ever, here's one "good" thing, in a schadenfreude (damn, Ari! Had to look that one up) kind of way: 007 got his heart broken once too.

And then they recast George Lazenby because he completely unraveled when Irma Bunt shot Tracy at the end of <u>On Her Majesty's Secret Service</u>. Not that Bond cried naked, hiding on the floor of <u>his</u> bathroom, but still.

Besides the giant plot hole of Blofeld just assuming Bond died in the avalanche while assuming Tracy survived, <u>and</u> the plot hole of Bond assuming Blofeld died when he got caught in the neck by that branch in their bobsled chase, <u>and</u> the biggest plot hole of all: Tracy showing up in that village at the base of the mountain where Blofeld's institute was to help Bond escape — after all, if her father knew the exact mountain in the Swiss Alps where Blofeld was the whole time, why did Bond have to break into that lawyer's office in Bern and then pretend to be Sir Hilary to find out Blofeld's location?

Besides all that, with his new bride dead in his arms, Lazenby–Bond loses touch with reality. In shock, he babbles about her just resting — when we've seen the bullet hole in her forehead. And then, in the final second of the movie, Bond lowers his head to her body and even though we can't see his tears we hear his <u>SOB</u>.

It echoes all the way through the end credits, as we imagine the red-eyed, perfect-nosed, snotty mess he's going to be...

And that was the end of Lazenby's one-film era as 007.

Crying showed weakness, so they had to bring back Sean Connery to save the franchise. The American public — the international public — couldn't handle their Bond crying. Real men don't — or at least, aren't supposed to. Even when their hearts are broken. It totally gets in the way of their saving the world.

So Bond stopped caring. Became the kind of man who doesn't cry, not even when he's being tortured. The kind of guy who laughs when he's being tortured —

Daniel Craig is such a badass in <u>Casino Royale</u>.

There's Dr. Sanchez's lesson: Bond keeps his cool, always. Doesn't cry. Ever. And he's able to do it because he's figured out how to not care. And that frees him up to make a difference in our world.

You didn't even make a difference to Kevin.

No, fuck it. Don't cry. Enough. So nobody's in love with you, boo-hoo. Get over it. Be a man.

Anyway, crying sucks.

Stop caring, Sam.

Just.

Stop.

Caring.

Be like Bond. Post-Lazenby Bond.

3

NICO

Nico walked into chemistry lab.

He was back, his second day at Lincoln High. He'd watched as these guys chugged their Red Bulls and tossed them in the trash. He snuck back mid-lunch, and with the coast clear, he had an assembly line going, draining the cans in the lab sink before crushing them and popping them in his backpack's wetbag. Then he heard the voice:

"I didn't peg you for Red Bull."

Nico froze in place, realizing what they saw: two cans on the counter and another in his hand. He probably looked like a total caffeine addict.

"Would you believe I'm trying to quit?" Nico said, turning with a half smile to see who it was. Clark. His friends shouted his name enough. Nico wondered if the can he was holding was the one Clark had drunk from earlier. He hadn't finished it. Nico ran through his options. Did Clark know he was taking them to recycle? Or was this maybe a chance to make a friend? First person to actually talk to him outside of class...

Clark grabbed the lab book he'd come in for and his eyes traced a line from the trash can by Nico's feet—with no Red Bull cans in it—to Nico. He flashed his teeth. "The Fairy Janitor. At least now we know what to call you."

Nico whipped the quarter-full can in his hand at him. Piss-colored liquid arced out and splashed across Clark's white polo shirt. He didn't even dodge the can, letting it bounce off his chest. His stunned look turned to murder.

And there was this second when they were both on the edge of smashing together to fight it out before the classroom door clicked open—then stopped as Ms. Cameron answered someone's question in the hallway. Neither of them were happy about the interruption.

Eyes narrowed, Clark said, "Watch your back, Fairy Janitor."

"You should watch your front." Nico shot back as Clark left.

He'd shoved the two cans he hadn't crushed yet back into the trash and snagged the one he'd thrown at Clark from the floor just as Ms. Cameron came in with a questioning gaze. Nico ignored it, and the long puddle of energy drink that looked like some dog peed there.

He'd promised himself he wouldn't get caught collecting cans at whatever new school he ended up at.

A squeal of the hydraulic brakes as the bus pulled to a stop woke Nico from the dream memory. Ironic that he wasn't going to any new school this time. But recycling was probably a good idea. He'd already learned recycling was recycling, no matter where you were. Tenth grade too. But making friends—maybe not so much.

THU 6 SEP
0725
SAN DIEGO CA

Nico got off the bus at Front Street and Broadway. The drugstore on the corner wasn't open yet—not that he could spend the $24 he had left.

He needed a phone. That would be $80 for a used top-of-the-line cell, another $40 for a prepaid month of unlimited: $120. Minus the $24, so he had to come up with $96. There were trash cans, and he could see two convenience stores selling liquor and sodas, which meant he could recycle like on a regular school day. At five cents a can that was 1,920 cans to the recycling center. The most he'd done was 200 a day on weekends, which was $10. That would take him ten days... Could he manage 640 a day? Three days sounded a lot better. And it wasn't like he was going to miss classes. But he'd also need money to eat. And somewhere to sleep. And a wetbag and maybe a backpack so he didn't come off like some homeless person—

Nico snorted at the thought. He kind of was. And given where he'd just been, it was awesome.

Day one of freedom. I can go anywhere!

A wave of guilt hit him. It was also day seventy for Bec, trapped back in Gold Wheels Preacher's Institute. Was she okay? How badly did they punish her for helping him escape? How was he going to get her free?

Nico pushed the thoughts away. There was nothing he could do for her right now—he had to help himself first. He needed to find a thrift store. And maybe a youth hostel, for at least a couple of nights. And maybe, before he got the phone, he could find a library with a free computer where he could log on and reach 321Boom and Power2People. Would they care enough to help if he made a real-world ask?

The pang of feeling all alone in the world gnawed at him, and Nico's fingers itched to message them. To connect—even though they didn't know much real-world stuff about each other. But the three of them shared videos online and had bonded in the vloggers lounge. They were friends who hadn't changed when Nico had been moved to foster placement number ten, and then eleven... But then he'd been dragged to Gold Wheels Preacher's Institute. That was eight days ago, and he hadn't spoken to either of them since then.

All the being tossed away added up, and up, and up, and each time Nico was recycled, he didn't feel worth as much. At least his No Obstacles videos were a world where he controlled everything, even if it was just for those few seconds of free-run stunt awesomeness.

321Boom, she did these movie-makeup tutorials, time-lapse transformations that, in the last one Nico saw, changed a blonde surfer girl into Jon Snow from *Game of Thrones*. It was a pretty recent reference, since 321Boom usually made him look up films from 1940s and '50s Hollywood.

Power2People, he did these wordless free-access internet and electric power videos for places all around the country. Each one zoomed in from a thousand feet up to show just where you could plug in your electronics and get online for free in small-, medium-, and large-town America. Power2People was a one-person silent revolution to make access a right—not a privilege.

Nico's last No Obstacles video was a split-screen edit of him running up the wall to flip upside down, next to Donald O'Connor doing the same stunt in one of 321Boom's old movie suggestions, *Singin' in the Rain*. He'd done it up Mrs. Parker's precious flocked paisley wallpaper, after she found that safe-space pride sticker in his math notebook and freaked out. After she decided that he wasn't Nico anymore but some predator. Some stranger, after twenty-two months of living there. Someone dangerous to the *real* kids in her care, who now needed to be protected—from him! He'd told her that being Gay didn't make him a pedophile, but she was all "God doesn't discriminate when it comes to perversions."

Discriminate. Air snorted out of Nico's nose, but his eyes stung. He hadn't even been allowed to say goodbye to the other foster kids. He'd stayed up the whole night, doing the wall-flip video, distracting himself online. And the next morning, before Omar, G., or the twins were even up, some social services woman he'd never seen before drove Nico and his stuff—in a black plastic trash bag—to foster placement eleven.

Recycled again.

At least *this* time Nico was in charge of where he was going. It made him want to come up with a new stunt. Make a new video.

He missed the other vloggers. Even if it was anonymous and he'd never seen their faces, they cared about each other—didn't they?

But connecting would have to wait. Right now, the air was salty and smelled of freedom. Nico let his feet carry him toward the water. He rubbed his neck, which felt naked. Blessedly naked.

A police car was parked where the road transitioned to a pedestrian path ahead, the officers talking to some uniformed Border Patrol guys. Were they looking for him?

Nico tugged the bill of his baseball cap lower and turned into the small park to his north. He kept it mellow—like he was just a tourist, out to enjoy the morning and catch a view of the cruise ships. As he crossed the geometrically angled patches of grass, a couple in their sixties cut through the parking lot ahead of him. They were each straining to pull two pieces of wheeled luggage, balancing other bags on top.

"Remember," the woman said, "just because it's all-you-can-eat doesn't mean you should eat it all."

"Dee, will you stop?" He complained. "Am I doing anything wrong right now?"

"I'm just saying, I've seen you with buffets."

"Thirty-two years, you think you could give it a rest."

The suitcase in her left hand hit a crack and the overstuffed beach bag on top thudded off. She stopped, voice shrill. "Harry, why didn't we send the luggage? Or at least take a cab?"

"Cabs won't go two blocks. Stop complaining, we're almost there."

"But it's heavy!"

Harry called over his shoulder, "Once we're on the ship, we only have to unpack once."

Nico got an inspiration. He trotted up to them. "Excuse me, ma'am?"

He dipped his visor like one of 321Boom's old-movie bellhops at a fancy hotel. "Maybe I can help you with your bags."

"Oh! Heavens be praised." Dee clasped her hands and gestured for Nico to take them.

Harry stopped and stared at Nico over half glasses, the kind they sell at drugstores. "You're not going to steal them, are you?"

"No." *Truth.* "My family's just up ahead. They took our luggage already." *Lie.* "I'm happy to help!" *Truth.*

"Let him!" Dee told her husband. "He's a nice young man."

Harry raised both hands in surrender. "Okay, okay."

Nico slung the beach bag over his good shoulder. *Damn, did she pack her collection of stones?* He rolled Dee's two other bags toward the sign that said: B Street Pier, Port of San Diego.

Breathing heavy, Harry called up to Dee, who was now walking two steps ahead of them. "You're not going to carry anything?"

"I have my purse! And we're going to need to give them our tickets and passports..."

Harry looked sideways at Nico. "We are such suckers."

On the other side of a parked bus, a kiosk with the SS *Aurora* logo advertised Sweet Sweet Aurora Coffee and Hot Chocolate—Free! Beyond that was another cop car, two police just leaning against it. They both had SS *Aurora* hot drink cups in their hands, watching the crowd go by. One of them glanced down at their phone.

Nico wondered if they were looking for him. He'd seen enough TV shows. Did Gold Wheels Preacher have them put out an APB? Was his Wanted photo everywhere? On that cop's phone screen?

He turned his face away from the police, making conversation with Harry. "What are you most excited about, for the trip?"

"Quiet." Harry closed his eyes for a moment, like just the idea of it was blissful. "Thirty-five days of quiet. No emails. No cell phones. No rain gutter emergencies."

Dee wheeled around, stopping them directly in front of the police. They were only eight feet away. *Keep going!* But Dee planted her feet and was glaring at her husband. "We are not going all the way to the Galápagos, to Tierra del Fuego, to visit penguins in Antarctica, just so you can have quiet!"

"True enough," Harry told her. "You'll be there too."

It was like they were onstage. Nico could feel the cops' eyes on the three of them. He fought the urge to look at them and stayed focused on Harry and Dee.

"Oh, you!" She batted at him with her purse, but not like she was trying to hurt him. Then, with a huff, she started walking again.

Harry chuckled and Nico joined in, painfully aware that he needed to seem like he was part of their dysfunctional family as they *finally* rolled past the police.

Thirty more yards, and Nico got the couple and their luggage to the short line for the check-in desk.

"I'll leave you here..." Nico said.

Dee elbowed Harry. "Tip the young man!"

"If I pay him, then his good deed just becomes an exchange of service for money. He won't *feel* like he did something good." Harry looked at Nico to back him up.

Nico kept his face impassive, like he didn't care one way or another.

Dee sighed dramatically. "You're being a cheapskate. He *did* something good. And good should be rewarded in this life. After all," Dee's voice downshifted to seductive, "I got rewarded with you..."

"Come here..." Harry beckoned her into a smooch that went on so long Nico started counting.

People were watching. At thirty-eight seconds Nico wasn't sure if he should stay or go. Was he going to get that tip after all? They didn't seem to care about the very public display of affection, or that Nico was waiting. He felt awkward just standing there. "I'll... just see you later."

"Wait, wait." Harry pulled away and fished a fifty-dollar bill from his wallet. He flashed it in Dee's face, then handed it to Nico. "It's a new Harry." He told her.

"Thank you, sir!" Nico stared at the money. That was a *thousand* cans and bottles. And it took him less than ten minutes. Which meant that now, his cell phone was only forty-six dollars away—920 bottles and cans. *Or...* He took in the crowds of people arriving to board the cruise ship... *Maybe just a few more tips.*

"Have a great trip!" he told them.

"I'm sure you will too!" Dee said.

What? Oh, they think I'm on the cruise with them! "I'm sure it will be great." He clutched the fifty-dollar bill. "Great." He had to stop saying the word *great.* But it was. "I'll see you later."

Dee waved as Nico headed into the crowd.

This could actually work.

11:03

It was already hot, and the throng of passengers just kept coming. Nico figured there must be thousands of people going on the SS *Aurora*. He picked up a discarded brochure and scanned the map of the ship. Thirteen levels—*decks*—lower numbers on the bottom, two main elevator banks. He folded it and stuck it in his back pocket. Maybe someone would ask him a question about the ship and he'd earn an even better tip.

He'd helped five more families. No one was as generous as Harry, but Nico was up to $126 total. Enough for his phone, with six dollars left over. Which was good, because he'd need to eat soon. And figure out somewhere to sleep. And come up with a plan for tomorrow, when there probably wouldn't be a cruise ship leaving...

For now, he was going to find more people to help.

The crew wore satiny red baseball jackets with their embroidered names on the chest, making them easy to spot—and avoid. They were super friendly and helping people with luggage too, but Nico didn't need them asking questions, or seeing him as competition for generous just-starting-on-vacation tips.

The two cops from earlier were strolling through the crowd. One kept checking their cell phone, then studying people's faces. Nico ducked behind a steel beam with a Y branch supporting the roof so they wouldn't see him. Resting in the crook where the riveted metal met was one of the crew jackets. Someone named Jacques must have gotten overheated and tucked it here while they went to do something else. Nico glanced around quickly. No one was looking his way...

He grabbed the jacket and slipped it on. He walked with purpose away from the cops, to the far side of the pier building. There were fewer people, which meant less chance for tips—but it also meant there were fewer crew to recognize that he wasn't *Jacques*.

Baseball hat off and *I'm here to be helpful* face on, Nico was pretty sure he looked like a crew member. He zipped the jacket to mid-chest. It made him feel official, like the police wouldn't give him a second glance. At least, that was the idea.

A woman saw Nico and waved him over. She stood next to a bearded man in a wheelchair—but he wasn't that old. Maybe thirty-five? Neither of them seemed happy. "Will you settle this for us?" She sounded angry. *No*, Nico realized. *She's frustrated.*

"I'll try." Nico told them, nodding hello to the guy in the wheelchair.

"Warren here doesn't want to be pushed on board."

Warren glared at her, stubborn. "Geena here doesn't want to let me—"

"Fall? Break a hip?" she cut him off, voice rising like she was about to sob. "Not be able to go on your dream adventure after all, because we're in some hospital because of your damn pride?"

Warren's voice got low, frustrated himself. "I was going to say, *do anything unless I'm wrapped in Bubble Wrap.* I don't want to board the ship like some invalid."

"You're not your old self, and I'm not strong enough to catch you!"

"I'm not porcelain!"

They fell silent, but the stalemate left them both fuming.

Nico addressed Warren. "This cruise is your dream?"

"Well, before ALS, I had other dreams." He let out a long breath. "But this way I'll still get to see lots of things I've always wanted to."

"Preposition." Geena corrected him.

"You'll have to forgive my sister, Jacques." Warren read the name off Nico's borrowed jacket and gave him a wry grin. "Geena proves you can take the teacher out of the English classroom but you evidently can't vice versa it."

"Very funny." Geena snapped.

"Was that a full sentence?" Warren shot back.

"It seems to me…" Nico said to Warren, "your sister really wants you to have your dream."

"See?" Geena was triumphant.

"But it also seems…" Nico inclined his head to her, "that for it to be your brother's dream, he has to have *some* of the adventure his way."

"Ha!" Warren shot her a *take that* expression.

Geena threw her hands up, confused. "So… what are you suggesting?"

Nico looked from her to him. "A compromise."

1118

The red jacket was a free pass into the boarding area. No one gave Nico a second glance as he pushed Warren in his wheelchair. Geena walked next to them, securing their passports and now-scanned tickets back into her tan fanny pack. She pulled her flowered blouse down over it, as if the pattern would hide the bulge on her hip. The corridor sloped up, turned, and sloped up again, but the actual ramp bridging the pier to the SS *Aurora* was more like a twenty-foot-long tunnel. Nico rolled them to a stop at the edge.

"Ready?" Nico asked Warren, flipping up the wheelchair footrests so they were out of his way.

"Ready." The knuckles of his right hand were white on the handrail as Warren got his feet on the red carpet. He put out his other hand for Nico to pull him up.

Geena seemed worried but just held the wheelchair steady as Warren made the effort to stand.

They were blocking one of the two pedestrian lanes, but nobody scowled or shot them dirty looks. They just merged over as Warren got his unsteady legs under him and let go of the railing, clutching Nico's left forearm. Nico put his right arm friendly-like around Warren's waist, ready to catch him as they made their own, slow way.

The first few steps were mostly on his own power, but by the time they reached the middle of the ramp Nico was supporting most of Warren's weight. "Halfway there. You got this," Nico whispered to him.

Warren's forehead was beaded with sweat. "I fucking hate this."

They both kept walking.

"Use it like fuel." Nico told him, judging the remaining distance. "Come on, three more steps."

Two.

One.

Warren's feet crossed onto the ship. Tremors went through his body as he stiffened to stand tall.

"Welcome aboard," Nico told him, echoing what the pair of crew members were telling the flow of passengers three feet south of them.

Warren's whole face lit up. "I did it, didn't I?"

"Yup." Nico gave the guy credit. He *had* done it.

Warren was still grinning, but he blinked hard. "Maybe I could sit now?"

"Sure." Nico spotted Geena swiping a tear from her cheek as she maneuvered the wheelchair just behind Warren. Making sure to keep his own face and jacket angled away from the real crew people, Nico helped carefully lower him into the seat. Once Warren was settled, they pushed into a lobby atrium six stories high that reminded Nico of a shopping mall.

"Let's find our cabins," Geena told Warren.

Nico offered her the wheelchair handles and stepped forward to say goodbye to Warren. "I should go…"

"No!" Warren grabbed Nico's arm. "Stay and help us. *Please.*"

Geena handed Nico their paperwork like he didn't have any choice. "We're in 1026 and 1028."

Why not? This had all the makings of one heck of a tip. "Okay," he told them, "Deck 10 it is."

11:38

"So, Jacques, tell us: what do we need to know about the ship?" Geena asked as Nico pushed Warren into the less-busy elevator down the hall from the atrium where they'd entered. They'd boarded on Deck 5, and he pressed the "10" button.

There were four other passengers riding up with them, and Nico wasn't sure how to cover that he didn't know anything about the ship besides what he'd seen on the brochure stashed in his back pocket. Were there facts on the flip side of the ship diagram? Could he pull it out and just hand it to Geena, or would that be weird? His eyes flicked to the ceiling, scanning for a service hatch, but he didn't see one. Maybe it was behind the light? They were all waiting for him to say something...

Warren spoke, saving him: "2,501 passengers, 859 crew, top speed 25 knots. Ten restaurants, three bars, a cinema, theater, casino, internet cafe..."

That last one lodged in Nico's mind. Could he get to the internet cafe and reach out to 321Boom and Power2People?

Warren kept rattling off facts: "Six pools, a spa, mini-golf course; there's even a rock climbing wall. Not that I'm going rock climbing anymore."

There was a moment of uncomfortable silence, the other passengers on the elevator avoiding looking at Warren.

"We should have you give the tour!" Nico laughed. It lightened the mood, but Nico could feel their eyes on him, still expecting *some* answer from the crew guy. What could he tell them? "There's so much, I'm still discovering things every day." *Truth.*

That worked. The doors opened on seven and the two women and young girl exited. When the doors closed again, the man remaining turned to Geena and pointed at Warren. "He knows his stuff."

Geena's tone was sharp. "*He* can hear you."

The man blanched. "I'm sorry, I didn't—"

"It's fine." Warren raised a hand to absolve the guy. "I have a lot of time to read."

The doors opened on Deck 9 and the guy bobbed his head nervously and darted out.

When the doors closed again, it was just the three of them.

"It's not *fine*." Geena snapped. "People don't speak to you. It's like they don't even see you because of the chair!"

"They're just scared," Warren said. "I'm a reminder of their own fragile humanity."

Nico thought about it for a second. Maybe he was right, but that sucked.

"But Jacques here isn't scared, are you?" Warren turned his face to Nico.

Nico met his gaze. "You're a human being, sitting down. It's not *that* unusual. I've even sat down a couple of times..."

Warren cackled. "Thank God for Jacques."

"One actual human being out of three thousand," Geena grumbled as the doors opened on their floor.

Nico figured that from her, that was a compliment. So he didn't correct her math out loud. But it was 3,360 passengers and crew.

He scanned the direction plaque to head the correct way as he wheeled Warren onto the Deck 10 landing. *And... we turn right.*

Rooms 1026 and 1028 were close, the second and third cabin from the elevator bank. Their key cards were in the door slots, luggage waiting inside. After confirming Warren's cabin was accessible for a wheelchair user, Geena headed to her room next door, saying something crabby about a nap.

Warren's room was bigger, a Junior Sweet Suite according to the engraved metal plate by the door. In addition to the bed and bathroom, it had a sitting area with a sofa, and a balcony. It was a nice setup.

"Will you wait a minute?" Warren asked him.

"Sure," Nico agreed. *Is that tip coming?*

Warren rolled into the bathroom, sliding the door closed behind him. The angled desk chair would be in his way, so Nico went to move it over by the sofa. Before he could, he noticed an extra key card to the cabin and the Welcome, Warren Bennett cruise itinerary printed out on the built-in desk. Nico scanned it. *Thursday, September 6, San Diego to Wednesday, October 10, Rio de Janeiro.*

His stomach rumbled.

All a person could eat for thirty-five days. And no cops...

Man, I wish I was on this cruise.

The extra key card was just sitting there.

Maybe I can be.

Nico studied the day's schedule for what he needed to know:

1:15 PM	Lifeboat station drill:
	Muster station L, Promenade Level, Deck 4
2:00 PM	Departure
2:45 PM	International Waters; Sweet Sweet Casino opens

The problem: according to the clock in the TV, there was an hour and twenty-five minutes to kill until the drill, and then Nico needed somewhere to lay low until 2:45 PM. He needed a way to be invisible.

The bathroom door slid open and Warren rolled out. Nico grabbed the desk chair and relocated it between the sofa and the stationary part of the balcony's sliding glass door, where it wouldn't be in the way.

Warren eyed his luggage on Nico's side of the bed, two old-style plaid suitcases with an enormous black duffel bag piled on top. He cleared his throat. "I'm sure you have a million places to be, but… is there any chance I can get your help settling in?

And… there's my solution.

"Sure, Warren. Happy to."

As Nico was unpacking and putting Warren's clothes in drawers, he got to a pile of three black V-neck T-shirts. Warren couldn't see Nico's hands from where he was propped up against the bed's headboard. Nico slid one of the T-shirts into the waistband of his jeans, hidden under his jacket. He needed something to wear that wasn't all bloody. He hoped Warren wouldn't notice it was missing.

When everything else was put away, Nico slid the nested empty luggage under the bed. He remembered what Harry told Dee. "That's the great thing about a cruise," Nico told Warren. "You only have to unpack once."

"I did sign up for the two-night Machu Picchu adventure," Warren said. "But I guess you're right."

Nico checked the time on the TV. "Let's get you ready for the drill."

Warren was settled in his chair when white strobe lights flashed in the cabin. A calm woman's voice came on over the wall speakers. "This is a lifeboat drill. Please make your way to your muster stations. This is a drill."

When they knocked on Geena's door, she wrenched it open, frazzled. "Why didn't you tell me there was a drill? I wouldn't have gone to sleep!"

Nico didn't say anything about the schedule on the desk. But Warren couldn't resist the dig. "Jacques and I were ready..."

Geena blew out an exasperated breath. "Even on vacation, you're impossible!" She made a point of ignoring her brother and talked to Nico, instead. "What do I need?"

"Just your key card," Nico told her. "And some shoes."

They waited for the elevator, while a stream of people passed them to take the stairs.

"Excuse me," a woman with a baby in a front-facing carrier and a little boy pulling at her came up to Nico in Jacques's red jacket. "Where are we supposed to go?" She held out her key card so Nico could read it. "Billy, boys who don't listen don't get dessert."

Billy froze like an exaggerated statue.

Nico pointed to the letter under the cruise ship logo. "Lifeboat Station D." He told her. "On the Promenade Level, Deck 4. You can take the elevator down with us."

"I think we need to work off some wiggles on the stairs." She waved thanks. "Okay, you heard the man. Six flights down!"

"Vroom!" Billy burst into action, pulling his mom to join the flow of people heading down.

"Use the handrail!" his mother reminded him.

Nico fielded three more questions by the time he got Warren and Geena to the crowd around Lifeboat Station L. He needed to lose the jacket before someone figured out he wasn't really crew, or worse, he bumped into the real Jacques.

"Time for me to go," Nico told Warren and Geena. "They'll be expecting me at my muster station." *Muster* sounded more crew-speak than *lifeboat.*

"Lots of other people to help, then abandon?" Geena snapped.

"That's not fair." Warren scolded her. "Jacques's been more than generous with his time."

Nico saw the crew member under the "L" sign spot Warren's wheelchair. The guy waved and made his way through the group of passengers toward them.

"You'll be in good hands." Nico told them quickly. "There are 859 of us, remember?" He gave Warren a wink as he started walking away. It had been *his* fact, after all. "I'll see you around."

Because Nico had something better than a tip in mind.

When he looked back, Geena was already talking to the crew guy, but Warren's eyes met his. Warren mouthed *thanks.*

Nico raised a hand and ducked into the interior corridor just as the crew guy glanced his way. He walked fast to the stairwell.

No obstacles.

Nico took the stairs two at a time, back up to Deck 10. Making sure no one was looking, he used the extra key card to let himself into Warren's cabin. He took off the crew jacket and stashed it inside Warren's duffel, inside the smaller plaid suitcase, inside the big plaid suitcase. He slid it all back under the bed.

In the bathroom, Nico peeled off the bloodied rock band T-shirt and checked out his back and shoulder in the mirror. He hissed silently. It looked like he'd been attacked by a cheese grater, and felt worse... At least he could keep it clean.

After throwing the bloody T-shirt in a random trash can on Deck 7, Nico was on the Promenade Level again. This time, he looked for all the world like just another passenger. He'd blend in until they made it to international waters. He just needed to find a place to sleep. He fingered the key card to 1028 in his pocket. It would help, but it wasn't like he could crash with Warren.

Baseball hat hiding his buzzcut, Nico joined the back of the crowd at Muster Station W. He was in Warren's clean black T-shirt with the purple sweatshirt resting over his shoulders like he was some preppy rich kid from a TV show. The crew member, a girl with floppy short locs, was explaining how they'd meet there in an emergency, and how the bright yellow lifeboats could hold everyone on board, and then some.

"Not like the *Titanic*," someone at the front of the crowd said.

"Exactly," the crew member agreed. "Safety first!"

"How do you get inside?" a ten-year-old in the front asked.

The crew member knocked the hard top. "Sometimes the waves are big, so this keeps everyone inside dry. The opening's here." She twisted a knob and a door slid open along the side, revealing rows of metal benches in a bright gray interior.

It felt like that moment, midair, when Nico knew a stunt would work. Like the one he'd come up with in Fresno, just before he'd been kidnapped to Gold Wheels Preacher's Institute. He'd leaped from one building roof to another, using the top of a moving truck as a bridge across the alley. Four feet on either side. Even with his body flying through space, Nico had been certain he'd done the math right—speed, time, motion—three quick steps on the truck roof and he'd jumped again... and nailed the second landing on the gravel roof of some storage building. It had all come together, like he was a real free-run stunt guy.

It had all come together, like this.

Nico eyed the lifeboat interior. *That can't be less comfortable than the cell in the Institute. And on this ship, I'm free.*

4

SAM

SAM WAS TUCKED INTO THE rabbit fur beanbag that still smelled of his grandmother's perfume from when it was her fur coat. He wasn't doing homework, just picking out tuneless notes on his ukulele, a pained experimental-film kind of soundtrack to staring out the window at the reflection of the neon Coca-Cola sign in the East River. In his mind, he was running through all the tells he should have noticed, but hadn't, about Kevin:

- Kevin not wanting to help with the gender-neutral bathroom fight at school.
- Kevin not really getting to know Ari or Frida, or coming along to any of Frida's Crank Shaft performances, or even wanting Sam to know his friends on the swim team.
- Kevin failing Ari's mismatched sock test: Last Monday, Sam had worn two really clashing socks on purpose (pink flamingos with top hats on one foot, neon green and blue plaid on the other). He made sure Kevin noticed, and said, "Wacky, huh?" The point was to see if Kevin could flow with the fun of it, or if he'd be a *tightly wound conservative killjoy*—Ari's

words. Kevin had stared at Sam's very un-Bond-like feet, then slipped off his own loafers, took off his black Polo socks with the single blue embroidered player at the top, and handed them to Sam—saying he'd rather go sockless than be seen with someone who looked like a thrift store clown. Ari had tried to get Sam to admit Kevin had failed the test—spectacularly—but instead Sam obsessed over the chivalry of that gesture. How Kevin had given up his own socks so Sam could have something nice. He'd thought it made Kevin boyfriend material! But looking back now, it was humiliatingly clear.

And the tells Kevin had been into him—into Sam as a person and not just as some guy to fool around with? *Bullshit. Like the whole Le Chiffre rubbing the scar over his messed-up eye when he's bluffing—but not bluffing—in* Casino Royale.

Sam's phone buzzed with a text, which lit up the screen saver: Kevin, all hot in his Speedos, some swim medal around his neck.

Shit. It hit Sam that he didn't even know what the screen saver on Kevin's phone was. The pic on Sam's phone was cropped to just Kevin, but you could tell by the arc of his shoulders that his arms were around some other guys on the team. *Other people.*

The thought hurt, but what was more painful was the idea that maybe he hadn't known Kevin at all. So how could Sam have been so into him? So stupid?

At least he could do something about this. Sam abandoned his ukulele and reached for the phone, ignoring the text from his mom asking if he'd met his college counselor that afternoon.

Predictable. Because there had been a cold snap early, some global warming weather-getting-more-extreme thing, trees in the Green Mountains were already changing color. So Sam's dad had offered to take him on a "Fall Foliage" father-son trip that weekend. And now, suddenly, Danica was trying to be super-mom. *Super-competitive more like it.*

He changed the screen saver back to Craig-Bond coming out of the water in *Casino Royale*, in those square La Perla Grigioperla Lodato light blue swim shorts. Sam had paid a crazy amount for a pair in his size. And those muscles! Daniel Craig's body was more linebacker than swimmer, but Sam wasn't complaining. Overall, much hotter than Kevin. Craig-Bond was a real man. And not a liar, liar, liar.

"Fuck you, Kevin!" Sam shouted. The sound bounced off his bedroom walls—it always resonated better in its current *lounge mode*, with his bed up and out of the way—and the echo made Sam think about his words… "Actually, no." The corner of his mouth tugged up despite himself—it was the first thing that felt funny since their breakup.

The phone in his hand buzzed again. Another text from his mom.

champagne cold boss hot
don't flip it

That… wasn't meant for him.

Sam read it again. And again. He could feel those seven words smashing around inside him like some earthquake.

Holy crap! Is she having an affair? With someone she works with? Someone who works for her?

Sam was up and pacing his room, crisscrossing the zebra-skin rug. Images from liquefaction videos online flashed through his mind. Houses, whole neighborhoods, just buckling, collapsing, the ground under them suddenly moving like waves on a hungry sea. Nothing can take that. Everything topples over. Crumbles. Dissolves into piles of bricks and trash and dust.

Breathe, Sam. Breathe.

He ran through possible explanations. Maybe the air-conditioning was broken at her office.

It's cold early this year.

Maybe the champagne was because she was selling the business after all this time.

She just hosted a party for her top staff to celebrate the sale last week.

But on Monday his parents had celebrated their twentieth wedding anniversary with a big splashy rededication of their vows. *That was only four days ago!*

There's probably a perfectly reasonable and innocent reason for that text, Sam told himself.

But maybe there isn't.

He dialed Ari.

"Q himself probably couldn't imagine how smart phones could make spying so easy," Ari said on the video call once Sam explained what he needed.

"So it'll just look like a regular app?" Sam asked, glancing at his phone as Ari controlled the screen from their side, rewriting some computer code that Sam didn't even know you could see on a cell phone.

Ari dipped their head a fraction of an inch. Today's tiny hat was a soft sculpture sushi-style avocado roll with orange rhinestones standing in for caviar. "Sensei helped me pick out the most boring icon. We're calling it Roomtone."

Sam's screen shifted and a pale gray square with a yellow *R* on it started loading on his home screen.

"Won't my mom notice this happening on her phone?" Sam worried.

Ari raised a brow. "I do get paid to do this."

"I know. I know." Sam put up an apologetic hand. "Sorry."

"I loaded it in the background on Danica's phone five minutes ago." Ari flipped through images on the monitor in front of them. "It's on page seven of her eleven pages of apps. She won't even notice it's there."

"How does it work?" Sam eyed the progress bar—40 percent left to go; 30 percent. When it finished, the Roomtone icon solidified. "It's loaded." Sam reported.

Ari clicked some keys on their setup. "Once we get your phones linked, it will be an open line, and you'll be able to hear everything her phone mic picks up."

"She won't be able to hear *me*, right?"

"Totally understandable fear," Ari acknowledged. "It's a one-way connection. Your mom's phone is just set up to narrow-cast, and yours is just set up to receive."

"Thanks for this," Sam said.

"I'm always here for you, Sam." Ari kept their eyes on their monitors. "Anyway, it's fun to do stuff together, right?" They risked a quick glance at Sam, but Sam was focused on his cell. Ari blinked a few times, forcing a smile. "Okay, we're ready. Press the icon to listen, close it to stop. Let me know what you find out?"

Sam nodded as Ari logged off.

He pressed the Roomtone icon, which added a narrow yellow outline to match the old-fashioned *R* inside it.

Suddenly Sam's phone was playing the audio from CNN—like always, his mom had the news on in the background. He could hear the clicking of keys on her laptop.

And as much as he loved James Bond, it hit Sam how weird it was that now *he* was a spy—on his own mom.

It wasn't even ten minutes before Sam made his first discovery: real spy work was boring.

So he did other things while listening on his earbuds: Lowered the bed, stripped the sheets so he wouldn't smell Kevin on them, and tossed them in the laundry closet. Put the whole thing together with fresh sheets and hoisted it back into the wall unit. Read his pages for history. Microwaved some sushi rice and unagi from Kurosaka—Ari's hat reminded him they had leftovers. Surfed videos online. And ultimately, decided to watch *Goldfinger* for like the hundredth time.

Connery-Bond was just discovering Jill Masterson's murdered-by-being-painted-gold body when Sam's mom had her first conversation—ripping into the PR company for not getting more national coverage of Sam's parents' Labor Day Renewal of Vows and Twentieth Anniversary Blowout at the top of the Empire State Building. Evidently, his parents and their 174 closest friends, plus Sam, weren't "celebrity" enough, and she wasn't happy about it. But as far as catching his mom cheating, or proving she wasn't?

Bust.

Bond was strapped to Goldfinger's laser table, bargaining for his life, when Sam got to hear his dad bailing on their weekend trip to Vermont.

"I'm tied up at the studio," Sam's dad told his mom. "It's looking like it's going to take all weekend."

"Michael." There was so much annoyance in her saying just his dad's name that Sam cringed. But it wasn't proof of anything. "My weekend's already booked solid." his mom said. "There are a lot of moving parts of the sale to manage."

"I'm not trying to screw this up for you," Sam's dad said.

But you'll screw up **our** *weekend*, Sam thought.

There was a pause, and then Sam's mom said, "He's almost

seventeen. I was on my own for two years by then. We did a shitty job as parents if he can't figure out one weekend to himself."

He thought about turning off the app, but no one said being a spy was going to be comfortable. Bond was nearly sliced in half by a laser beam! So instead, Sam kept listening. He tried to focus on the movie as Bond met Pussy Galore at gunpoint. *That name! And the smirk on Bond's face!*

Bond was trapped in the basement holding room, braced—hands and feet—against the walls above the doorway, ready to ambush the guard when someone came into Sam's mom's office and she said, "That took you long enough."

Sam paused the scene.

A man—not Sam's dad—spoke. The voice was scratchy, and weirdly familiar. "You'll never have to work again."

Sam's mom replied, "What would I do if I wasn't working?"

"You've earned a break, that's all."

Sam tried to place the voice… Then he remembered, *her assistant Jesse.* There was that toast he'd given at the anniversary party, congratulations on behalf of everyone at Sam's mom's company. It had sounded like he'd been shouting and lost his voice, and it was just coming back. Four days later, he still sounded that way. Sam guessed maybe that was Jesse's thing, a fake gruff voice that didn't match his delicate features any more than his lumberjack beard went with his skinny suit and tie.

Sam's mom answered Jesse: "Look who's talking, running up to New Haven when the contract's already all negotiated."

"Not signed yet. Someone very wise taught me buy-in works better in person."

"They'll sign."

"And then," Jesse answered, "I'll take a break if you will."

"That sounds like a dare." Sam's mom sounded amused.

"Okay," Jesse said. "I… dare… you."

There was a pause. A rustle of fabric.

Sam boosted the volume to not miss anything. His mom's voice was muffled, but he could just make it out: "Do I have to fire you so this isn't sexual harassment?"

Sam stared at his phone, pulse racing.

"I already signed the NDA," Jesse said.

The silence dragged.

"Mmmm." Sam's mom said, "Buy-in *does* work better in person."

"Want me to pour that champagne?" Jesse asked.

Sam's mom scoffed. "Shut up and kiss me."

Busted. So, so busted.

Breathing fast like he'd just gone for a run, Sam closed the app. He didn't want to hear any more. He didn't think he could stand it.

Don't you fucking cry! Don't.

One Good Thing

In <u>Goldfinger</u>, Pussy Galore (!) tells Connery–Bond on the private plane to America that she's "immune" to his charms. That and her Pussy Galore's Flying Circus girl pilots make it pretty clear she's a lesbian. But 31 minutes and 20 seconds of screen time later, Pussy and Bond are sort of play–fighting in a barn on Goldfinger's Kentucky stud farm (ha!) and Bond forces a kiss — consent, anyone? — and suddenly she's pulling him in closer to her. We know they're going to be doing it…

After the fade–out, Pussy is Bond's secret ally, betraying Goldfinger and swapping out the Delta–9 gas for air freshener — foiling the villain's plan to kill all the US military surrounding Fort Knox with her all-girl team of crop dusters. "What made her call Washington?" Bond gets asked by his CIA buddies after the nuclear bomb to irradiate all the gold is defused (countdown clock stopped on the perfect "007").

As an answer, Bond kind of smirks, and his body language is all, _Yeah, I have a magical penis..._

His actual line of dialog is some throwaway bullshit about how he must have awakened a "maternal" instinct in her.

WTF?

There was nothing maternal about that fade-out, unless we were supposed to think Bond got her pregnant.

Was there no actual lesbian on the production team? Had no one, of the hundreds of people who worked on the movie, ever even met a lesbian? Was it supposed to be some super-orgasm that changed Pussy's mind? _So_ the sexist, heteronormative bullshit of the Bond mentality, where all a lesbian needs to make her straight is a magical penis. A roll in the hay (literally) with a _real_ man. Like all you'd need to be straight is a roll in the hay with a real woman. _No thank you._

Could they even get away with this shit today, or would the Queer community cry foul?

Did they, back in 1964? Five years before Stonewall... Maybe not.

Why call her "Pussy Galore"? Like the only thing about being Queer is how we have sex. Like we don't have hearts that love.

And break.

Maybe "Pussy Galore" was to keep it all about sex. It was all about sex for Kevin.

That actually hurt to write.

Stop being such a pussy, Solomon! Pussy Galore.

Is it all about sex for your mom and Jesse? Ugh. You don't want to even think about your mom having sex.

What about love? Your mom and dad took vows — twice! For God's sake, the second time was just Monday. Twenty years together! Maybe it's like Pussy's allegiance to Goldfinger. Bond's magical penis wooed her away...

So your liar mom's allegiance to your dad was no match for the liquefaction power of Jesse's magical penis?

Ick.

<u>So</u> ick!

What else could it be? An easy internet search confirmed it. Jesse is 16 years younger than your mom. He's only 15 years older than you. If he was Gay, <u>you</u> could date him.

Double ick.

Pussy's change of heart is this giant plot hole in <u>Goldfinger</u>, unless you believe in the magical penis theory.

So, one good thing? Maybe it's good to know that some people have a magical penis. And you're either wary of that, or you make sure you're the one with that magic down under.

Bond would absolutely have some quip about Australia here. "Thunder from Down Under" is some male stripper show in Vegas. Thank you, internet. But even that's pretty clearly marketed "to the ladies."

Where's the Gay Aussie stripper show?

Like you'd be brave enough to go to that. Fun to think about though.

But really, even the way Bond walks—that swagger—it's like he <u>knows</u> his penis is magical.

Confidence radiates off him in waves.

He's so freaking handsome. Dapper. Sexy. Craig-Bond coming out of the Caribbean Sea in <u>Casino Royale</u>. Water rolling down his abs. Tanned skin. Muscles everywhere. Crazy, crazy hot.

Everybody wants him. And Bond knows it. And he kind of pretends he doesn't notice. He just owns it, in everything he does. Even how he walks.

You could try walking across campus like that. Hear every person at St. Bacchus laugh at you. Even the books in the library would laugh.

No one laughs at Bond.

Why?

Because he's got magical penis swagger. Just another tool (ha!) he uses to save the world.

Something to add to Frida's list of things you can't buy:

MAGICAL PENIS SWAGGER

Goes hand-in-hand with being the strongest guy in the room—and that's not muscles, or being able to knock out the biggest henchman—that's about not giving a flying fuck. About anyone. Or anything. Except the saving-the-world mission.

Add it to the list:

STOP CARING

Dr. Sanchez would appreciate that you have a goal. Two goals, actually. <u>Bond-goals.</u>

God knows you're never going to tell her what they are.

So how do you get to be that person?

And what the hell are you going to do about Kevin? Your mom? Your dad?

You've got to tell your dad... Don't you?

5

NICO

Gold Wheels Preacher glanced at the computer tablet in his hand and, seeing something he liked, touched the screen.

Nico was back in the Institute, tied down to the barber chair in the intake room. Past his long hair, the corner of Nico's eye caught the door frame light change from green to red. He could feel the cold metal of a necklace against his skin.

It was happening, all over again...

"Welcome, Number Seventy."

Nico wasn't going to answer to Number Seventy. "My name is Nico. But you should call me Nicolas."

"Interesting artifice... Your real name is Peter."

"My real name is Nicolas Hall."

Gold Wheels Preacher double-checked something on his tablet. "Peter Josefs."

Nico narrowed his eyes. *I know who I am.* Just because the people formerly known as his parents called him Peter, didn't mean that was his name now. *A name is something that has meaning.*

"I'm not going to argue with you." Gold Wheels Preacher set the tablet down and opened a cupboard. "Here, you'll be called Number Seventy."

With a flourish like some bullfighter he fastened a black nylon cape around his own neck, then took out electric clippers.

Nico was defiant the only way he could be. "I'm not going to answer to Number Seventy."

"I hear your soul struggle." Gold Wheels Preacher adjusted something on the clippers. "The eternal battle, between Heaven and Hell."

"Which side are you on?" Nico asked.

Gold Wheels Preacher seemed surprised by the question. "Yours, of course." He turned the clippers on. "The more you move, the worse it will come out. But that doesn't matter either. For man looketh on the outward appearance, but the Lord looketh on the heart. Samuel 16:7."

As cut hair fell past his eyes, Nico decided there was no point in struggling. He was tied down, and Gold Wheels Preacher was going to cut his hair no matter what. He might as well avoid looking like an idiot. But why make it easier for him? No. Better to keep still. Let him think I'm no risk, then when he least expects it, *POW!* I'll be gone.

So he held still, except for his leg. Vibrating as fast as the clippers.

It was a buzzcut. There was no mirror, but Nico could feel the air of the room get cooler all over his head.

Finished, Gold Wheels Preacher stood back. Cut hairs itched down the back of Nico's T-shirt. Stuck to his bleeding wrist.

"And now, your training," Gold Wheels Preacher said, like he was talking to a dog. It wasn't winning Nico over.

Gold Wheels Preacher put away the hair-cutting tools and came back with a pair of red-handled wire clippers. As the metal point came close Nico leaned away, which prompted an innocent "I'm not here to hurt you."

Liar.

Five snips and Nico was free. His wrists too. He let out a breath it felt like he'd been holding since Fresno when those guys tackled him. Kidnapped him here. Gold Wheels Preacher turned to put the wire clippers back in a drawer. The doorway was open—

Go, Nico! Now!

Nico burst forward and his neck started to tingle. In two steps he was even with the doorway and—

Nico forced himself awake a split-second before Gold Wheels Preacher zapped him.

The dream memory had left him drenched in sweat and gasping like there was no air in the lifeboat. He let out a groan, trying to push away the memory, the pain of being electrocuted by the collar, the darkness, the anger—and most of all the guilt, knowing that he'd left Bec and all the others behind.

He checked the time on his phone: 4:41 AM.

There was no going back to sleep now.

FRI 7 SEP

0522

SS AURORA: INTERNATIONAL WATERS 120 MILES WEST EL ROSARIO DE ARRIBA MEXICO

No Obstacles: Hey.

321Boom: Hey!!! You okay? We were worried.

Power2People: I told her you probably just lost your phone.

321Boom: and I told HIM you were too responsible for that

Power2People: accidents happen

No Obstacles: It wasn't an accident, but yeah, no phone. Sitting in an internet cafe.

321Boom: You should have let us know you were safe.

No Obstacles: First chance I've had. A lot's happened.

Power2People: They moved you again, didn't they?

Nico's fingers paused above the keyboard. He checked, but he was still the only person in the Sea-Wide-Web lounge. How much did he want to tell them?

No Obstacles: They did, but it didn't work out. So I
    moved myself. Kind of on my own now.

321Boom: You are NOT on your own. We're here.

Power2People: What she said.

Nico bit his lip, but typed what he was thinking anyway.

No Obstacles: Here where? The vloggers lounge?

321Boom: and wherever else you need us to be. Heck,
    I'm retired, I can hop on a plane.

Power2People: I can be there in whatever the speed
    limit allows.

321Boom: Do you need us to come to you?

Power2People: Do you want us to?

Nico looked out the row of round windows to the water stretching to the horizon, and took a shaky breath. It wasn't *come live with me*, or *let us be your family*. 321Boom probably lived in one of those fifty-five-and-older gated communities. Power2People featured a different town or city in every video, so he might not even have a home.

Or... maybe they just didn't care *that* much. After all, Nico was kind of a stranger.

But offering to help by coming to him was something.

It's probably all I can hope for. More than I deserve. He blinked until his vision got clear again. The connection, even if it wasn't the dream, was something to hold on to.

He needed something to hold on to.

> **No Obstacles:** Thanks. I'm OK for now. Can we just keep talking?
>
> **321Boom:** Sure, hon.
>
> **No Obstacles:** What's been going on? Catch me up.
>
> **Power2People:** Did you know that up to half of the eggs in a starlings' nest aren't genetically related to their parents? I was reading about these DNA tests. Turns out these birds drop their eggs in someone else's nest, and then those parents raise them along with their own.

At least all those birds got a family, and a nest.

But then, Nico considered, he was sitting in a cushy orange desk chair on a luxury cruise ship, and there was a breakfast buffet that opened in thirty-two minutes. Not a bad temporary nest.

SUN 9 SEP
1143
SS AURORA: INTERNATIONAL WATERS 60 MILES WEST MANZANILLO MEXICO

Day seventy-three for Bec. Keeping count, like some guilt vigil, seemed the least he could do. The nightmare memories didn't stop. And Nico couldn't do much more than try to keep himself from being caught. Even though he used a different lifeboat every night, and he timed it to be super late when he went in and super early when he snuck out, his heart raced every time. He needed more clothes, or a way to clean these. He needed to take another shower, but he had to wait for Warren to go ashore to know he could use the cabin again without getting caught. He needed to fit in with the rest of the passengers but he didn't have a bathing suit and wasn't going to take off his T-shirt again because of all the scars. The one time he *had* taken it off led to endless questions about his fictional "skateboard accident."

At least there was food—ridiculous amounts of it, multiple buffets for every meal—and tables with open seating. He avoided the pizza. It reminded him too much of the bribes to squeal on each other in Gold Wheels Preacher's Institute. But the rest of the food was amazing. The challenge was, sitting alone attracted too many curious strangers. *Where's your family? Where are you from? What cabin are you in?*

So when Warren spotted Nico at the pasta station for lunch and rolled over to him with "Beautiful day, isn't it Jacques? Care to join us?" Nico said yes. An hour without having to make up any new lies sounded good.

Warren wheeled himself forward, but someone grabbed Nico's arm as he followed with Warren's and his own plate. "Yoo-hoo!"

It was Dee. "Harry!" She elbowed her husband next to her. He was lost in the sketch pad open in front of him. "It's our young friend!"

"Hi!" Nico cursed himself for not having seen them earlier. For not avoiding them. He needed to be more invisible.

Harry gave a "Hmm" of acknowledgement, then went back to sketching what looked like a rain gutter with flaps.

"You enjoying the cruise, hon?" Dee gushed.

"It's great." Nico realized she thought he was a passenger, but Warren and Geena thought he was crew. *Yikes. Got to keep them separate.*

Dee made a *tsk* sound and pointed to the plates in Nico's hands. "I don't want your food to get cold. Are those for your family?"

"Uh, yes." Nico felt hopeful that he'd be able to get away.

"Well, come on! I want to meet them!" Dee was up and had her hand on Nico's shoulder before he could come up with a way out of it. "I don't think you ever told us your name?"

"Jacques." Nico told her. At least they'd all be calling him the same thing.

They arrived at the table and Nico was grateful it was just Warren.

"A friend of yours?" Warren asked.

"I'm just so happy to meet Jacques's people." Dee pumped Warren's hand. Her eyes took in his wheelchair. "You have a special boy, right here."

Warren seemed about to ask Dee what she meant, so Nico jumped in with a question of his own. "Where's Geena?"

"She's signing up for the singles miniature golf round robin after all." Warren snorted. "Though it seems an improbable place to meet Prince Charming."

"Don't knock it." Dee said. "I met my Harry at an indoor glow-in-the-dark miniature golf party, and we're going on thirty-three years! Yoo-hoo!" She called across the dining room to Harry, who waved without raising his head, busy adding something to his sketch. Dee reddened. "It's good to have your own interests. That keeps it fresh."

Nico put down their overflowing plates. "Well, it was good seeing you, Mrs...."

"Oh, you just call me Dee. Everyone does." She glanced from Nico to Warren and back again. "I don't want to take away from family time—we all know how precious that is. You two sit and enjoy—" Dee's eyes widened at Warren in his wheelchair. "Oh, I hope I didn't just offend!"

"No, it's fine." Warren assured her. "I sit a lot these days."

"Well... enjoy." With an awkward finger wave, Dee headed back to Harry.

Once she was gone, Warren turned to Nico. "Family time?"

Nico shrugged like there was no accounting for wacky strangers. "She calls everybody 'family.' I helped her and her husband with their luggage the day we left San Diego, and she practically adopted me!" Nico tried to chuckle, but the sound caught in his throat, choking him.

"You okay?"

After a sip of water, Nico managed, "Just went down the wrong way."

But then he couldn't shake the thought: *No one's ever wanted to adopt me.*

1328

"It would suck to be a pawn," Nico told Warren, taking one of Warren's off the chessboard with his own knight—two up, one over, in an L.

They'd gone from lunch to Warren teaching Nico chess in the Deck 10 library. With only one self-serve shelf of books, the space seemed more about overstuffed chairs and fancy game tables than reading. But it was just down the hall from Warren's cabin, and they had it to themselves.

"Sometimes," Warren observed, "it sucks to be the knight." And with his bishop he took Nico's knight off the board.

Damn. He had to be more careful.

Nico squinted at the setup, trying to do a better job at predicting the future. Or, better yet, steer it. If he moved that pawn, and Warren fell for it, Nico's queen could take Warren's bishop.

"How was Cabo yesterday?" Nico asked, trying to distract Warren from the maneuver. Nico hadn't gone, figuring the less he used Jacques's crew jacket, the better. And it had given him the chance to duck into Warren's cabin for a quick shower.

"Honestly?" Warren glanced up from the board. "It sucked. They couldn't find their *one* sand wheelchair. And the launch boat couldn't get me closer than two hundred yards down the beach from the arch in the cliff. I can't walk two hundred yards. Not anymore."

Warren didn't take the pawn, and instead his rook was suddenly threatening Nico's queen.

Nico pushed her to safety.

Warren pursued with his rook, keeping her in danger. "It was the one thing I wanted to see, up close, with my own eyes. Everyone else got off the boat, staring at me like I'm some freak. I made Geena get off so she could at least take pictures and tell me about it. And then I had to sit there in the sun. Waiting for everyone to do what I can't anymore." He turned to stare at the "Free Library" shelf, dog-eared novels finished by previous cruisers and left behind to make room in their luggage for souvenirs. "I finally made them bring me back to the ship."

Nico knew that if he'd been there, he could have helped. Given Warren a piggyback ride. Something. But he hadn't been, because he was too busy protecting his own skin. "I'm really sorry."

Warren shrugged. "Sometimes, it sucks to be Warren."

Nico saw a move he hadn't before. "Sucks worse to be your rook!" And he took it with his one remaining pawn.

MON 10 SEP

0823

SS AURORA: PORT ACAPULCO MEXICO

Day seventy-four for Bec.

Nico had been working on his second refill at the breakfast buffet when Geena found him and insisted he come talk sense into Warren, who was holed up in his cabin.

"You'll miss the cliff divers," Geena scolded her brother.

Warren picked listlessly at his room service breakfast. "I'll see it on YouTube." He was wearing jeans and one of his black T-shirts, a match for the one Nico had *borrowed* and was still wearing, with the little red embroidered rectangle on the sleeve. Except Nico's wasn't smelling so fresh. Dressed alike, Nico guessed that he and Warren probably seemed like the siblings.

"Why are we even here, then?" Geena snapped. "Isn't it so you can experience these things yourself?

"I don't enjoy being a spectacle, okay?" Warren shot back.

Like in Cabo. And Nico had already told them that he couldn't go ashore with them here in Acapulco either. But Warren sitting in his cabin meant that Nico wouldn't get to use this place... So no shower, or getting to stop checking over his shoulder for suspicious crew members all day. And he'd been planning to wash the T-shirt and jeans in the shower and dry them with the hair dryer. Laundry, stowaway style.

"The cliff divers are supposed to be pretty incredible," Nico said.

"Why don't you two go?" Warren focused on shredding his croissant into little pieces, like he was going to feed a miniature bird.

Geena threw her hands up. "If it's this pity-party or Acapulco, *I'm* going ashore."

After the cabin door slammed shut behind her, they just sat there, silent.

"Anything I can do?" Nico asked.

Warren didn't answer, just tore flakes of pastry smaller and smaller.

Maybe, Nico thought, he could go with Warren without wearing the crew jacket, like he was just a passenger too. "I can try to shuffle my schedule to see if I can get the morning off. Then, I can come along to help out."

There was more silence, and Nico felt compelled to fill it: "I would have given you a piggyback ride to see the arch, if I'd been there."

"Like that wouldn't have been humiliating." Warren deadpanned.

Nico flinched. He was right. "What I mean, is... I would have tried to help."

"I do have a question." Warren's sharp eyes locked on Nico's. "It's our fourth day at sea, right?"

"Yes." Nico wasn't sure where he was going with this.

"So how come I've never seen you in anything but jeans and a black T-shirt?"

What did he know?

"The exact same T-shirt I have. From this store in Israel. Castro." He pointed to the embroidered red rectangle on his own sleeve. "It seems quite the coincidence, doesn't it?"

Nico tried to keep it light. "We both have good taste."

"Jacques."

He suspected something. *Shit.* But Nico didn't have to admit to anything.

"Why don't you and I go swimming while the crowds are exploring Mexico?" Warren said. "You can use one of my swim trunks. You know what drawer they're in better than I do."

1006

The adult pool on Deck 11 was empty, only an older woman sunbathing on a lounge chair with a silk scarf over her face. Nico wheeled Warren right up to the stairs leading into the water and parked the wheelchair sideways. He couldn't get his T-shirt wet as it was his only one, so Nico pulled it off, grimacing as the newly scabbing skin stretched. Maybe the water would be good for it.

Together, they got Warren standing, pulled the robe off his shoulders, and with Nico's arm around the older man's waist and Warren gripping the handrail, they stepped over the white plastic edging onto the first step. The day was hot, and cool water washed over their toes.

"Stairs are a bitch," Warren hissed. "ALS is too. But in the water, everything is a little easier."

"We'll do it together, okay?" Nico told him, counting down the steps as they took them. "Three. Two... And we're in."

Warren floated free of Nico, wriggling in the liquid supporting him. He dropped his head under the surface, making Nico tense, but then Warren moved his arms and legs to propel himself forward. He rolled onto his back to breathe, starting a series of slow kicks to the far edge. He turned and followed the curve of the oval pool back to where Nico stood chest deep in the water.

Warren was no Olympic swimmer, but it was pretty beautiful all the same, seeing him in charge of his own body again—even if it was just for this moment.

Nico lowered down to get his cuts under water. He closed his eyes, enjoying the contrast of the sun's heat and the water's coolness.

As Warren approached Nico on his next lap, he whispered. "I'm not going to tell anyone. But you need a place to sleep. And some different clothes. I think we can help each other."

Nico's eyes flew open, but Warren didn't even break his pattern of small kicks. Nico turned to see if the woman on her lounge chair had heard. He couldn't tell.

"We'll talk about it later," Warren said, kicking steadily to make another round of the pool.

Shit!

1924
ACAPULCO MEXICO

It was just before sunset, and their outdoor table had a great view of the cliff where divers were supposed to do their thing every half hour. A piano player on the restaurant's patio played soft rock over the clatter of silverware and glasses around them.

Leg bouncing with nervous energy, Nico focused on rolling up the sleeves of the borrowed green plaid shirt Warren had insisted he wear. *When is he going to bring it up? Is he just playing with me? Did he already rat me out?*

But if Warren had told the ship's crew about Nico, he wouldn't be sitting there in clean clothes, drinking a bottle of orange soda with a fancy dinner on its way. He'd be arrested. In some jail. Or on his way back to Gold Wheels Preacher and the Institute.

"So…" Nico said. It was like the chess game, waiting for Warren to make his next move.

"So," Warren echoed, a smiled playing on his face as he took a slow sip of wine.

Nico's eyes traced a path through the other tables to the street. If this went wrong, he'd run. But where the hell could he go in Acapulco? All he had was $126 in his pocket. He'd get to a computer. See if 321Boom or Power2People could help.

So whatever happened with Warren, this wouldn't be checkmate. There was always another move, even if it was just to flip the board and start over. He'd started over lots of times.

Finally, Warren set down his glass. "The sofa bed, sharing my clothes, and cabin. For your assistance with daily swims and excursions like this."

Negotiation. Nico could do this.

"And you don't tell anyone," Nico said, rolling down the sleeves so he had something to do with his hands. The plaid shirt fit pretty well. "Not Geena, no one."

"And you help me with meals and mobility so Geena gets a break. God knows, the way this is going…" Warren glanced down—at his body or the wheelchair, Nico wasn't sure. "Some part of this needs to be a vacation for her."

Thirty more days of all he could eat, a safe place to sleep, avoiding a million questions from the other passengers, and helping a nice guy who needed the help—there was no downside Nico could see. He'd have to figure out what to do when they reached Rio de Janeiro, but until then... "Deal."

"I'm glad we agree." Warren raised his wine glass, gesturing to Nico's soda.

They clinked to the arrangement.

The piano played a flourish and everything went silent around them. They turned to watch a guy maybe ten years older than Nico in Speedos pause at the top of the cliff like a statue, silhouetted against the sherbet-colored sky. Then he leaped off, arms out like some exotic bird flying down sixty feet to splash into the water below. The tourists around them applauded, and Nico and Warren joined in.

"I wish I was that brave," Warren said as they watched the next diver, a young woman in a one-piece racing swimsuit, climb barefoot up the jagged cliff face to a different invisible launch point.

Nico thought of Warren going on this trip when his body was falling apart on him. He had checked it out online. ALS was a nervous system disease, where your muscles get weaker and weaker and eventually stop working. Doctors were working on it, but there was no cure.

Another dive, this time with a midair twist that had the tourists around them gasp. The diver sliced into the water and applause burst around them.

"There's lots of ways to be brave," Nico said.

Warren stared at him. "Was it jumping off a cliff that got you all scarred up?"

Of course, Warren had seen his back, in the pool.

Maybe he'd tell Warren someday. For now, Nico just said, "A different kind of cliff."

"Or maybe..." Warren swirled the last sip of wine in his glass and signaled to their server. "It was a different kind of brave?"

6

SAM

"So you think I'm doing the right thing?" Sam spoke low, knowing Frida could hear him through the earbud. He turned on the run-down block west of Hudson where his dad had his art studio.

"Wouldn't *you* want to know?" Frida asked.

Sam thought about how humiliating it had been when Kevin told him he had been fooling around with other guys, and how much worse it would have been if it had dragged on longer. If he'd been made a fool of for even one more day.

Didn't someone owe his dad the truth? And if his mom wasn't going to do it… "Yeah."

Sam paused outside Circus of Porn, staring across the street to the windows of his dad's fifth-floor studio. The shades were pulled up from the bottom halfway, which meant his dad was there. Ever since his dad started working with Yolanda, this creativity coach, trying to get his fine artist career un-stalled, he'd been spending more time here than in the art restoration room he had at home.

A hot guy with a yoga mat strapped to his back checked Sam out as he walked by, but Sam wasn't going there.

"Do you want me to stay on the call?" Frida asked.

"No." Sam took a deep breath. "I got it from here. Thanks for holding my hand this far."

"Anytime. Romantic crises are kind of my thing."

Not mine, Sam thought as he hung up and crossed the street. Then again, he wasn't also a drag king slam poet with thousands of views for each uploaded performance.

He redialed as he climbed the stairs of his dad's building.

"That was fast."

"No, haven't done it yet. Just, you're not going to do a whole Crank Shaft thing on this, are you?"

"I'll change every name. Always have to protect the guilty."

"You mean innocent."

"I'm not convinced there's anyone in that category."

"Frida…" He knew there was no winning on this one. *Her life, her art.* He just hoped she'd be kind. Then again, Crank Shaft wasn't known for kind.

"You're stalling," she pointed out.

"Talk to you later."

"I know."

Sam hung up again as he passed the fifth-floor doorway and headed to the roof so he could peek through the skylight. If his dad was on break, he'd go down and knock. If he was in the middle of a painting, Sam could wait. He knew that technically it was more stalling, but this way he wouldn't get him all crabby from interrupting his "creative flow," if it was flowing.

It wasn't a roof for sunbathing, more just to access the air-conditioning units, so Sam picked his way across pipes and loose TV cables to get close enough to the sloped glass skylight to see in. He hunched down and peered into the artist loft.

His dad was standing there. *Naked.* Covered with a million colors of paint. At least he was facing the other way. Yolanda, in a sweatshirt and jeans, was circling him.

What the...? The thought stalled out as Sam saw his dad was painting his own body. Yolanda paused, her face just inches from Sam's dad's.

Sam's dad dipped his head toward hers. *Is he going to kiss her?*

Yolanda stopped him with a coy finger to his mouth.

"Paint me first," Sam heard her through the skylight's ancient glass. Yolanda pulled off her sweatshirt—she wasn't wearing a bra—and Sam lurched away.

Creativity coach? More like sex coach. Holy crap!

He tried to slow his breaths. *Get it under control, Solomon.*

His legs felt unsteady as he made his way back to the stairs, trying to not make any noise.

Is their whole marriage some kind of bad joke? What about the whole retaking their vows? Do they even love each other anymore?

And then, the thought stopped him cold in the stairwell: *Did they ever love each other, or was it always just an act? An accident, like some accidental pregnancy? An accidental marriage?*

Was I an accident?

Am I the only reason they're together?

Sam forced himself to keep moving, out of the building, to the subway, onto the train uptown.

He stared out the window at the dark tunnel rushing by and swiped at a tear, pissed at himself for being so weak. For caring so much.

Bond wouldn't freak out; 007 goes into every situation with a plan.

Everyone was gathering at Mais Monsieur that night for Sam's birthday dinner.

What's your plan, Solomon?

1813
UPPER EAST SIDE MANHATTAN NY

Sam was walking into the apartment when his grandmother video-
called him. He sighed. It was talk to her now or later. At least he knew
he would never tell her about his dad—her precious son—fooling
around. Was he supposed to tell his mom? Did their cheating cancel
each other out?

He pressed talk and propped his phone on the wooden tray filled
with his dad's colorful spice jars. They never cooked with them—it
was more about the decoration. He grabbed some almond butter and
pretzels and sat on a leather stool.

His grandmother's face wrinkled with a wide grin. She started
clapping and singing in Hebrew, "Hayom yom huledet, hayom yom
huledet, hayom yom huledet le Sa-mi-ka! Hayom yom huledet, hayom
yom huledet, hayom yom huledet le Sa-mi-ka!"

"Thanks, Savta."

"It's really machar, but I don't want your father to think I forgot."
His parents had decided when Sam was a baby that, living in
Manhattan, 9/11 wasn't the best day to celebrate. Sam hadn't even
known September 10 wasn't his real birthday until the rabbi let it
slip when they were planning his bar mitzvah back in seventh grade.

"What do you want for your gift this year?" his grandmother asked.

Sam shrugged. "I don't know."

"I used to tell your father, if you don't make your needs known,
you have very little chance of having them met."

He covered his mouth and spoke through a mouthful of food so
he wouldn't get a lecture on how his Dad didn't teach him any table
manners, not to mention his mom. "When I figure out what I need,
I'll let you know. Promise."

"Next year, we know the gift. You'll be eighteen—chai—lucky number! And you'll be in charge of Saba's hotel." She gave him a sly expression. "Unless, of course, you meet some nice girl first and get married. Then you won't be a minor and we can make it a wedding present!"

"Savta. We talked about this. A nice boy."

"The right girl might change your mind…"

"You think the right girl could change *your* mind?" Sam deadpanned.

Her laughs came in waves, and Sam couldn't help but laugh too.

"I'm not so into dating, Samika."

"Why not?

She made a sour face. "Who's the pushy grandmother here?"

"I love you, Savta."

"I love you! I miss you! But I don't miss the cold."

"I miss you too."

"Happy birthday, early." She blew him seventeen loud kisses, pressing her lips so hard Sam could see the lipstick on her fingers. "And don't think you're getting out of getting a present!"

"I don't need anything."

"When you think of what it is, Savta will be right here. Or, maybe by the pool. But I'll have my phone!"

"Thanks. Love you."

"Oh. My Samika." She put her hand over her heart. "I love you too." Her eyes were wet as Sam disconnected the call.

He felt a little better, but he had to get his head in the game. He didn't have a lot of time.

1900

Sam was downstairs in time to watch Zoltan pull up in a silver Lamborghini, with a cherry-red McClaren right behind him. The McClaren was driven by Cyn, one of Zoltan's team of drivers. Sam wondered if they were dating. Zoltan was hot, for a guy in his thirties. He rocked the shaved head thing. Different than Ari with their tiny hats set "just so" on the polished surface. Zoltan's version was more testosterone style.

Sam heard the echo of his grandmother's words when he came out to her last year. "You're so handsome." She'd touched his cheek. "What a waste."

"I promise you, Savta. It's not wasted."

That got her laughing. Got them both laughing.

He was pretty sure Zoltan wasn't wasting it either.

Zoltan hopped out and dangled a key fob from each hand. "Man of the hour... Which will it be?" Sam had driven both cars before, and Zoltan knew they were among his favorites.

Sam snagged the key to the silver Lamborghini and told himself Ari and Frida would be fine in the tiny backseat. It wasn't that long a drive to the restaurant.

Zoltan started over to the McClaren.

"Wait. You're letting me take it myself?" Sam heard the surprise in his own voice.

"A hundred and four hours of driving the best of the best? It's made you the best." Zoltan had the passenger door to the McClaren already open. "Go get your friends, drive around, have fun. I'll need it back by midnight."

"What am I, Cinderella? Two AM"

"One AM"

"One thirty?" Sam hoped he wasn't pushing his luck.

"Happy birthday, Sam."

1948

CENTRAL PARK WEST MANHATTAN NY

Sam pulled up fast and smooth outside the restaurant, with Frida in the passenger seat and Ari stretched across both backseats behind them. Heads turned. Two valets jumped to their doors. People on the sidewalk paused to stare.

As they walked into the restaurant, Sam saw some guy take a selfie in front of the Lamborghini. His Lamborghini, for the night.

He felt so Bond.

The plan was set: Total parental humiliation. Leading to confessions. Apologies. Tears, maybe, at least from his dad. And then, reconciliation. A second shot at love. His parents' marriage, version 2.0.

Beyond getting Ari's help to hack two fake texts, Sam hadn't told his friends the plan. He'd been too afraid he might lose it. Hyperventilate. Collapse in a puddle of tears. Or something else totally not Bond-worthy.

Time to suck it up and be a man.

"Solomon. Sam Solomon," he told the host, who found them on the reservations list and beckoned for them to follow. With Ari and Frida flanking him, Sam tried to walk like he had magical penis swagger as they headed through the dining room. He was wearing the *buy yourself a new outfit, anything you want* birthday treat from his parents: a new Tom Ford light blue suit tailored to fit him perfectly. He was feeling Bond-level dapper as he pulled at his shirt's white cuffs, flashing the Craig-Bond *Casino Royale* palladium S.T. Dupont 5174 cufflinks, square with curved lines.

"You okay?" Frida asked him. "You're walking funny."

Her words deflated his confidence. "I'm fine," he said, but it came out snippy. Sam tried to get the swagger back, but maybe with less shoulders? Was he being too girl-on-a-runway? Ari sauntered forward, their dramatic origami-style black blouse giving them huge shoulder wings with these nearly transparent billowy sleeves. With a tiny soft-sculpture birthday cake with a candle as a hat, they acted like they were a movie star and everyone in the room was paparazzi. Frida, in a simple navy dress with small multicolored flowers sprinkled across the fabric and her favorite black boots, strode the carpet like a boss. Like she was going to get up on a slam poetry stage—even if she wasn't in drag—and bring the house down.

Sam felt super self-conscious the last twenty steps, like he'd completely forgotten how to walk. *How does Bond hold himself? Does he move his hips? How can this be so hard?*

When they arrived at the table by the fountain that overlooked the dining room, Sam saw that the two extra settings he'd requested were already in place. He chose the chair with the best sight line to the restaurant entrance and sat, relieved to not have to force the walk any longer. The host held out the chair to Sam's right for Frida, and Ari just stood there by the chair on Sam's left, waiting for the same courtesy. The host, maybe on purpose, never even looked Ari's way, and hurried back to some people waiting at reception.

His friends froze. He didn't have to guess why. Frida out of guilt that she'd been offered a level of graciousness just because she presented as a woman that Ari didn't get—and that she'd taken it. Ari at being snubbed *yet again*.

Someone had to be a gentleman. Save the day, at least in a small way. Sam could do that.

He stood back up, gave Ari a slight bow, and pulled out their chair. With an elegant lift of their chin, Ari took their seat.

None of them said anything about it. Friends didn't have to.

"My gift first!" Ari said, breaking the awkward moment. They pulled a sleek jewelry box from their bag and set it in front of Sam.

Frida pouted like she'd wanted to go first, but Sam knew it was just for show. He put on the best game face he could manage, but he was completely on edge about the whole plan. He told himself this was a good distraction: Inside the gift box, a chunky matte-black bracelet with stones cut at geometric angles absorbed all the light hitting it. The inside gleamed like the polished surface of a grand piano.

Sam didn't wear a lot of jewelry, so it was pretty much the last thing he expected. "It's nice." Sam tried it on. It was masculine, in the same way hot yoga instructors wore leather cord necklaces.

"Onyx?" Frida sounded as surprised as Sam. "Or is it hematite?"

"Hematite?" Sam teased her. "Is that an actual thing or are you making it up?"

"I had a geeky gemstone phase when I was nine, okay?"

"It's not stone—it's a prototype." Ari explained. "Since I can't convince you to give up your cell phone addiction, at least now you'll be able to have some privacy. Flip it to the shiny side to turn it on."

Sam shot them a questioning look, but twisted the pieces around and slipped the bracelet back on his wrist.

"There are cameras everywhere in this city," Ari said. "The bracelet picks up the Pantone-matched colors around you and broadcasts them randomly. Like a color shield. It masks you from surveillance."

Sam gave a low whistle. "Very Q department."

Ari pulled at the chiffon on their wrist to reveal the same bracelet on their own arm. "Your cell phone location will still be trackable, by both Wi-Fi and GPS, but with that on, at least you won't show up on every ATM, elevator, and cell phone camera in Manhattan."

Frida scrambled to the other side of the table and motioned for Sam and Ari to pose as she lifted her cell to take their picture.

Sam put up bunny ears behind Ari's birthday hat of the day.

Mouth open as she stared at the photo, Frida walked it over for them to see. The fountain and diners and view of Central Park in the background were clear, but where Sam and Ari should have been was a smudge of colors, like someone had gone into Photoshop with a paintbrush tool and smeared all the pigments together.

Frida whispered, "It's like an invisibility cloak!"

"A digital one." Ari shrugged. "People will still be able to see Sam in real life."

"It's the coolest gift ever." Sam gave Ari a hug, saying softly in their ear, "Thank you."

Ari was blushing as Sam pulled away, but Sam didn't notice. Frida clocked both things as she plopped back in her chair on Sam's other side. "Well now *my* gift is like some consolation prize..."

"It isn't—" Sam started.

"Hello, everyone." Sam's mom interrupted them. "Sam, Frida, Ari." After handshakes for his friends and a shoulder squeeze for Sam, she settled into the chair the host held out for her. The host skillfully avoided Ari's death stare before returning to the entrance. Sam's mom eyed the two extra settings. "Did you and Kevin make up?"

Sam shook his head, taking advantage of a mouthful of warm bread. He struggled to swallow past the thought of getting back together with Kevin. Would he even want to, now that he knew who Kevin was—a total player who had played him? *The answer is **no**, Solomon,* he told himself, but he wished he *felt* over it. He had to stop feeling so Goddamned much.

"Then who's joining us?" Sam's mom asked.

He tried to play it Bond-cool. "You'll see."

Sam's dad arrived a few minutes of small talk later, freshly showered, kissing everyone on the cheek—including Sam's mom—and passing out compliments like party favors. Sam had trouble looking at him. At either of them.

When Sam's dad noticed the extra settings, his eyebrows lifted. "Did Savta fly up?

Sam shook his head again. "It's a surprise. We should start—they won't be able to join until dessert."

"Seventeen and full of surprises, huh?" Sam's dad caught eyes with Sam's mom. "That's our Michelangelo."

Sam decided it wasn't the time to bring up that he'd outgrown the nickname.

"So we discussed your gift," his dad said.

"You're impossible to shop for, you know that?" his mom added.

"Like mother, like son," his dad snarked.

She put up a *stop* hand. "Just tell him."

"Seems like you loved the driving lessons. Zoltan says you're doing really well, even with some of the most powerful engines."

"Are you getting me a car?" Sam got excited despite himself. If he'd known it was to *own*, maybe he would have gone with the McClaren! But the Lamborghini was incredible…

"Well, no," his dad admitted.

"Of course not." His mom shook her head, and disappointment flooded Sam. She kept talking: "It's Manhattan, after all. But we did get you another year of lessons with Zoltan. Two hours a week. Quite the price tag, but then, you do have caviar taste."

"Who do we blame for that?" his dad snipped at her again.

It would have been nice to get a car that was really his, but maybe he'd just think of Zoltan like his own Q department for amazing Bond-worthy vehicles. *Don't bite the hand that gives you a Lamborghini key fob.*

Except he was about to bite it pretty hard.

"Thanks," Sam told his parents. "I do love driving those exotics. It's a great gift."

His dad nodded. Clearly the second year of sports car access had been his idea.

Sam started to feel a little bad about what he'd set up. They were *trying*, weren't they?

"Gratitude." His mom spread her arms out wide. "What a nice change of pace."

"Way to piss on the moment," his dad said.

His mom rolled her eyes as she picked up her menu. "Will you stop? You're like a dog with a chew toy tonight."

Their sparring made Sam feel ungrateful. And not that guilty anymore about what he had planned.

"Can we order some Bollinger R.D.?" Sam tried. That was Bond's choice of champagne.

"You're seventeen, not twenty-one." His dad shook his head. "Don't push it."

"It's a stupid law," his mom said. "Actually, the drinking age used to be eighteen."

That got them onto a discussion of how old you had to be to vote, to drive, to join the army, to drink, and how none of it was consistent or made any sense. No one brought up the age of consent for sex, which Sam thought was just as well… No one wants to talk about sex with their parents (or their friend's parents), and anyway, that wasn't the point about sex he was aiming the evening toward.

Dinner was a seven-course chef's tasting menu, and Sam tried to focus on the food and completely premature conversation about colleges he might be interested in touring, but his eyes kept going back to the entrance.

Yolanda showed up during the cheese course, seven minutes early. Frida was still choosing a goat brie from the cart. Sam's dad's creativity coach wasn't dressed for Mais Monsieur, in jeans and a newly paint-smeared Penn sweatshirt. She seemed so out of place. In another situation, with clothes that weren't a screaming reminder of what he'd just seen, Sam might have felt sorry for her.

The text he'd had Ari send her from his dad's number said, I have something very important to ask you. Tonight. 9:30 pm. And gave the restaurant address.

Sam's mom was agreeing with the server that the fig bread was a better match than the olive for the pule, this donkey-milk cheese from Serbia. Sam watched as Yolanda spoke to the host and he pointed to their table. She started over hesitantly, but Sam's parents hadn't seen her yet. Interesting that the host let her walk in on her own. Maybe being escorted, like holding out the chair, was only for women who were dressed up and playing the part.

Jesse showed up then, all hipster beard and skinny designer suit.

The text Sam had Ari send him from his mom's number was more her style: Important. 9:30 pm. And then the address.

Jesse's eyes tracked Yolanda walking to their table. He spotted Sam's mom and started over too.

Sam cleared his throat and asked the server, "Can you give us a minute, please?"

"Of course." They kept their eyes down as they wheeled the cart away.

Sam's dad protested, "But I didn't get my cheese yet!"

Sam ignored that and let his eyes travel from his dad to his mom. "I thought we'd invite the two people who were missing from the big family celebration. Since you're sleeping with them."

BOOM.

Yolanda walked up at just that moment. "Michael?"

BOOM.

"You said it was important," Yolanda told Sam's dad. "But you didn't tell me it was going to be so fancy." She brushed at some dried paint on her sweatshirt.

Jesse arrived at their table, nodding to Sam's mom as he stood by her side. "Danica."

BOOM.

Everyone was silent.

His parents had heard Sam, that was for sure. His plan was working perfectly...

Sam looked at each of his special guests in turn. "Jesse, Yolanda, why don't you sit and join us for some cheese and dessert?"

Sam's dad's lips were a tight line.

Sam's mom's eyes darted around their neighbors. Maybe regretting the table by the fountain she always insisted on because it was the one that was like being onstage.

Neither Yolanda nor Jesse sat. Sam thought they both looked really awkward.

Good.

His mom spoke first. "I don't know what you're talking about."

His dad worked up some anger. "You have a lot of nerve..."

And then, louder than he intended, Sam shouted, "Oh, just shut the fuck up! You're both cheating!"

Silence. Across the whole restaurant.

Sam glared at his mom. "You're cheating on him with Jesse."

Sam's dad turned on her. "Jesse?"

Sam couldn't keep his words Bond-cool as his anger boiled and he turned on his dad. "And you're cheating on *her* with your 'creativity coach'!"

Sam's mom went sarcastic. "That's not very creative."

"Like sleeping with your assistant is?" Sam's dad fired back.

"I'm vice president of digital—" Jesse stopped talking at Sam's mom's raised hand.

"Don't..." Sam's mom trailed off, noticing everyone was watching them. Not how she wanted to end up in the society pages. She set her jaw and her face was New York tough. "This is a completely inappropriate, not just time and place, but discussion."

"Really?" Sam's laugh sounded bitter even to his own ears. "Why? Because you're so busy selling this 'happy marriage' thing to the press? To your friends? To me?"

Sam's mom stood up. "You've certainly chosen an interesting way to celebrate your birthday, Samuel." She locked eyes with Jesse, then walked away. Jesse hurried to stay by her side as she wove through the tables and left the restaurant.

Sam's dad got up then too. "I think that's the right idea, actually. Ari, Frida, my apologies, but we won't be staying either." He set his napkin by his plate and took Yolanda by her arm, like a proper English gentleman in some *My Fair Lady* revival. "You can use the emergency credit card to settle the bill," he told Sam. And then he led Yolanda away like she was the fanciest woman there, dressed for the opening day of the Royal Ascot races.

And with Ari and Frida staring at him, Sam just sat there, not able to figure it out. His plan had totally failed.

They left with the wrong people.

One Good Thing

Hubris. Like those stupid Bond villains. Some big grand plan, which they always explain just before they're about to kill 007, which then gets foiled. Your plan got foiled, Solomon.

My plan got foiled.

"Why don't you sit and join us for some cheese and dessert?"

God, I sounded like Dr. No, or Blofeld, or Goldfinger.

But I'm not the villain — I'm supposed to be Bond!

Happy birthday to me, I guess. It's late. Technically already September 11 — the world's worst birthday if you're growing up in New York City, in the ghost-shadows of 9/11. The Twin Towers forever collapsing in everyone's eyes when they hear you share the anniversary. Life and death, the combo platter.

Maybe it's fitting — my life is a disaster.

Frida's gift was a visit to this old recording studio just above Times Square. The music engineer (who was probably there in 1964) told us about watching Dionne Warwick record some of her hits. I didn't get the gift part until Frida signaled him, and suddenly this old Bond track started playing out of the control room speakers.

A Bond theme I hadn't heard before.

Turns out it was the first version of the theme song from _Thunderball_, "Mr. Kiss Kiss Bang Bang."

Such a kindergartener reduction of what Bond is all about.

Shirley Bassey recorded the song first. Her version sounded like the lyric was "Mr. Kiss Kiss Ban Ban." The producers did kind of ban it, replacing Shirley with Dionne.

In Dionne's version you could understand the lyrics better. Though I had to look up _demoiselles_. Google popped up this famous painting by Picasso of five nude prostitutes in Barcelona. Art and paying for sex, all tangled up together.

Like Dad and Yolanda.

But then the movie producers scrapped the song entirely, saying the song needed to be about the villain, not the hero. Not Bond.

So they hired Tom Jones to sing "Thunderball."

Which is why no one's ever heard of "Mr. Kiss Kiss Bang Bang."

There was one last audio file Frida had for me. A completely wack jazz version of "Mr. Kiss Kiss Bang Bang" by Ann-Margret. Like some 1950s remix, or a lost song from the musical _Chicago_. Listening to it, you could almost see the Bob Fosse hand movements and bowler hats and dancers in sleeveless black shirts.

Same song, three different ways. And then it was trashed.

Like your dad and mom's marriage.

It's after 3 AM, and neither of them are home yet.

What the hell did you do?

7

NICO

"Number Seventy..." Gold Wheels Preacher waved Nico up the stairs.

It was all happening again.

"Why do you keep calling me that?"

"You're my seventieth patient."

Nico wasn't sick. Or violent. But arguing wasn't going to help him learn anything. So he stayed quiet as they headed down a long stone corridor, toward the security camera mounted ten feet high on the far wall.

"The monks, when they built this, thought seventy symbolized perfect spiritual order." Doorless cells lined both sides, each one with a narrow bed and small window and a single teen inside. Nico thought some of them were younger than he was, like eleven-year-olds, but most seemed like they, too, were in high school. Every doorway and window glowed with red lights. Everyone wore the same highlighter-yellow jumpsuit with a metal collar. Everyone's hair was buzzed or growing out from being buzzed. And they were all barefoot on the cold stone like he was.

They watched Nico and Gold Wheels Preacher silently as the monologue went on. "But Acts chapter one tells us that after Jesus was resurrected and raised up to sit at the right hand of God, 120 true believers gathered in Jerusalem to choose, with the Lord's help, which of them would take Judas's place as an apostle. The construction you saw? We're adding fifty beds—120 will be our new auspicious number. And who knows? Maybe one of you, with the proper guidance, will prove to be Matthias."

Gold Wheels Preacher stopped outside the last cell on the west side. It was empty. He touched the tablet and the cell's doorway light turned green. His eyes motioned Nico inside.

Nico couldn't see any option. Holding that tablet, Gold Wheels Preacher could zap him whenever he wanted.

The moment Nico was past the stone archway the light changed to red. Nico's neck tingled with low-level electricity and he moved faster inside the cell until it stopped.

"Pray without ceasing," Gold Wheels Preacher said. "In every thing give thanks: for this is the will of God in Christ Jesus concerning you. Thessalonians 5:17 and 18." And with a self-satisfied jut of his chin, he disappeared around the bend in the corridor.

Nico felt relief—and panic—swirl inside him. With Gold Wheels Preacher gone, at least he didn't have to worry about getting zapped in the next few minutes. But now he was trapped like some animal. He started to move, but the cell was so small. Not even three steps wide before he walked into the cot. Four steps deep. Fuck! How am I going to get out of here?

A wave of not feeling but **knowing** he was completely alone threatened to pull Nico under the surface. Telling him to give up. Let go. No one would ever love him, or care about him. He should just lay down on the prison cot and never get up. Drown.

Nico snapped awake from the dream memory. He was gasping, and tried to be quiet so he wouldn't wake Warren on the bed just three feet away.

Fuck. Nico put his head in his hands. He was exhausted. He looked at the time on the TV screen. Not even midnight. He had to try to fall back asleep.

But all he could think of was that it was day seventy-four for Bec.

TUE 11 SEP
0849
SS AURORA: ANCHORED OFFSHORE HUATULCO MEXICO

"Look at you, dressed and ready!" Geena was surprised when Warren and Nico knocked on her cabin door. "This cruise is doing you good!" She yawned, still in pajamas. "Jacques, I see you'll be suffering Warren's company while I take an Aloha Spa day."

"Happy to," Nico told her. "Anyway, I have a good excuse—it's my job." *And now, that's kind of true.*

1114
CLUB AZUL HUATULCO MEXICO

After the breakfast buffet, Nico and Warren went parasailing. It took some extra convincing, and Warren signing a second waiver, but they finally got pulled aloft like a kite—the bright yellow smiley-face parachute above them catching the wind as the speedboat at the bottom of the cable roared through the calm bay waters. They were harnessed in side-by-side, their seats hanging from the metal bar that junctioned it all together.

They climbed up and up…

Warren's hand was tight on Nico's arm as the cable unspooled below them.

"We got this," Nico told him.

"Geena would never let me come up here!" Warren's voice was a shaky shout.

"Good we didn't ask her," Nico cracked.

He noticed they were higher than some birds with extra-long wings, who weren't bothered by them at all. Like they were just some other huge, friendly bird. Maybe that was what the smiley face was all about.

"She hates heights!" Warren said, way louder than he needed to.

"What do you think about heights?" It was so quiet, Nico figured they could whisper and still hear each other. He'd expected to feel like they were fighting the wind, but instead it was like they were part of it. It was oddly... calm.

"I don't know. I hate the idea of falling," Warren admitted.

"I think everybody does."

Warren gave Nico a sideways glance. "Even the cliff divers?"

"They weren't falling, they were diving," Nico pointed out. "And technically we're not falling either."

The cable ratcheted to a stop, tugging them forward. They'd reached eight hundred feet.

"We're flying, aren't we?" Warren's elation was contagious.

"Yup," Nico told him. "We're flying!"

The world stretched out under them: river spilling into the bay, red tile roofs, turquoise pools, golf course beyond. Nico tried counting beaches. There were supposed to be seven altogether but he actually counted eight.

It's beautiful here.

All too soon they were reeled back down into the boat. Warren's face was flushed. He'd had an adventure, and Nico had helped make it happen. It was hard to stop grinning.

The boat pulled back onto the sand where they boarded, and the parasail guys helped Nico lift Warren over the edge and settle him in his wheelchair on the thin wooden dock with jet skis tethered on the other side. Warren took the fanny pack from his waist and clipped it back through the chair's arm, where it usually lived. Then he fished out an extra forty dollars for each of the two parasail guys.

Nico and Warren waved their thanks as the guys pushed their speedboat back into the water.

A woman in a blue skirt suit watched them, her face friendly as she walked down the wooden path from the beach bar. In heels.

"That was the first time I've seen them take up a wheelchair user," she said.

"It didn't really matter," Nico pointed out. "All we were doing was—" He was about to say *sitting*, but Warren was right there. "Flying." He couldn't help the grin.

Warren chuckled. "You know," he told them both. "Someone once told me that everyone starts out life disabled and finishes life disabled, and it's only a lucky few that are *abled* for a short period of time there in the middle."

They were all quiet for a moment. Nico had never thought of it like that, but he figured it was true. Babies needed help. Old people needed help. So it shouldn't be that big a deal that Warren needed some help too.

"Still, it's good progress for us," the woman said.

"Your English is pretty great," Nico told her.

"¿Como es su español?" she asked him.

Nico shrugged. All his Spanish was pretty much courtesy of Dora the Explorer and her cousin Diego.

"That we can fix." She sized Nico up, but not in a gross Gold Wheels Preacher way. More like she was impressed with what she saw. It make Nico stand a bit taller.

"I like the initiative. Making sure your friend got to go up. If you ever want a job..." She handed Nico a business card. Beatriz de la Silva. Manager, Club Azul. Huatulco, Oaxaca, Mexico.

"Thanks." Nico pocketed the card. "I'll keep it in mind."

"Do," she answered. And with a tug at the hem of her short blazer, she walked back to her hotel.

Warren turned to Nico, and all Nico could do was shrug. Warren chuckled, and Nico joined in. Once he'd fallen back asleep he'd had a decent night's rest on the softest-ever memory foam pull-out bed, a great breakfast, a day with no worries about being caught, a crazy job offer, even an eight-hundred-feet-in-the-air flying experience. Things were looking up.

"Let's see about getting a drink, shall we?" Warren waved them to the thatched roof bar.

As Nico pushed Warren forward it hit him, a wave of guilt so strong that his knees buckled and the wheelchair rolled off the wood planks onto the sand.

"Whoa. We need to see about getting you some driving lessons," Warren teased.

"Sorry." Nico pulled the wheelchair back onto the path. Told himself to pay attention.

They settled at an outdoor table in the shade. Talking up a storm, Warren happily ordered them drinks with paper umbrellas. Nico played along, wanting to let Warren enjoy this moment to the fullest.

But inside, he couldn't stop thinking about how he'd been flying free… and for Bec, it was day seventy-five in Gold Wheels Preacher's Institute.

SAT 15 SEP

1422

SS AURORA: INTERNATIONAL WATERS 300 MILES
WEST PANAMA

Nico was on his seventeenth attempt to do the corner flip on the climbing wall. He wasn't getting enough height. Was it the ship's movement that was messing him up? He was sweaty, which, now that he could clean up in Warren's cabin, felt good, but he had to nail this if he was ever going to post another stunt video.

Maybe I need more runway. With more speed, maybe he could get the height he needed. Nico walked all the way back onto the blue rubberized track and started sprinting for the climbing wall... until Geena rolled Warren right into his path. Nico slowed his launch to a jog in place.

Geena scowled. "You don't work much, do you?

Nico shrugged. "Shifts."

She shoved a piece of paper at Nico. "Can you explain this so easily?" With a sigh, Nico stopped to read it. It was addressed to Warren.

Dear Mr. Bennett,

A conflict in your excursion plans has come to our attention.

The upcoming three-day off-ship visit to Cuzco and Machu Picchu is, unfortunately, unable to accommodate passengers with limited mobility.

As this excursion is contracted with a third party, we have no control over this decision. While we have appealed, they insist it is purely a safety issue, and as such we have little recourse. As a gesture of goodwill, they have refunded your payment (including the $600 "nonrefundable" deposit), and the entire amount has been credited to your shipboard account.

Please accept my apologies, and the enclosed voucher for a world-class lomi lomi massage in our Aloha Spa.

Sincerely,

Jacques Montagne

Excursion Director

SS *Aurora*

Holy crap. Jacques? Keep it together, Nico told himself.

"How could you do this to him?" Geena glared at Nico.

"I wouldn't—it's a different Jacques!"

"Not likely," Geena said.

Nico kept his face a mask of calm as he lied. "He goes by Jack, actually."

She wasn't convinced. Nico looked at Warren, who seemed numb. "You okay?" Nico asked him.

The words came out listless. "Seeing Machu Picchu was kind of the whole point of this trip. The starting point anyway." Warren smacked the arm of his wheelchair, and like a flame turned to high, was suddenly shouting. "I wasn't in this when we made the reservation!"

Silence. They were all just quiet.

Warren stared at the rubberized deck, his flame dying back to embers.

Nico wanted to help. Somehow. "Don't give up on it," Nico told him. Told both of them. "Let me see what I can do."

1435

Besides a ten-year-old playing video games, the Sea-Wide-Web lounge was deserted. Like every day when he connected with 321Boom and Power2People, Nico signed in with Warren's name and cabin number. It took him less than five minutes to find another tour company, one that specialized in wheelchair tours of Machu Picchu. He opened a DM chat with them and ten minutes later they had a reservation.

TUE 18 SEP
0300
CUZCO PERU

Geena was vomiting in the bathroom of her hotel room. The rest of the group was gathered awkwardly outside the closed bathroom door: Nico, fingers of his right hand drumming against his jeans; Warren in his wheelchair, oxygen tubing hooked over his ears and delivering full O_2 into his nose since they got off the plane the day before; and their Wings for Wheels guide, Paolo, the ends of his waxed moustache curving up against gravity even at that hour.

"How long has she had the altitude sickness?" Paolo asked.

Warren turned to Nico. "Two hours? Four?"

"She had a headache at dinner," Nico pointed out. "But even then, she didn't want to take the pills."

Geena shouted from the other side of the door. "Every symptom I have was also a possible side effect of that drug! Why would I take it when I can feel this horrible naturally?" She retched again.

Nico and Warren had both taken the medicine and didn't have any side effects. But it seemed mean spirited to say it.

"Would oxygen help?" Warren lifted his tubing, willing to share.

Paolo shook his head. "Once it starts, the only cure is to go back below her line."

"I want her to see Machu Picchu," Warren insisted.

Paolo kept shaking his head side to side. "The train goes up. Miss Bennett, she needs to go down."

The toilet flushed.

Geena moaned as she pulled the door open. She listed dangerously against the doorway. "Just get me out of here. Back to the ship."

"But you wanted—" Warren started, but Geena cut him off.

"The Galápagos. Islands. Sea level." With tired hands, Geena retied her hair into a low bun. "That's what I want to see. I don't care about your ruins. Ohhh…" She whirled out of sight, the door slammed, and they heard her puke some more.

Nico grimaced, sorry for her and relieved he'd taken the anti-altitude-sickness pills like Paolo suggested. They were at 3,350 meters above sea level, and most people felt it at 2,400 meters. Geena just thought she was above it all. Nico smirked at the pun, then quickly got his face back to neutral. He didn't want Warren thinking he was laughing at her being sick.

"The first flight to Lima is at ocho—eight." Paolo said.

"Wait." Nico asked. "Won't the plane go higher too? Shouldn't you drive her down, keep her as low as possible?

"The plane is fast, and cabin pressure will be…" Paolo paused for a moment, Nico guessed to translate the number: "Two thousand meters."

Warren did the math as fast as Nico: "1,350 meters less than here."

"Below her line," Paolo agreed. "But your train is at ocho y media—eight thirty. Paolo cannot be two places at once." Paolo glanced at his old-fashioned pocket watch and wound the top. "There are two men to meet you from the Vistadome train. They know to lift Mr. Bennett and the chair around the sacred city. Meantime, Paolo can take Miss Bennett to hotel by the Lima dock. She will feel better lower. Then Paolo meets you here tomorrow morning and brings you to Lima before quince—3 PM, when ship goes." He eyed each of them in turn. "This is a good plan?"

Nico glanced at Warren to check.

Warren gave a thumbs-up.

Nico agreed. "Yes."

1208
MACHU PICCHU PERU

They climbed toward the highest point, hard-to-see birds chittering to remind them they were in the jungle. But not jungle like Nico had imagined a jungle. These were mountains. Paolo's guys were yoked, carrying Warren and his wheelchair with the oxygen tank like it was no big deal. They didn't speak much English, but it didn't matter—it was as if Warren had memorized the guidebook.

"Consider the stonework!" Warren ran his hand along a wall as they passed. The stones were a crazy mix of sizes, and the angles where they met were like a solved jigsaw puzzle. Warren's voice was reverential, like he was in church. "How they're joined together with no mortar in between, and it's perfect."

There was a roped-off area ahead, with a rock formation that seemed like they'd started to carve out a hot tub but stopped halfway through. A column of rock stuck up from the back of it. Nico noticed the top lined up exactly with the mountain ridge in the distance.

"The stone is called Intihuatana," Warren explained. "They used it to track the sun's movements. This whole city is about the Sun God."

"How old is all this?" Nico asked.

"Six hundred years, give or take. They thought these mountains were sacred too. A good spot to build a sanctuary to the sun."

Twenty minutes later, Warren was directing them up the stairs of a rounded tower.

"This was their Temple of the Sun." Warren's eyes gleamed as they entered a round-walled room with a giant carved stone bench in the middle. It occurred to Nico that maybe it wasn't a bench but a bird. An abstract bird.

"They built this on the mountain ridge so nothing blocks the view. Take in the windows," Warren directed.

Nico checked out the two vertical windows in the walls, not much more than geometric holes. They didn't seem that special. Then again, it was all ruins. Was he supposed to imagine some six-hundred-year-old curtains? Stained glass?

"Perfectly positioned." Warren motioned forward so the men would carry him to the east window. "At dawn, the sun shines directly through this window on the longest day of sunlight, the summer solstice!" He gazed out, imagining it. "Brilliant."

"And this one?" Nico asked about the window facing north. "Winter solstice?"

"*Ding ding ding!* We have a winner!" Warren was jubilant.

There was a burst of snickering laughter behind them. A handful of tourists had started to come in but stopped when they saw Warren.

Warren flushed with embarrassment. It made Nico want to charge them, fists flying. Instead, he shot them deadly looks, but they escaped back outside with their whispers and giggles.

Warren didn't want to stay long after that.

Minutes later, Paolo's guys carried Warren up a stone path that climbed a series of terraces. Warren leaned his head Nico's way and whispered, "I hate being on oxygen. It's bad enough being in a wheelchair."

"You'd hate throwing up and having a brain-splitting headache worse," Nico told him.

"People are staring."

They were.

"Dude, fuck them. You're like an Egyptian king—"

"Incan," Warren interrupted.

"Fine, Incan king, getting carried around on one of those throne chairs. These people..." Nico dismissed the jerks. "Peasants."

Warren cracked the hint of a pained smile.

"Imagine you're an Incan king and you're touring your city in style."

The trail switched back as they climbed, and Warren glanced out over the ruins. "My city's seen better days."

At the top terrace, Paolo's guys settled Warren down. The smaller man motioned for them to enjoy the view, then mimed that he and his partner were going to get a drink. Warren gave a thumbs-up and dug in the fanny pack to give them a ten-sol note, about three dollars. They ambled away, over to a woman set up with a plastic cooler about fifty yards farther on.

Nico sat on the ground next to Warren and they stared out over the ancient city. The other tourists were far enough away that they had quiet. Nico didn't usually like being so still, but the sun spilled over them, despite the clouds clinging to the mountains that seemed so close all around. It smelled of moss, and rich earth, and... a llama that wandered by, a yellow tag in its ear.

"You want to ride?" the guy holding the llama's rope asked them.

Nico checked with Warren, who shook his head. Nico did likewise, and the llama and its human moved on.

It was hard to imagine what the ancient grid of stones and grass was like six hundred years ago, but even in ruins, Nico had to admit it was pretty impressive.

He breathed in the silence as it stretched, comfortable, for a long moment.

"Today's my birthday." Nico surprised himself by saying it.

"Happy birthday!" Warren slapped him on the shoulder companionably. "If you'd told me earlier, I would have got you something!"

Nico allowed himself a half smile. Why had he told Warren at all? He hadn't told 321Boom or Power2People when he talked to them two days ago. Maybe he'd said it because he needed someone else to know. Someone else to acknowledge it for it to feel real. He was seventeen, and completely alone in the world—if you didn't count two internet friends.

He just needed to feel a little less alone. He forced the smile all the way. "Seeing this *is* a present."

Warren let out a shallow breath. "Life is so fucking ironic. You've got your whole life ahead of you. Me? Eight months. Tops." Warren kept his eyes on the postcard view. "And from everything I've read, the last six months are going to be... not what I want. That leaves me two months to wrap up a lifetime of living. We'll get to Rio and I'll have twenty days. Geena's set on us going back to Seattle so I can be 'surrounded by friends,' but I don't want any of them to remember me like that. Like this." He lifted the oxygen tubing sneaking up to his nostrils, then let his hand drop. "Maybe another cruise. The Caribbean? There are worse places to die..."

Nico studied him. With the beard it was hard to tell, but even if he was double Nico's age Warren was too young to talk about dying. But he was sick. "I wish there was a cure."

"I'm still going to visit the Sacred Rock." Warren gestured to the far side of the ancient city. "Stretching your arms out on it is supposed to 'concentrate great energetic power.'" He laughed, but it was weak and wheezy. "I could use some of that. Maybe it will buy me an extra week."

Nico didn't know what to say. "I'm sorry."

Warren shrugged. "Hey, today's a good day. It's your birthday, and I have one more thing checked off my bucket list... Let's take a photo so I can show Geena what she missed and totally rub it in."

Nico swiveled the wheelchair, put Warren's cell in selfie mode, and snapped a photo of the two of them smiling—the ruins of Machu Picchu behind them. Just as he touched the button, Warren flashed a peace sign.

1328

The short woman who approached them a few minutes later had two string-mesh shopping bags with white motorcycle helmets inside. "Would you like to see what it looked like in the time of Pachacutec?" She held up the bags. "Virtual reality."

It was pretty much the last place Nico would have expected it, but maybe that was what was so cool about it. Where else would be the perfect place to see what this was like in its heyday?

Warren negotiated her down to a hundred soles (thirty dollars) each, paid her, and Nico and Warren both put on the helmets. Dark goggles and fat headphones completed the headset experience, but Nico didn't like the idea of not being able to see or hear anything in the real world, so he pulled the right headphone off his ear.

A fanfare of music played from Warren's helmet, and then the same loud music started in Nico's. The goggles lit up with a bird's-eye view sweeping down through a cloud and discovering an ancient city, perched on a flattened mountaintop—the same one that was below them. It was like a video game, how the people loped along in funny steps as the bird's-eye view landed on a colorful street, a market with stalls of fruit and pottery and woven blankets. Nico turned and the view of the crowd and market shifted to reveal a full 3-D world that made him a little unsteady. He was glad Warren was sitting down.

There was a low *click.*

But not from inside Nico's helmet. He tilted his head back to look past his chin and saw a small pair of hands pull past with the black fanny pack from Warren's wheelchair—with his money, phone, and passport inside it!

"Hey!" Nico shouted, struggling out of the helmet. *How low do you have to be to steal from someone in a wheelchair? Someone dying?*

The woman just stood there, but the thief was running, and Nico threw down his helmet and tore after him. Not even twenty yards and he was short of breath. *Altitude. Not used to the altitude.*

But it was all levels.

The thief would have to switch back and run right under him to get away.

He imagined it was a stunt. Breathing fast and shallow, Nico clambered onto the short stone wall. *Three... Two...*

On *One*, Nico jumped down the ten feet and knocked the thief over like a bowling pin. They both went sprawling, but Nico managed to wrench the fanny pack out of his grip.

The thief's eyes were wide as he and Nico stared at each other in a face-off. Nico realized his eyes were probably wide too. Because the thief was just a kid. Eleven, maybe twelve years old at most. Not any older than Squirrel Boy. Bec was on day eighty-two. How many days had Gold Wheels Preacher locked up Squirrel Boy before he betrayed Nico for a fucking slice of pizza? Who knew what kind of hell *this* kid's life was?

Nico's fury drained away.

Gripping the fanny pack tight, Nico flung his arms wide. "Get the hell out of here!"

The kid spooked and ran.

Winded, Nico walked back to Warren. Paolo's two men were there, holding the virtual reality woman by the arms. She was arguing with them in a language Nico didn't understand. It didn't sound like Spanish. The taller one turned to them: "She says the boy not hers."

Warren turned to Nico. "We should call the police."

Nico handed over the fanny pack, huffing the words out. "Is it all there?"

Warren checked. "I think so."

"No harm, no foul," Nico told him. "We got it all back."

"You could have been hurt! And he's just going to steal from the next dumb tourist!" Warren was shaken.

We can't go to the police. They'll want to see our IDs... Nico shook his head. "Let's keep this day a good memory, okay?"

"No one ever listens to the guy in the wheelchair."

"I hear you. I just don't agree." Nico turned to Paolo's men. "You can let her go."

Released, the woman pulled Warren's 200 soles from a fold in her brightly pattered skirt and pushed it at Nico. "For good memory, yes? Lo siento. Lo siento."

Nico wanted to believe her. "Thanks."

He took the money and handed it to Warren. "How about we go see that sacred rock you were telling me about?"

1918

CUZCO PERU

Nico started to push Warren around the corner to their hotel but stopped abruptly. A car with Policia on the side was parked on the sidewalk right by the hotel door. A policeman sat inside, watching people come and go.

Not good.

"Actually, I *am* hungry," Nico said like he'd changed his mind, going straight down the alley instead. "How about we grab some food before heading back to the hotel?"

1934

Maybe they aren't looking for me.

Who are you kidding?

Nico was freaking out in the bathroom of Diamantes Verdes, an organic restaurant Paolo had recommended that was only a five-minute walk from their hotel. The hotel where police were waiting to pick Nico up. Arrest him.

Take me back to Gold Wheels Preacher.

Over my dead body.

What am I going to do?

Hands shaking, Nico splashed his face with water. He stared at his reflection in the mirror.

I'm not going back.

1938

It was still early Peru-time, so the restaurant was almost empty. When Nico got to their table, Warren had his phone to his ear. He must have finally gotten reception again.

Nico didn't say anything, just sat opposite him, leg jackhammering the terra-cotta tile under his chair. He stared at the wine-bottle candleholder. It was a slow-motion melted wax volcano, a riot of colors from maybe fifty candles. A green candle was lit now, dripping twin rivers of moss-green lava onto the rest.

"My voicemail," Warren said, setting the phone on the table. He hit the speaker icon.

Geena's voice, sounding agitated: "When the police get there, don't try to stop them. Jacques is not who he says he is. There's only one Jacques on the crew, and he's here in Lima, standing right next to me!" Warren pressed the red *end playback* button.

"So now everyone else has caught up to what you and I already know—you're not Jacques." Warren paused as the woman who had seated them brought them a basket of fried yuca with dipping sauce.

Nico nodded thanks.

Once they were alone again, Warren said, "You have nightmares every night."

He noticed? Nico had thought he'd been quiet about it.

"And you've been avoiding the police—twice just today. Do you want to tell me what's going on, or should I take Geena's advice and let you explain everything to the police at our hotel?"

Nico thought it through. He could tell Warren, and if it didn't go well, he could run. Sprint out that door, head down the alley, lose everyone trying to find him in the turn of streets... Unless Warren already called the police?

"Do they know?" Nico asked.

"They don't know we're back in Cuzco," Warren said.

Nico believed him. But his body stayed tense—coiled to spring into action. "Okay."

"Why don't we start with your real name?"

Nico took a steadying breath, realizing it was getting easier to breathe at the altitude. He was getting used to it. Adapting. That's all he had to do. Keep adapting and he'd be fine.

"Nico—Nicolas Hall. That's my real name." It wasn't legal, but it felt real when he said it.

"Nice to meet you, Nico," Warren said.

"They think I'm still Peter Josefs, but I never liked that name." It would be more honest to say it hurt too much to be called the name his parents had chosen for him, after they wanted nothing to do with him. After they threw their Gay son away, like an unwanted bottle destined to be recycled again, and again, and again through a system that didn't want him either. Then he remembered what Gold Wheels Preacher called him at the Institute. "Or, I guess, Number Seventy."

Warren listened quietly, nodding encouragement, as Nico told him the whole story. It lasted most of their meal.

"So I can't go back," Nico finished.

Warren shook his head. "Not without a team of lawyers."

They were both quiet. Nico was full, but he kept eating. *Who knows when my next decent meal will be?*

Warren nodded to himself, like he'd decided something. "Where will you go?"

Nico didn't know. Then, he remembered that woman who worked at Club Azul. "Maybe Huatulco. See about that job?"

Warren scratched at his beard. "Mexico is eight countries away. "You'll need a passport to get there, which I'm guessing you don't have."

Nico shook his head. "I don't even have a driver's license. And even if I did… They're looking for Peter Josefs."

Warren dug around in his fanny pack, then set his passport on the table in front of Nico. "They're not looking for Warren Bennett."

Nico stared at him. He was serious.

"You can say you shaved the beard, and anyway, it's a terrible picture from eight years ago." Warren pulled out a pen and started signing a stack of checks. Traveler's checks. A hundred dollars each.

"Go cash these right away. I'll tell them that you heard the voicemail and ran. They'll be searching for you here in Peru, and you'll be on your way to Mexico. As me."

He signed the last, fifteenth, check and put the pile on top of his passport. One thousand five hundred dollars.

Warren pushed the whole thing into Nico's hands. "I'll stay here until the place closes, then have the hostess get me back to the hotel. Paolo can see me to the ship."

"Are you sure?" Nico asked.

Warren nodded. "It's a new day. A new birthday, my friend. Have all the adventures you can, while you can. Live for you. And maybe, a little for me too."

"Warren, I…" Nico didn't have the words. And even if he did, he didn't think he could get them past the giant lump in his throat.

"You're Warren now." Warren's eyes held Nico's. "So get the hell out of here. And live!"

8

SAM

"I JUST DON'T GET WHY neither of you wants to even try!" Sam's heart pounded so loudly, it was crazy his parents couldn't hear the sound bouncing off every surface in their kitchen.

They'd both been there when Sam dragged himself out of bed. He'd called this emergency family meeting. It would make him late for school, and his birthday was all shot to hell, but none of that mattered.

Sam's dad fiddled with the display of spices, changing the colors around, while Sam's mom's eyes kept drifting to her upside-down phone, like she'd rather lose herself in emails than listen to her son's meltdown.

"So you thought humiliating us in public would solve things?" His mom wasn't known for her sense of humor, and this was no exception.

"I thought…" Sam struggled with what he should say. He knew he was being too emotional, and it wasn't helping. "At least it's all out in the open now."

Sam's dad kept his eyes on the spices as he moved them around. "Not every closet door is supposed to be opened, Sam."

Sam blinked hard. "So you knew? About each other?

His parents looked at each other, faces hard and unreadable. His mom exhaled through her teeth. But they didn't say anything else.

Had they known? Or did they feel as unsteady about things as he did?

"Hey!" A wave of angry heat rose inside Sam. "This affects me too!"

"Does it, Sam?" His mom picked up her phone and walked toward the apartment door. Without a backward glance, she grabbed her laptop satchel and left. The door shut behind her with a quiet *click*, but Sam felt it like a sonic boom.

He turned to his dad, who slid a final spice jar into place and stood, heading to grab his downtown studio bag from the closet.

"Dad!" Sam spoke to his back. "Don't you care? Am I the only one who gives a crap about your marriage?"

His dad didn't turn around. "That's just it, Sam. It's *our* marriage." And then he left too.

Sam stared at the forty different kinds of dried spices in their clear glass jars. Cayenne pepper opposite basil. Lavender flower buds opposite saffron. Smoked paprika opposite blue cornflower petals. It was a color wheel, with each spice arranged by their specific gradation of color, like those fancy watercolor pencil sets that broke it all down into so many intricate differences. It was an idea—a plan—perfectly executed in under ten minutes.

Maybe that's the thing, Sam thought, feeling sick about it all. *Perfect plans only work on things, not people.*

One Good Thing

I'm not the villain. I'm the hero. Right? Right.
So now I have to rescue them, back to their marriage.
What would Bond do?

"He's got a license to kill..." Gladys Knight sang it for the movie with Timothy Dalton as Bond.

I'm not going to shoot Jesse and Yolanda. But I do need to get rid of them. Or just get Dad and Mom away from them for long enough to remember that they love each other more than they want sex with these new people.

Rekindle the romance.

Sounds like an ad for a terrible Hallmark card. _Caught your parents cheating on each other? Help them back to that honeymoon state of mind with our Rekindle the Romance line of greeting cards and scented candles!_

There's a commercial.

But actually, they never had a honeymoon.

Mom had that dream about going around the world on a sailboat. That would be plenty of time away from Jesse and Yolanda for them to fall in love with each other again.

It might work.

It could work.

So I've got a goal. A Bond hero mission.

It's not saving the world, but it's saving _my_ world. Maybe that's enough.

THU 13 SEP

2142

LOWER EAST SIDE MANHATTAN NY

The crowd whooped it up as Crank Shaft took the stage, no one cheering louder than Sam and Ari. Frida's performance persona man-spread his way onto the stage, looking gruff as he ran a hand over his mustache and scraggly goatee, down his open button-down denim shirt showing lots of chest hair, to rest at his crotch on not one but *two* bulges in his jeans.

"Two penises seems appropriate for a truly toxically masculine man" was Frida's explanation back when she came up with it, and while Sam imagined there was some therapist just dying to connect Crank Shaft's double endowment with Frida having two dads, he hadn't said anything. It wasn't like *he* appreciated Dr. Sanchez's "insights" into what he did. And the double penis was a hoot when people noticed.

The house lights shifted and Crank Shaft was hit by a spotlight. The red *recording* lights around the stage came on, and Crank Shaft started their slam poetry piece… Part of the brilliance, Sam thought, was that Frida didn't change her voice at all.

"Mr. Maître d', I'm here to expose your hypocrisy."

Sam whooped. He and Ari shared a glance. They knew the inspiration for this one.

> *You grade each person's gender presentation,*
> *and reward the conformists with straight As and basic*
> > *human courtesy.*
> *Pretty dress?*
> *A woman.*
> *Tailored suit?*
> *A man.*
> *But the second we play with gender expectations*
> *your grading cheat sheet of two options is useless,*
> *and you're left with no tools except rudeness.*

The pink neon words buzzed to life behind Crank Shaft as he said the phrase:

"Pull out my friend's chair, bitch."

The audience knew their role and said it just a fraction of a second after Crank Shaft.

"They're a better human than you'll ever be."

The neon lit up again and everyone joined in, *"Pull out my friend's chair, bitch."*

"You're not the arbiter of what's valuable in humanity."

Sam thrilled at the crowd saying it along with them: *"Pull out my friend's chair, bitch."*

"In fact," Crank Shaft mused,

> *Pull out **all** our chairs, or let everyone sit themselves.*
> *We don't need your gender performance hierarchy.*
> *Ticked off at you, Mr. Maître d'.*
> *This is Crank Shaft. Peace out.*

The stage went black, and then the neon words PULL OUT MY FRIEND'S CHAIR, BITCH lit up pink, the only light in the whole bar. Crank Shaft was gone, and the crowd erupted in applause.

2217

"So the trick is going to be making the sailing trip *their* idea," Sam was telling Ari when Frida pulled up a stool to join them.

"You were great!" Sam told her.

"Crank Shaft was great," Ari amended.

"Thanks. Makes me wish I had the neon that night at the restaurant."

"I hear you," Ari agreed.

"What sailing trip?" Frida asked Sam.

"Bond Boy here has another plan," Ari said, with a gentle tap on Sam's arm.

Sam realized he was fiddling with the Benson & Clegg Plain Slim Rhodium Tie Slide on his skinny tie, just like Craig-Bond sported in *No Time to Die*. He dropped his hands. Bond wouldn't fidget. And another thing: "Bond doesn't give up! I'm not going to either."

"So this is about your parents?" Frida asked.

"It's a beautiful step-by-step process," Sam told them. And it was.

FRI 14 SEP
1717
METROPOLITAN MUSEUM OF ART MANHATTAN NY

After school, Sam took his dad to see the Gauguin show at the Met. All the glamour of Tahiti, through the eyes of the famous painter.

"The colors!" his dad kept saying, painting after painting. Sam let him talk, even asking what was so special about the colors. The lecture went on, gallery after gallery, his dad so excited to have Sam as an audience.

Sam waited for the perfect moment, then asked, "Do you think Gauguin would have been as good if he hadn't gone to Tahiti?"

His dad considered. "Being a true artist means you see with fresh eyes, and your art helps others see things anew." His gaze lingered over the peacock and dog in the foreground of *Le Sorcier d'Hiva Oa* (*Marquesan Man in a Red Cape*). "Immersing himself in different cultures, first in Tahiti and then in the Marquesas, most likely helped Gauguin do that."

"Must be nice, to see everything like it's new," Sam said.

His dad's eyes drank in the stream and grassy field beyond the figure in the red cape, maybe imagining where it went. Maybe imagining standing right where Gauguin stood to create a painting of his own, a Michael Solomon original...

Sam let Gauguin's brushstrokes make the argument for him. He wouldn't rush his dad, even though a lifetime of being dragged along to museums came with an instinct to pull off the Band-Aid as fast as possible and just get through it. Wait at the end of the show on a bench near the gift shop, lost in some video on his phone. There was always a gift shop. But this time, he told himself he'd stand there for as long as his dad wanted. Let his dad move away from the painting first.

To kill time, Sam checked out the painting, noticing the long hair and the white flower tucked behind the main person's ear. He wondered if Ari would feel some connection across space and time. Did this Marquesan, back in 1902, see themselves as a "man," or was that just Gauguin's colonial labeling at work? Sam checked on his phone—*sorcier* was French for *wizard*. *Marquesian Wizard in a Red Cape* would be a better translation. But even *wizard* was a pretty gendered word.

His dad finally got his fill of *Le Sorcier d'Hiva Oa* and they moved on through the exhibition. Sam didn't say anything else. He didn't need to.

<u>One Good Thing</u>

First hook — set.

When Bond has a plan, he's relentless. Single-minded. Focused.

Be like Bond.

SAT 15 SEP

0652

UPPER EAST SIDE MANHATTAN NY

Sam had the storage bin with his mom's childhood scrapbooks out on the living room's hide rug. She was ten back when she started cutting up travel maps of South Pacific islands and drawing ink lines across the pale blue water, like a connect-the-dots drawing.

The maps were interspersed with magazine photos of sailboats and clippings about Krystyna Chojnowska-Liskiewicz and Naomi James, the first women to sail solo around the world back in 1978. They took different routes, and many of the articles made it sound like a race, with the Polish Krystyna beating the New Zealander Naomi by something like six weeks.

"I remember this!" Sam's mom picked up a scrapbook on her way through to the kitchen. "What are these doing out?"

Sam had gotten up early to be in the middle of it all when she walked by. "Savta and I were talking about how many countries you and Dad had been to by the time you were my age, and I got curious."

"I didn't get to travel until college," his mom said.

"But you wanted to, right?"

"Hmmm." His mom didn't glance up. "You mind if I take this?"

Sam shrugged. "It's yours." He managed to hold back the silent *Yeah!* fist pump until she left the room.

<u>One Good Thing</u>

Second hook — set.

MON 17 SEP

1335

THE ALICE AUSTEN: HUDSON RIVER WEST OF LOWER MANHATTAN NY

It was a weird in-service day at St. Bacchus, and Sam and his parents were on the boat for a half-day sail, as a school fundraising raffle prize that his parents just *happened* to win. There wasn't any raffle, and Sam had paid cash to rent the boat himself—so they'd never know. The fact that he'd convinced them both to come felt like a minor miracle.

With the captain and one crew member doing all the work, Sam and his parents got to just hang out as the sailboat's hull slapped a path through the light waves as they made their way down into the bay. Sam ignored the Statue of Liberty off to the right and instead, out of the corner of his eye, he watched for the moment.

Maybe it was when the salty air blew through his mom's short hair and she didn't try to smooth it down, closing her eyes for a moment and just letting it be. Letting herself just be.

Or when his dad couldn't stop staring at the sunlight glinting off the dark water under them, getting lost in the shifting patterns of light and color.

Whatever it was, about an hour into it, with Long Beach off to their left, Sam could tell it had happened. Along with the spray of the ocean, he could feel the silence that had felt so sharp between his parents smooth at the edges.

Good Thing

Remind them how much they both like sailing, and travel. Check.

And a moment of togetherness that felt healing? Double-check.

Now for them to make it their idea...

TUE 18 SEP
0625
UPPER EAST SIDE MANHATTAN NY

Sam's parents were both waiting for him in the kitchen before he left for school. It was *beyond* unusual. His dad awake. His mom home.

It made Sam wary as he approached and dropped his backpack to the floor. "What's up?"

"We're not sure how you're going to feel about this..." his dad started, glancing at Sam's mom for support.

She put down her cell phone. "Your dad and I are going on an extended vacation. I've hired a yacht and crew, and we're doing the trip I always meant to. Sailing around the world. With selling the company—the timing couldn't be better."

"I'll be able to paint every day." His dad cleared his throat. "But here's the thing, Michelangelo: it means you'll have a few months of being on your own, for school."

His mom shot his dad a *don't sugarcoat it* expression. "Maybe more than a few months."

"You can fly out and meet us!" his dad said. "We already booked a week at a resort in Mexico over your winter break. And then, who knows? Maybe Easter Island, for Easter?"

Sam raised an eyebrow. "No surprise they didn't call it Passover Island."

"They called it Rapa Nui," his mom corrected.

"We're just... worried about you," his dad said.

"It sounds like an amazing adventure." Sam bobbed his head, a little unprepared for the reality of being a reverse empty-nester. *But this was the plan, right?* "Go for it," he told them.

His dad seemed surprised, like he'd prepared more arguments and didn't know what to do now that he didn't need them.

Sam's mom seemed pleased. Sam was proving to her that he wasn't a little kid anymore. That he was all grown up.

His parents glanced at each other, and he could see their excitement. *Together. They were doing it together.*

He'd done it.

One Good Thing

Does Bond ever feel lonely?

He ends practically every movie having sex with whichever Bond Girl has managed to survive.

Except, of course, Lazenby-Bond.

But all the rest? Mission fulfilled. Booty call landed. Heart... empty?

Or is even asking that totally unworthy of Bond?

Feeling lonely, when they've only just told you they're going, is stupid. They're not even leaving for another week.

And you wanted this!

Maybe having your own Bond Boy would help — though getting used and then thrown away isn't the best gig. Bond Girls would know. I would know, thank you very much, Kevin.

You're caring way too much, Solomon, and your feelings are totally messing things up. Again.

You did it. Obviously, that's the one good thing. The plan worked.

It isn't any more ridiculous than the plot to <u>Moonraker</u>, where Roger Moore as Bond goes to California to Drax Industries to track down a missing space shuttle. That's where he meets undercover CIA agent Dr. Holly Goodhead, played by Lois Chiles. (Dr. Goodhead. How the hell did they get away with those Bond Girl names?)

Bond follows a clue to Venice, Italy...

Which leads to an orchid poison clue...

Which leads to a secret base in the Amazon...

And then Bond and Dr. Goodhead stow away on a space shuttle flight to a secret space station in orbit around the Earth...

Where they have to defeat Drax and save the world.

So it shouldn't be any big surprise that Dad's artist fantasy at the Met...

Which led to Mom's childhood dream...

Which led to an afternoon sail—clue after clue after clue—all worked to put Dad and Mom on a trip around the world to save their love.

Only when he completed <u>his</u> mission, Moore-Bond got to have floating-in-outer-space zero-gravity sex with Dr. Goodhead.

And you've got nobody.

TUE 25 SEP
0644
UPPER EAST SIDE MANHATTAN NY

"Don't come to the dock this afternoon." Sam's dad tried to be upbeat as he packed face cream in the leather Dopp kit, but his eyes were misty. "It'll be easier to say goodbye here. Now."

It sounded like his dad had lost some earlier argument and was repeating Sam's mom's words back like he was reading them from some interior sketchpad.

Sam stood awkwardly by the door to their primary bedroom, backpack by his feet. He glanced at his parents' bed, his dad's clothes strewn all over the comforter, while his mom's two bags were packed and ready to go on the upholstered bench. He hoped his dad wouldn't cry. This was hard enough.

In front of the bathroom mirror, Sam's mom dripped saline into her eyes to get rid of the redness, catching the runoff with a washcloth. Synthetic tears for the one out of the three of them Sam knew wasn't holding back real tears. She'd pulled another all-nighter. "We'll video-conference every Saturday, as long as there's a satellite connection. And you can reach us on email."

"You're not going to be checking your emails!" Sam's dad said.

She put a hand up in defense. "Everybody relaxes in their own way. I don't judge *you*."

Sam thought that was borderline hysterical, since his mom was *all* about judgments. Eyedrops done, she started to put on makeup.

"So you've got the emergency credit card?" his dad asked.

"In my wallet, always." Sam patted his pocket.

"Watch," his dad instructed, opening the bathroom vanity in front of him and picking up a can of shaving cream. Old school, like something he'd had from before he'd grown the tight beard. He twisted the bottom, and Sam saw it wasn't shaving cream. It was a secret stash. "*Emergency* emergency credit card, and $2,000 cash, in twenties. Just in case."

"Real emergency, Sam," his mom added.

"Like a tsunami," his dad said.

"Don't jinx us!" His mom squinted as she applied eyeshadow.

His dad screwed the false bottom back on and placed the shaving cream in its spot by the orange razor. "There's no real limit on that. Family password."

"Got it," Sam said.

"Reach us on WhatsApp if you need anything." His dad was the worrier. "Raul knows to keep an eye on you. And Savta's just down in Florida."

"He'll be fine, Michael." Sam's mom sounded out of patience. She pressed her lips together to smooth out the plum-colored lipstick.

"I'll be fine, Dad." Sam said it aloud, which helped him believe it was true. His mom believed in him. He had to believe in himself too. He repeated it, trying to sound more sure of himself. More Bond-like. "I'll be fine."

His dad tossed the full Dopp kit onto the bed and crushed Sam in a hug. "I know you will." He pulled back. "We'll see you at winter break in Mexico, okay? Plane ticket's all set." His dad held Sam at arm's length, like he was memorizing him for some future painting. It made Sam fidget. "Our Michelangelo. December will be here before you know it!"

"Don't be late for school," his mom said, coming out of the bathroom and kissing the air by Sam's cheek. "And you." She pointed Sam's dad back to the mess on their bed. "Finish packing!"

"If I didn't know better, I'd think you were trying to get rid of me!" Sam tried to say it as a joke, but it came out like his feelings were hurt.

His mom gave him a tight-lipped smile, and suddenly Sam understood. Rushing him out, saying goodbye here and not at the dock, it was all to avoid a big emotional scene. It was what his mom had always taught him: if you have to pull off a Band-Aid, do it fast.

Saying goodbye was the Band-Aid.

He'd never been completely on his own before. Their other vacations Savta had flown up, or he'd stayed the weekend at Frida's. But this was different. They were going to be away for *months*.

The other thing that was different was that he was seventeen, and they were finally treating him like an adult. So he had to act like one. Which meant no scene.

He could give his mom that, a goodbye gift of sorts. He'd tough it out, Bond-tough.

Bond wasn't the kind of guy who slowly, painfully pried up the edge of his Band-Aid and cautiously, bit-by-bit wrenched out each hair stuck to the adhesive, making the whole thing a torture session that, follicle-by-follicle, took forever—he ripped the whole damn thing off in one go. *If* he even bothered to cover his wound in the first place.

So Sam swung his backpack over a shoulder, like he wasn't all torn up inside, and headed out. He turned at the door to the hallway. His mom was already on her phone, answering some text or email. His dad was testing color combinations of shirts and shorts.

They weren't standing next to each other, but they were going on this trip together. *That means something, doesn't it? Everything?*

"Have fun, okay?" Sam told them.

"You too," his dad said, not looking up from trying two different pattered shirts against green seersucker shorts.

"Yeah," Sam said. And then, before there was any chance for his emotions to betray him, Sam ran out of their condo, taking the stairs sixteen flights down to force his body to focus on something else.

Lungs heaving, Sam burst into their building's lobby and made a beeline for the door, avoiding looking at Raul in the doorman alcove. Then he was out on Eighty-Seventh Street, jogging to the subway on Lexington and Eighty-Sixth.

With every step, Sam told himself he was Bond-tough. That he didn't care. That his face was wet because it was starting to rain, dammit.

But the sun, just breaking through the already muggy sky, didn't believe him.

"So what's *Alba Andorrana* mean, anyway?" Sam asked, after the past week's travelogue of his parents crossing from North Carolina's Cape Lookout to their first islands in the Bahamas. The laptop with its camera was at the foot of their bed on the yacht whose name was clearly in another language, and his dad and mom sat side-by-side against the repurposed surfboard headboard with its odd handgrips.

Sam sat on his own bed—he hadn't put it up since they left, leaving his room in perpetual lazy mode. And when he leaned back against his dark blue leather padded headboard, the other side of the video call didn't feel like they were 954 nautical miles away.

At least they were in the same time zone, for now.

"*Andorran Dawn,*" his mom answered. "It's Catalan. Remember we went skiing there? Andorra?"

"They have Gay marriage," his dad added.

"That's cool," Sam said, but thought getting married wasn't something any of them particularly needed. Maybe he'd read up on Andorra, see if they had a pride celebration he could take Ari and Frida to.

He remembered to ask about his parents. "And you're both good?"

Sam's dad nodded.

"This time's been like..." His mom focused past the camera to something Sam couldn't see, and her whole face lit up. "A gift." She seemed more relaxed than Sam had ever seen her. Like she wasn't thinking about work in the background of everything else. Like she was actually on vacation.

"That's great!" Sam felt amazing. Maybe they were going to be okay. Which meant they might stay together. And if that happened, it would be because of him and his wild James Bond plan.

They needed more good times and new memories, just the two of them. "You shouldn't waste your time together talking to me. Go do stuff!" Sam said.

"We were going to go snorkeling before it gets too hot..." his mom said.

"What about school?" Sam's dad protested. "We want to hear about what's going on for you. You're studying Shakespeare this semester, right? Are you going to be doing *Romeo and Juliet*?"

"It's actually *The Tragedy of Romeo and Juliet*, Dad. And we don't get to it until December. But all that can wait. I'm safe, everything's good here. Go!" He thought but didn't say out loud, *Try to make your marriage **not** a tragedy*. What he did say was "Enjoy the time together! We'll talk next week."

SAT 13 OCT

1002

UPPER EAST SIDE MANHATTAN NY

"Your mother's convinced that the first person to invent a roller coaster was a sailor." Sam's dad was wearing a neon orange life jacket over a black short-sleeve shirt with small green palm trees sprinkled across it, and Sam knew he'd chosen the shirt to complement the life jacket.

The laptop with its camera was in its spot at the foot of his parents' bed, and it started to tilt back at the same time Sam's dad pitched forward—the sailboat was climbing another giant wave. The upper part of his dad's body tipped out of the frame as the laptop camera showed part of the cherry-stained wood of the cabin ceiling, then dropped back as the boat crested the wave's top and tilted downward.

"This ride's insane!" his mom whooped like she'd shed twenty years, and jumped into the frame next to Sam's dad as the boat careened downward. She seemed good. Exhilarated. They both did.

Sam spun himself around on the kitchen stool, wishing he were on an exciting adventure too. "Insane?" he teased when he was facing the laptop again.

"Not what you kids say?" his mom asked.

Sam shook his head. "How come you're not in a life jacket? They just made it a tropical storm, didn't they?"

His dad grinned. "It's no longer *depressed*. Get it? It was a tropical *depression*..."

Sam rolled his eyes at the dad joke.

"Funny." His mom patted his dad's knee, then answered Sam. "I'll put one on when I go up top. They're not exactly designed with a woman's body in mind..." She shrugged, and Sam noticed how she'd left her hand resting on his dad's leg. *A good sign.*

The screen tipped back again as the boat climbed another wave. Back, and back, his parents tilted out of the frame until all Sam could see was the cabin ceiling.

"It's a big one," he heard his mom say.

"Hold on!" His dad's voice.

"The laptop!" his mom cried as it flipped over into the air, giving

Sam a split-second glimpse of their cabin door just as Jesse burst through, shouting, "Captain needs everyone on deck! Now!"

With a loud *crack* the laptop struck the floor and the video call window on Sam's screen went dark. A notification replaced the image: CONNECTION LOST.

Sam just sat there, trying to process that last second.

Jesse?

If he was there, that meant...

Yolanda probably was too.

Sam knew he should be more worried about his parents' safety: Were they all right? Had the yacht capsized? Or was it just the video had disconnected, or his mom's laptop had busted?

Shit!

Shit, shit, shit!

He was up and pacing the kitchen, trying to figure out what to do with himself. It was hard not to be furious. They were lying to him the whole time. They weren't getting back together. They weren't even *trying*, not if they had their lovers along with them...

That's why they didn't want him to come to the dock!

It's why they were so easily convinced to go on the trip in the first place.

They hadn't played neatly into his plans... Instead, *he'd* been played.

He hadn't made any difference in saving their marriage—except, maybe, helping them make it worse by being so stupid. So gullible. So totally unlike Bond.

Sam hit the video call *redial* button and gripped the marble counter edge to steady himself. If they picked up, he'd know they were okay, and then he could hang up on them. Feel righteously angry, without having to worry if they were fighting for their lives or drowning somewhere off the coast of the Dominican Republic.

The line rang, and rang, and rang. Sam counted fifteen rings. Twenty. Thirty.

No one picked up.

Sam stopped the call. Toggled online and searched for the latest on Tropical Storm Xiomara. Nothing useful. Just that it wasn't quite a hurricane. Yet.

Shit.

One Good Thing

Love is such complete bullshit.

Bond knows it. After Tracy, after George Lazenby, Bond doesn't put his heart into any relationship. Lust — sure. Loyalty — yeah, Craig-Bond was loyal to Vesper, but she betrayed him to save her other lover.

But he didn't give her his heart.

That's off limits.

And when he gave his heart away one more time — it cost him his life at the end of <u>No Time to Die</u>. They're going to have to reboot the whole series.

Craig was the best Bond.

Anyway, an off-limits heart is how Bond gets to be such a hard-ass.

That's how he keeps going.

It's what makes him a hero.

<u>He doesn't care.</u>

One good thing?

I got nothing. Just emotions. Just pissed-off, freaked-out, messed-up emotions.

Fuck!

SUN 14 OCT

1441

UPPER EAST SIDE MANHATTAN NY

Sam's cell rang. Where the numbers should have been it just read UNLISTED. He'd seen enough TV shows—calls from numbers you don't know are never good news. Police. Or coroners.

Stop it.

It rang again. Ari and Frida looked at him, then at his phone sitting on the living room's Noguchi coffee table.

Sam had been up all night, all day so far, freaking out. Ari and Frida were there for him, but there wasn't much they could say.

Whatever it was, he needed to know. He dropped the knot pillow he'd been wringing like a big deflated soccer ball and grabbed his phone before it could ring again. "Hello?"

"We reached you!" His dad!

"Are you okay?" Sam's voice nearly cracked.

"Yes, bit of a scare, but we made it to the harbor in Cockburn Town. I'm calling you from a landline."

"How's Mom?"

"She's down at the airport, trying to figure out shipping her laptop for repair and then getting it sent to a future port."

"So you're both okay?" Sam asked again, even though it sounded like they were.

"Everyone's safe," his dad reassured him.

Sam nodded to an anxious Ari and Frida, who were visibly relieved.

But then the word his dad used played again in Sam's mind: *Everyone.* And Sam realized his parents didn't know *he* knew about Yolanda and Jesse being there with them. They maybe thought the laptop hit before Jesse came in the door. That Sam was still blissfully unaware that they were cheating to the second degree. Cheating squared.

Should he let them have it? Scream everything he was feeling?

No.

Bond would stay quiet. Use it as leverage. Save it for the right moment.

Sam swung his leg back and kicked the knot pillow hard, aiming to get it through the kitchen to the hallway beyond. See if he could get it to the apartment door this time. Indoor soccer with his mom's interior decorator crap. The pillow caught on the waterfall edge of the kitchen island and skidded to a stop just below the microwave drawer.

And all Sam said was "I'm glad."

One Good Thing

They're alive.

In Cockburn Town. No kidding. It's the capital of the Turks and Caicos Islands.

Like a James Bond movie pun come to life.

The villain would live in Cockburn Town, for sure.

So it makes sense Dad and Mom are there. The liars.

9

NICO

Through the glass wall of the cafeteria, they all watched Gold Wheels Preacher pay the bearded bicycle delivery pizza guy.

Nico was back. Again.

Clouds shifted and suddenly the crushed glass behind the three-wheeled delivery bicycle with the hot box in back sparkled in the sunlight. Nico clocked it as one more barrier, making sure all the barefooted prisoners weren't going anywhere.

"Maybe it's extra today," one kid said quietly at the table next to them, staring at the pizza exchange.

"Maybe it's just torture," someone else responded.

Nico glanced at Bec, but she gave a microscopic shake of her head and kept her lips pursed.

Gold Wheels Preacher entered the glass door and almost posed, pizza box on his hip. His eyes swept the room like he was taking attendance. Satisfied, he said, "Time for grace."

It was the first time Nico heard everyone speak. Even though the words were religious, it was nice to hear talking, seventy voices strong. It was so silent in the cells. They finished, "...through Christ our Lord. Amen."

Nico thought they would start eating then, but no one did. No one's eyes left Gold Wheels Preacher as he set the pizza box down on a smaller table off to the side. He pulled out a slice, cheese stretching dangerously close to falling to the floor. He put the tablet on the table, pinched the cheese to pile it back on the slice, then picked up his tablet again. He weaved his way between their tables. "Meat lovers today." Gold Wheels Preacher took his time, describing it like a commercial: "Beef, chicken, bacon, sausage, extra cheese..."

One pizza. Seventy of them. Nico knew there couldn't be more than twelve slices in that box, so Gold Wheels Preacher wanted them all to smell what most of them couldn't have. And it smelled like real food. Nico stared at the glob in his bowl. That kid was right. It was a kind of torture.

Gold Wheels Preacher asked, "Who has something worthy of meat lovers?"

Five hands went up.

"Number Twenty-Four." Gold Wheels Preacher called on a kid whose growing-out hair poked the air like porcupine quills.

"Four unauthorized words each, Number Fifteen and Number Eighteen. While we were waiting for you to get the pizza."

"Really?" Gold Wheels Preacher said, but he didn't sound surprised. "Anyone else?"

Two hands up.

"Number Thirty-Seven." Gold Wheels Preacher called on her.

"Thirty-Six was jerking off again."

"Fuck you!"

"And unauthorized talking, just now. Two words."

One hand up.

"Number Seven?" Gold Wheels Preacher called on him.

"I think Number Ten is tearing pages out of her Bible. I keep hearing ripping sounds."

"We'll investigate that," Gold Wheels Preacher said.

"The pages were missing when I got here!" Number Ten protested.

Six hands flew up. Gold Wheels Preacher called, *"Number Nine?"*

"Number Ten, unauthorized talking. Eight words."

Five hands dropped, disappointed they didn't get the credit for squealing.

"You know what? Fuck you all!" The girl they'd been calling Number Ten was up and moving fast to the small side table. *"You want pizza so mu—"* She stopped mid-word. Frozen, hand only a foot from the pizza box, which Nico guessed she was about to hurl at someone. Instead, a wet spot moved out from the top of her leg, dulling the neon jumpsuit down to her left knee. Gold Wheels Preacher hadn't touched his tablet, hadn't moved. Nico spotted Sports Radio Guy on the other side of the glass. He was staring at her, hand on the monitor in front of him. He'd done it from in there.

Nico shifted his eyes back, just in time to see the girl crumple to the floor.

The cafeteria was silent.

No one moved to help. Her eyes were closed. Nico watched her stomach. It rose the slightest bit. Fell. Rose again. She was breathing, at least.

"Anyone else?" Gold Wheels Preacher sounded bored.

Cautiously, the squirrely junior-high-aged guy next to Bec raised his hand. One of the few Black kids there. Maybe not even junior high. Maybe only eleven years old. Bec shot Squirrel Boy a warning look, but he ignored it.

Gold Wheels Preacher called on him, *"Number Sixty-Seven?"*

"I heard Number Seventy talk. When you brought him in. Four words."

Nico stared at his bowl, fighting the urge to fling it across the table at the kid. But then he'd just end up zapped in a puddle of his own piss.

Gold Wheels Preacher shifted into lecture mode. *"Observation. Vigilance. Self-control. These are the qualities we nurture."* He stepped over the girl on the floor. Her eyes were open, but she still wasn't moving.

Nico stopped listening, caught Bec's glance and sent his eyes over to the pizza table. He pointed his plastic spoon at her and shrugged. She shook her head. Nico saluted her with his spoon. Sixty-three days and they hadn't broken her to betray someone else.

They won't break me, either.

Nico snapped himself awake. He wasn't broken, but he didn't feel whole, that was for sure. He tried to close his eyes again, but all he could see were little origami animals made from torn-out Bible pages. The girl they called Number Ten was so lonely, she'd made company for herself the only way she could. Nico knew what that kind of lonely felt like. How deep it went.

There was no point in trying to sleep any more. He got up and started his morning workout. At least he was seeing the lawyer that afternoon.

SUN 23 DEC
1434
HUATULCO MEXICO

"US-Mexico extradition laws are clear."

"Wait. What?" Nico didn't understand why the lawyer wasn't answering his question. What progress had he made in the last two weeks to free Bec and all the others from Gold Wheels Preacher's Institute? "Do you mean they'd need to be Mexican citizens for us to do anything?"

"No." Raymond Viceroy, Esquire, finished counting out the $500 cash Nico had given him for the hour of his time—more than half of Nico's last paycheck—and slipped it into the slot in his mahogany desk like it was a giant antique piggy bank. "I mean if they find out about you, the Mexican government would be only too happy to hand you over to the American authorities."

Nico's blood went cold. "That's not what I hired you for."

"You have to admit, it's suspicious." Viceroy leaned back in his chair. "An American who won't show me his passport but says he's Warren Bennett pays my $2,500 new case fee in cash. Where's a kid getting this kind of spending money?"

Nico wanted to snap that he wasn't a kid, but he needed to see where Viceroy was going with this. He settled for a silent glare.

"There's no bank account in his name, but a teller at Cambio Efectivo was only too happy to gossip about the American teenager cashing his paychecks—at a terrible exchange rate, I might add—for US dollars. Paychecks from Club Azul."

He could run again. But if Viceroy knew he worked at Club Azul, where could he go? He'd spent all of Warren's traveler's checks just getting to Huatulco. After rent for the apartment he shared, buying just enough clothes to get by, paying back the mountain bike, and all the money he'd given this lawyer... all he had managed to stash away in the core of one of the cinder blocks that, together with some planks of wood, made up the shelves in his room, was $187. It was 3,740 recycled cans' worth, but it wouldn't get him far.

His leg jittered and he forced it still. Could he even recycle bottles and cans for cash in Mexico? Would he be homeless again? He felt panic at the edges of his mind, but then thought of something he'd seen on TV. "You can't say anything! Attorney-client privilege."

Viceroy ignored the objection. "So I dug deeper. Looked into *Warren Bennett's*"—he added air quotes as he said the name—"credit scores. And it turns out there's an identity theft alert *and* traveler's check fraud alert on a Warren Bennett, deceased, past resident of Seattle, Washington. Nice place, by the way. You ever been?"

Deceased.

Nico knew he shouldn't be surprised, but now wasn't the time to think about it. He practically spit the words out. "Did you do anything I asked? You said you had to figure out if we had standing to sue in US court!"

"Son. I'm teaching you a lesson about leverage here. I know you're not *Warren Bennett*"—air quotes again—"and now *you* know I can bring your life crashing down around you. Your friends in that Institute should be the least of your worries. After all, now I'm curious to connect the dots." He picked up a Sharpie and literally drew dots on a yellow lined notepad as he spoke. "What happened to the real Warren Bennett? What's the connection with this Institute? Who. Are. You?"

Five dots. Four arranged like a diamond, with one farther out. Viceroy connected the three dots in the middle with a long line, then drew shorter lines connecting the outer dots with the tip. He turned the pad so the arrow pointed at Nico.

The quiet in the small first-floor office was laced with threat.

Viceroy showed his capped teeth. "Curiosity is a hungry beast. Keeping mine fed with other things…" He shook his head in mock regret. "I'm afraid that's going to be a costly endeavor."

Blackmail.

"How much beyond the three thousand you already stole from me?" Nico asked.

"Glass houses," Viceroy said with a dismissive wave of his hand. "I'm sure I've spent six hours on this already. Let's call it a retainer. One thousand dollars cash every month, or… I expect the police on both sides of the border would be very interested in what my curiosity might discover. Just like me."

Nico didn't want to believe this was happening. Weren't lawyers supposed to help right wrongs? Fight injustice? "You're really not going to help me get them out?"

"Haven't you been paying attention?" Viceroy patted his paunch. "Minors have no rights under the law. But here's the good news: Eventually, you'll all be eighteen. And then they can't hold you, unless a court finds you mentally incompetent. Or criminal. But you and I wouldn't know any criminals, would we?" He stood, lips stretching around his too-white-to-be-real teeth. "I have a golf date with a young woman hoping to be the next Mrs. Viceroy, like that will ever happen again. Not that I'll stop her from trying to convince me. Retirement is good for the soul, don't you think?"

1445

Outside the lawyer's office, Nico stomped out his rage on his way to the Club Azul van he'd parked down the street. He'd been played. Stolen from. But he didn't have any leverage against Viceroy.

Nico got in the van and leaned his forehead against the steering wheel. Warren was dead.

He let his mind go to what was worst of all: for Bec, it was day 178. All this time, and he wasn't any closer to getting her free.

10

SAM

THE MOMENT THE AIRPORT SHUTTLE cleared the blue stucco archway, something large hit the van roof. One of the dozen other tourists from Sam's flight from Mexico City let out a startled scream, but Sam's eyes followed the quick footfalls above them to the front windshield, catching a glimpse of a figure leaping from their still-moving van to the stone wall alongside them, a fast-moving silhouette against the brilliant blue of the ocean. Their driver narrowed her eyes and gunned the engine, the van and figure racing the length of the bumpy driveway.

Sam and the others were shaken like ice in a blender.

"Whoa!"

"Slow down!"

But the van didn't.

The figure leaped back on the hood an instant before the van's front tires hit a drainage channel cut across the driveway twenty feet from the hotel entrance. The nose of the vehicle bucked down and then up, and the figure shot toward the flagpole on the van's other side.

Everyone inside the van rushed the land-side windows to watch whoever it was swing counterclockwise on the flagpole rope like some modern Tarzan. Their feet pumped three quick steps on the circular driveway and then, still holding the rope, the figure was running *sideways* across the doors and windows of a line of parked cars, back toward their van, building speed until the rope pulled them aloft, swooping past their windshield to soar up... and land light on their feet on the roof above the hotel entrance.

It was another three seconds before the van's brakes screeched to a stop just outside the front doors.

Not like Tarzan, Sam thought. *Like a real-life James Bond!*

Their driver pushed the door lever open and raced down the stairs like she was spoiling for a fight.

Sam and the rest of them were on her heels. He wanted to see who this Bond person was.

The sun was behind the figure, and Sam squinted to get a better look. A guy. Not that much older than Sam. The guy threw his arms wide. "Welcome to Club Azul!"

American accent, Sam noticed.

The driver shouted up at him. "¡Uno de estos días, voy a ser más rápido que tú!"

"No hasta que este camina se repavimente," he said, leaping down ten feet to the driveway like it was nothing. Sam liked the sound of the guy's voice, in both languages. Really deep.

"Camino." Their driver gave the mystery guy a playful shove that told Sam they were friends. "Sorry for the bumpy ride, everyone," she told them without actually sounding sorry at all.

"We'll get your luggage to your rooms." The mystery guy headed to the back of the van and started unloading the bags.

Their driver started toward the hotel lobby. "Follow me and we'll get you checked in."

The mystery guy cleared his throat, to remind her of something.

She turned but didn't stop walking—now backward—through the sliding doors. "And then Warren can tell you about our Azul Adventures, if you're interested."

Warren. Sam memorized the name.

As everyone else followed their driver inside, Sam stayed where he was, holding his silver mesh ukulele gig bag (not that he'd ever had a gig) and watching Warren stack all the suitcases, duffel bags, and backpacks.

I'm interested.

Warren glanced up at Sam at just that moment.

Sam flushed—it was like his thought had been heard. Their eyes locked, and Sam felt his stomach drop. In a good way. Good-terrifying. The guy was crazy hot. Short hair, longer on top. Amber eyes, that were maybe a little sad. Or was that just aloof? Like Bond, not giving away too much... A light green Club Azul polo that hinted at a rocking body. He'd never be interested in someone as boring as Sam. He'd want someone who knew all the secrets of the world. Someone who walked with magical penis swagger, too.

Sam could feel his face heat up at the thought of Warren's...

Totally out of his league. He'd need to be someone else to have a chance.

Warren smiled at him. Just the slightest upturn of his lips on the left side. Just enough for Sam to notice. "Hey," Warren said.

The word rumbled through Sam, toppling over all his carefully constructed interior walls. A velvet earthquake.

"Hey," Sam said back. "I like adventure."

Was that bold, or did I just sound like a three-year-old?

Warren's smiled widened. "Well then, we'll get along great..." He reached out to shake, and Sam worried his own palm was suddenly sweaty. "Warren," he introduced himself. "I run the adventure program here." His grip was *all* magical penis swagger.

Bond. James Bond. The words went through Sam's mind.

"And you are...?" Warren prompted.

"James," Sam heard himself say.

"Good to meet you, James."

"Yeah," Sam breathed.

Warren's eyes twinkled. They weren't just amber, they were rings of color—gray on the outside, then green, and brown before the darkest black of his pupils.

Warren raised an eyebrow. "I'll need my hand back for the luggage."

"Oh!" Sam's face flamed with heat. "I'm—" *No. Bond isn't the kind of guy who apologizes.* So he just said "Yeah," even though he'd just said it, and released his grasp. "I should go check in." Sam turned to disappear up the stairs when Warren called out after him.

"I have to deal with the luggage, but come find me later, by the pool. We'll hook you up with an adventure or two."

Sam turned but didn't trust his words. He just gave Warren a single macho nod with what he hoped was magical penis swagger, and escaped through the lobby's automatic doors.

1551

"Are they here yet?" Sam asked the woman at the registration desk as he handed over his passport.

She checked the computer screen and shook her head. "You're the first to check in. Hold on. There's a package..." She headed to a back room.

Weird. His folks were supposed to have arrived early that morning. Maybe they were stashing Jesse and Yolanda at some local hotel first, to keep up the subterfuge. Where did yachts even dock around here?

The registration person was back with a FedEx envelope. Addressed to him, in his dad's handwriting.

Instinct told him he shouldn't open it there in the lobby.

Ten minutes later he was in the entry hall of Azul Turquesa, the two-bedroom suite his parents booked for them. His two Globe-Trotter Green Vulcanised Fibreboard suitcases, like Craig-Bond had in *No Time to Die*, were already there, next to the side table with an orchid and a plastic-wrapped basket of fruit. He wondered if Warren had dropped them off, and tore open the envelope.

There was a card, a Frida Kahlo self-portrait, a monkey and cat over each of her shoulders, from some museum. His friend Frida's favorite. Inside, his dad's precise script:

> Dear Sam,
>
> We hope you're not too disappointed, but we're not coming to Huatulco after all. Your mom found out about this *Rededicate the Flame* couples retreat in Costa Rica, and we thought that since we're trying to… Well, it seems a good opportunity.
>
> We still want you to have an amazing vacation—it's why we didn't tell you while you were still in New York. We didn't want you to stay home alone. This is *your* vacation.
>
> Use the credit card, take every excursion, buy yourself something nice, lots of things, and stay an extra week if you want—it's all our treat!
>
> Have an amazing Chanukah/Christmas week.
>
> Love,
>
> Dad and Mom

He'd signed it for both of them.

One Good Thing

Fuck them.
I honestly don't care. Fuck!
Okay then.
A week on my own.

16 12

The fourth time Sam "wandered by" the Azul Adventures cabana between the pool and the beach, Warren was there.

"Hey." Sam walked up, trying not to overthink the magical penis swagger.

Warren was whispering with another hotel employee, the one who'd driven Sam in. She gave him a sympathetic hug, saying "We'll talk more later," and then left with a stack of towels.

Warren shook off whatever it was and put his focus all on Sam. "James!"

He remembers me! Sam felt a thrill, and then a hesitation that Warren remembered him as *James*.

But it reminded Sam that he had to be a different person. He picked up the laminated menu of Azul Adventures, pretending to study it but really watching Warren in his peripheral vision as he came toward him.

"What do you recommend?" Sam asked.

Warren shrugged, and Sam watched his chest muscles move under the snug Club Azul polo, light green with blue piping. "You said you like adventure, but it depends on you. Man-made loud and fast—jet ski. Nature-made loud and exhilarating—the waterfall zip line hike."

Sam tried not to stare. "Is there a jump? At the waterfall?" The image of Brosnan-Bond bungee jumping off a 750-foot dam in the opening to *GoldenEye* flashed through his mind. He wouldn't mind a chance to feel like Bond.

Warren leaned on other side of the counter, face just two feet from his own. Was he flirting? "Thirty feet, off the third zip line. It's awesome."

Thirty feet wasn't 750, but even Bond had to start somewhere. Sam leaned in a little too.

"I've got some shots from the last tour." Warren used the mouse to scroll through photos on the computer screen set up at the end of the counter. Stills of tourists hiking past huge foliage, wearing bright orange zip line harnesses, climbing steps carved into some hillside, and then of falling water flashed by, but Sam had already decided he'd see it all in person. So he used the time to drink in Warren's features as Warren's attention was on the screen, almost like his dad did before he drew something. Sam would love to draw Warren. Not that he drew. But he could always start!

"It's about an hour hike, and by the time we reach the waterfall, you've earned it. I'm leading that adventure this afternoon at 4:30, if you want to come."

Sam managed to not shout *ABSOFUCKINGLUTELY!* He told himself to be cool. To be *James*. So he just gave a single nod. "Sign me up."

"Room?" Warren asked, clicking to a registration screen.

"It's the turquoise suite."

"Azul Turquesa?" Warren said, his Spanish accent sounding flawless to Sam. "Will the rest of your party be coming too?"

Sam pushed down the swell of emotions—*No*. He wasn't going to give into them. He was James fucking Bond, and like his dad said, this was *his* vacation... He forced a casual shrug. "Party's just me. Parents bailed at the last minute."

"You'll enjoy it, the Azul Turquesa," Warren said. "It's big. Lots of space. Beautiful."

"Yeah," Sam kind of breathed, thinking, *He's beautiful.*

Two people were waiting behind Sam to sign up for adventures, and he couldn't figure out any good reason to stall longer.

"Okay." Warren gave him that killer smile again as he checked his watch. "We're leaving in sixteen minutes. We'll meet in the lobby, by the fountain."

"Okay," Sam repeated like an idiot. He knew he was grinning like one.

One Good Thing
So maybe this week in Mexico won't be tragic.

11

NICO

SUN 23 DEC
1648
OAXACA MEXICO

HE HAD SIX TOURISTS WITH HIM: two preteens, their single mom, the cute guy from New York whose dark hair made this adorable swoop, and college-age soon-to-be newlyweds who Nico kept expecting to sneak off into the brush to get a jump on their wedding night. From the moment outside the van when he had them all put on the simple safety harnesses, Rob and Mercedes couldn't keep their hands off each other. It was driving the single mom crazy.

Focusing on work was a good distraction from freaking out about Viceroy blackmailing him. And trying to figure out what the hell Nico could do about it… He tried to be as present and friendly as he could.

Forty-five minutes of hiking and two zip line runs in, they arrived at the zip line that would carry them out in front of the waterfall for the drop into the deep pool.

"Okay, here's the jump," Nico told them.

Rob and Mercedes weren't listening. Again.

Nico explained it anyway. "It's important to go one at a time—glide to the stopper and then let go—it's a clear drop to the pool below. And remember, don't put your hands or anything near the line!"

The single mom raised her hand for Nico to help. "You don't have to, Ezra," she told the younger of the two kids, who clung to her. What was he, eleven? Nico flashed on Squirrel Boy from the Institute. He didn't want this kid to be scared. He hated when kids were scared.

"Hey." He lowered himself down so they'd be eye-to-eye. "No worries. We'll let the people who want to do the jump go, and then the rest of us will walk the path down. Same beautiful waterfall, and we'll all end up there together. Okay?"

Ezra answered with a timid "Okay."

Suddenly, Mercedes gave a "Whoop!" whipped off her bikini top, and tossed it onto the line ahead of her. In just cutoff shorts, she gripped the handles dangling from the track pulley and jumped.

"Wait!" Nico shouted, turning just in time to see Rob leap and grab her around the waist. Mercedes screamed in delight as he came along with her, the extra weight bowing the taut metal line as they rolled out fast, traveling eight feet—then jerked to a stop.

Mercedes screamed again, but Nico could hear the fear in it this time.

The fabric of her bikini top was jammed in the track pulley wheels, but they weren't past the giant boulders ten feet under them. "Hold on, baby," Rob said, and started to climb up her body to get his hand next to hers on the handhold. Mercedes shrieked, "You're going to make me fall!"

Nico snagged the loose orange and green return rope from where it trailed on the ground and tried pulling them back, but the pulley wheels were locked.

Nico did the math. When their strength gave out, they'd hit the rock under them, then slide twenty feet down to the waterfall's deep pool. Unless they landed really bad, it wouldn't kill them. Maybe a broken arm. A twisted ankle. Some abrasions. No one would drown. But it would kill Nico's no-injury record, screwing things up for him in the one place they'd been good... Nico shook the thought off—the main thing was he didn't want Rob and Mercedes hurt, even if they were idiots for not listening.

Moving as fast as he could, Nico grabbed another track pulley from his backpack, clipped the short rope from it to his harness, and snapped it on the line. "Hold this." He tossed the new return rope to the cute guy from New York who was just behind him. Next, he measured out five feet of two different ropes and knotted them to carabiners on both ends, attaching one side of each to his own track pulley. Lines set, he was ready to go fishing.

"Pull on my mark," he told the guy from New York, who gave him a confident nod. Nico launched himself out.

Rob and Mercedes both screamed as the line dipped at the new weight on the stainless steel cable. Rob had his legs around Mercedes to help hold her up, but she was crying now, and his biceps were visibly shaking with effort.

In seconds Nico was there, the harness leaving his hands free. He reached past Rob to clip a safety line to the top loop of Mercedes' harness, figuring she'd been hanging on the longest. But before he reached it Rob kicked at him in a panic. "Don't pull on me! You're going to kill us!" Rob let go with one hand to claw at Nico, hand catching in Nico's backpack and ripping the zipper down, spilling the contents to the boulder and the pool below. Mercedes screamed as Rob's legs lashed around her and Nico lunged headfirst to clip the carabiner to her harness as she fell—and the safety line caught her. She dangled three feet below them, heaving sobs.

"Mercedes!" Nico yelled. "Grab the rope. All you need to do is stay upright. The rope will hold you."

Rob was shouting over him, and he kept climbing on top of Nico as Nico struggled to right himself. It felt like wrestling an alligator, trying to get the second safety line hooked onto Rob's harness loop.

"Calm down!" Nico ordered, but Rob's pupils were dilated in panic and he wasn't hearing anything.

"Don't put your hands on the line!" Nico shouted. All he needed was for his track pulley to run over the guy's fingers and mangle them. Rob's elbow hit Nico hard on the chin as he grabbed the zip line's metal wire.

Nico got one hand into the harness belt over the guy's shorts and used all his strength to bring his hands close enough together to snap the safety rope to the loop. He got it there, and clipped the carabiner shut. Nico allowed himself a huge sigh of relief.

Neither of them would fall now. None of them would.

"Rob, you need to let go of the line." Nico used his calmest talking-a-guy-off-a-ledge voice.

Rob's whole body was shaking. Below them, Mercedes sobbed, but she was holding the rope, upright and safe. Nico looked up. Rob's hands were on either side of Nico's pulley track—trapping them there.

"I've got the safety line on you." Nico told him. "It will hold you like it's holding Mercedes. But they can't pull us back until your hands are somewhere safer."

"I'm not letting go!" Rob squeaked the words out.

"Dude. You won't fall." Nico reached his hand up. "Come on, take my hand." Rob stared at him, and Nico kept his face calm, sure. "I got you." He kept his hand an easy grasp away from Rob's fingers on the wire.

A long minute passed.

Finally, hand quaking, Rob reached down to Nico's outstretched arm, holding on to him like a scared child clutching a teddy bear bigger than themselves. The instant Rob let go with his other hand Nico called back to the others. "Pull us in!"

They did. Four feet from the launch point they had to stop to let Mercedes get her feet on the rock under her. The tourists formed a chain with the New York guy at the lead, reaching out to grab her hands and haul her up to safety.

Once Mercedes was back on the dirt trail, the New York guy and the others heaved on the return rope, and then Nico felt the trail under his own feet. Hands peeled Rob off him, and then Rob and Mercedes were in a messy pile of tears and apologies: "I'm sorry, baby. I'm sorry." Rob took off his shirt and put it around Mercedes so she wouldn't be topless.

The mom and her kids whispered to each other.

Nico glanced over at the guy from New York. *James*, he remembered. "Thanks for helping."

"Sure." James scanned the pool below them. "Did you need any of that?"

Nico eyed the metal wire strung across the river. "I'll need to get that jammed track pulley off the line. I had a knife in there I was planning to use. But I think I need to get those two back to the hotel first."

"No, we want to see the waterfall!" Mercedes spoke up. "We don't want to ruin this for everyone else."

Too late for that, Nico thought.

Rob still seemed shocked. "You saved our lives."

"Not really," Nico said.

"Shut up. Really!" Rob insisted.

"Everyone helped." Nico waved his hand to the group. The boy, Ezra, seemed pretty freaked out. "Come on. Let's all walk down. The waterfall's really beautiful."

Nico led them along the path to where it opened up. Five streams of water sheeted off the rocks above, like nature's most amazing bathtub.

Rob and Mercedes sat quietly on a dry boulder off to the side, holding hands like an old couple just happy to be alive.

The mom and her kids jumped around in the sheeting, bubbling froth, shouting to each other and taking a million selfies.

On a rock ledge, Nico kicked at the water under him, his mood a storm. What was he going to do, about everything? If he got fired for this and couldn't pay Viceroy? He didn't want to run again. Could he even still use Warren's passport if he was dead? He was dead! How was Nico not going to end up right back in Gold Wheels Preacher's tiny cell?

He felt James walk up next to him, but neither of them spoke. What part of any of it could Nico say out loud to some helpful guy just here on his vacation? He settled on "No one's ever supposed to be in actual danger. I'm going to be in a lot of trouble."

James shook his head. "We'll all vouch for you. And anyway, they did everything you said not to."

He looked up to say thanks, but that he really didn't think it would help—the words never left his lips. James was holding out a pair of swim goggles. "Come on. Let's find your knife."

Nico shook his head, not able to help the half smile on his own face. "You do like adventure."

12

SAM

MON 24 DEC
1538
CLUB AZUL HUATULCO MEXICO

THE FIVE JET SKIS PULLED into their spots on the left side of the thin wooden dock that was only two feet above the lazy waves. Sam hung back on his own jet ski about ten yards out, letting the other tourists thank Warren as he tied each craft in its spot. The dad whose eight-year-old daughter had ridden behind him pressed some bills into Warren's hand as he shook it, and then everyone else finally walked up to the beach.

Warren, looking awesome in his board shorts and body-clinging rashguard, waved him in. At first Sam had been disappointed Warren wasn't wearing tight blue square swim trunks like Craig-Bond, but it was probably better they weren't twinsies.

And when Sam had seen Warren wet, he realized there was nothing to be disappointed about! *Damn.*

Sam shook off his daydream of Warren without those layers— Warren was waiting, leg bouncing with all this extra energy that Sam thought made him seem even more of a James Bond action hero.

Sam powered his jet ski up to the last spot, cutting the engine and coasting in the last two feet in a way he hoped had swagger.

Warren grabbed the tether rope and made a quick knot. He put his hand out for Sam to clasp and hauled him up to the dock.

Sam peeled off his wet life vest, and then the T-shirt like Craig-Bond wore in *No Time to Die*, an Orlebar Brown Grey Melange Tailored Fit Crew Neck that was plastered to his skin. When he got it over his head, he saw Warren's attention was on the pile of life vests the others had dumped on the dock's wood slats. He sort of wished Warren had been looking at him.

"I can help you with those," Sam offered.

"Thanks," Warren said.

Arms full, they walked side-by-side to the supply shed, a few palm trees back from the sand.

Inside, they were finally alone. Sam reminded himself that James Bond takes initiative. That if he didn't say anything, nothing would change. He'd do a bunch of adventures with Warren like any other tourist at Club Azul—every adventure Warren had led since he arrived—and then go home daydreaming about what might have happened if he'd just been brave enough to say something. There were no scheduled adventures until tomorrow afternoon. This was the moment!

But what if Warren laughed at him? What if he smiled at everyone that way? What if he was secretly a homophobic jerk, who was only nice to Sam for his job? For tips?

But what if this guy was everything Sam hoped? Afternoon sunlight slanted through the gaps in the shed's walls, and golden light caught Warren's strong profile as he hung up the last of the life vests he'd carried in. *Maybe a moment like this was how they came up with that girl dipped in gold in* Goldfinger. *But this is so much better...*

Sam wanted to be brave. Be like Bond. For once. So as he handed over two dripping life vests, he forced the words out: "What are you doing for Christmas tomorrow?"

Warren did that half-smile thing that made Sam crazy. "Just another day in paradise."

Not for the first time, Sam thought the angle of Warren's lips, the stubble on his cheek, the rings of colors in his eyes... It should all come with a warning label—*DANGER! TOO HOT!*—but he was willing to risk getting burned. He handed over another life vest.

"Christmas Day is going to be pretty quiet. We don't even offer a morning adventure. Just the afternoon snorkel trip, and you're the only one signed up for that so far." Warren moved some paddles used for stand-up boards. "Most families just want to spend the time together." He got quiet then. Maybe Warren didn't do Christmas. Or maybe he didn't have family to be with.

Neither did Sam.

"I don't really have anyone here." Sam admitted, hanging up the last two life vests. "My parents are in Costa Rica, and my friends are all back in New York. Well, actually, neither of them are. Ari's in Switzerland with their dad's family, and Frida's off skiing..." Why was he telling him all this? *Get to the point.* He gave a nervous laugh. "I guess I'm kind of not sure what I'm going to do with myself."

Shit. That wasn't Bond-like at all.

Warren looked at Sam then, really stared at him. Sam could feel the heat radiating off his own face, and dropped his eyes to his feet. He lowered his navy blue cotton Carhartt baseball cap with the logo removed, just like Craig-Bond had in *No Time To Die*, hoping Warren wouldn't notice him blushing in the dim light.

"Maybe..." Warren started, but then stopped.

"What?" Sam raised his eyes.

Warren shook his head. Got busy restacking the dry life vests, though Sam could tell they didn't need restacking. "We're not supposed to socialize with guests."

Sam managed to not shout, *BUT THAT'S EXACTLY WHAT I WANT!* He tried to play it cool. Sort of. "If I *wasn't* a guest, what were you going to ask?"

Warren's turn to blush.

Sam was convinced it was the most adorable, sexy thing ever. And then Warren's eyes trapped Sam's. Those rings of color, drawing him in. "I can't."

"You going to make me check into a different hotel just to hear your answer?" Sam didn't break their gaze.

"You can't go to a different hotel. It's Christmas Eve."

"It's Christmas Eve and…" Sam prompted.

He could see Warren's Adam's apple bob. Was he nervous too? And then Warren said it: "Have dinner with me?"

YESYESYESYESYES!!!!!!!!!!!!!!!!!!!!!!!!!!

Sam couldn't even channel James Bond to play it cool. He just started laughing, and pretty much shouted "YES!"

Warren laughed then too.

One Good Thing

He's coming over at 6. Room service so no one sees us socializing. You've got a date, Solomon!

I've got a date! A real live actual First Date!

In less than two hours… Shit. Okay, off to buy Warren something for Christmas while the lobby shops are still open.

More later — much, much more, I hope!

1800

A knock at the door to the suite. Sam looked through the peephole. Warren, right on time. Which made Sam silly happy, thinking maybe Warren was as into this—into him—as he was into Warren. Or maybe, Sam reminded himself, it just meant that Warren didn't want to spend Christmas Eve alone. He couldn't let himself get lost in the daydream—Warren was right there!

Sam flung the door open. "Hey."

"Hey," Warren said back, leg bouncing with extra energy. He was so easygoing in his jeans and short-sleeve gingham shirt, red and blue lines making purple squares on white.

Sam had been going for a classic Bond look but now felt overdressed in his light blue Turnbull & Asser shirt with the two-button turnback cocktail cuffs like Connery-Bond wore in *Dr. No*, and the deeper blue Tom Ford O'Connor windowpane suit pants like Craig-Bond wore in *Spectre*.

But it was too weird to run and change. Sam told himself to fold up his sleeves as soon as it wasn't obvious. Short-sleeve shirts were always too big at the sleeves on Sam, needing tailoring, and he noticed how tight the fabric was around Warren's biceps. Naturally. Because the guy was crazy buff. *Stop staring, Solomon.*

"The food's already here." Sam waved Warren in, shutting the door behind him. He'd ordered dinner before he went shopping, and the round rolling table in the living room was packed with room service plates with their silver domed covers. So Warren wouldn't have to hide when it came. So they wouldn't have a reminder that he wasn't supposed to be there, wasn't supposed to socialize with guests. So Warren could feel more like a guest too.

Seemed more important than hot food.

"How many people are joining us?" Warren asked, but Sam could hear the joking tone.

"Yeah. I didn't know what you like, so I kind of ordered a bunch of stuff: pad Thai, eggplant Parmesan, pesto pasta, filet mignon, swordfish, and chicken Marsala."

Sam watched Warren's eyes scan the spread, then the huge gift basket from Sam's parents that was on the coffee table, filled with fancy chocolates, a colorful macaroon tower, swirled chocolate caramel apples, mini brownies, and handmade marshmallows.

It had come with a printed-out note:

> Dear Sam,
> Here's to a sweet Christmas—and Chanukah (nice how they overlap this year!)
> We're having a great time, and hope you are too.
> Know how much we love you.
> Love,
> Dad and Mom

Sam had stashed the note away in his Dopp kit—Warren still thought he was *James*. And it was bullshit anyway. If they really loved him, he wouldn't be here alone. But he wasn't alone, Sam reminded himself, staring at the real-life James Bond right in front of him.

Warren let out a low whistle.

"A guilt basket from my parents," Sam explained.

"Gift basket, you mean?"

Sam stuck by his first answer. "Guilt. I'd already ordered the fresh-baked cookies and chocolate strawberries before it got here, so dessert-wise, we're pretty covered."

"I'd say."

Sam felt embarrassed. Was it all too much? "I know it's early for dinner..."

Warren waved that away. "I'm starving."

They dug in, Warren settling on the eggplant Parmesan and Sam the pasta.

When they were nearly done eating, Sam turned the conversation to Bond. "I'm guessing you're a big fan of the Bond movies?"

"Huh?" Warren glanced up from a final bite of breaded eggplant.

"Bond. *James* Bond." Oh, he'd practiced that line so many times in the mirror.

Warren shrugged. "Not really. Should I be?"

"You've seen them though, right?"

Shaking his head *no*, Warren tasted the parsley garnish and made a face.

Sam knew it was bitter. He'd eaten enough bitter herbs at Passover Seders. "*Goldfinger?*"

Warren took a long swig of iced tea. "Nope." He wiped his mouth on the back of his hand.

Sam couldn't figure out how the guy who was the most like James Bond that he'd ever met didn't even know who 007 was. "We have to fix that." Sam grabbed the remote and set up the movie to stream on the living room's giant flat-screen TV. He smiled. "It's one of my favorites."

They got to that great scene where Connery-Bond is tied spread-eagle to a gold table, laser beam about to slice him in half—from the crotch up—and all defiant, he calls out, "Do you expect me to talk?"

Sam could totally imagine Warren having balls of steel like that. He almost said it out loud but didn't want to step on Goldfinger's line.

Goldfinger chuckled evilly, "No, Mr. Bond. I expect you to die!"

One of the best moments ever, but when Sam looked over at Warren on the lounge chair next to where he was on the couch, Warren kind of rolled his eyes. "Of course he expects him to talk! Otherwise it's going to be a really short movie."

"But it's cool, right?" Sam said.

"If he wanted him dead, Goldfinger could have just shot him," Warren pointed out. "Or if he wanted him to talk, he could have just shot near Bond's, you know..." Warren glanced at Sam's crotch and Sam's whole body flushed hot.

"But then it wouldn't be a Bond movie," Sam pointed out. "There's always something incredibly cool."

"I guess," Warren said, focusing back on the screen.

They both groaned when the nuclear bomb countdown stopped on 007… And then, after's Bond's snarky line about it being "no time to be rescued," when he and Pussy Galore got back to making out as the end credits rolled, they were talking about the final fight between Bond and Goldfinger's henchman Oddjob.

"I think it was a plan. Like a chess move," Sam said. "Distract him, and then *zap!*"

"You play chess?" Warren asked.

"Barely. My savta—grandma—she watches all these chess competitions, but I don't know…" Sam said, then realized maybe Warren asked because *he* liked chess. "You?"

"Still learning," Warren said. "But I think he tried to hit him with the hat. When that didn't work, he got lucky. Did the math fast and made it happen."

"What did you think was cool?" Sam so wanted him to like it too.

"Some of the stunt fights were," Warren admitted. "When he hid on the ceiling and dropped down on the guard."

"Yeah!" Sam agreed. "Like you on the zip line! You ever thought about doing stunts for movies?"

Warren was silent for a moment, and Sam worried that he'd said something wrong. But then the corner of Warren's lips ticked up just enough for Sam to recognize the hint of a smile.

"Let me show you something." Warren snagged the remote from the coffee table in front of them, navigating online to a *No Obstacles: Free-Run Wall Flip* video.

Perfectly synced, the split screen showed Warren and Donald O'Connor running up a wall and flipping over in midair.

"Wait! That's you?" Sam's eyes were wide, and he made Warren play it twice more. "That's incredible!" Sam gushed. "Do you have more?"

Warren showed Sam his other five videos that were online.

Sam was up and circling the room, more and more excited. "Warren! You're really amazing at this! How did you learn how to do those? Where's the video of the one where we came in on the van, where you swung on the flagpole rope?"

Warren blushed, making Sam's heart race.

"I still haven't done that video. The stunt took a lot of practice, and we've only just got it down. Hardest part was timing the van's dip to launch me high enough. And parking the cars just right for the sideways run. Shira's been a really good sport about it. Everybody here has been."

Sam told himself to not be jealous of Shira getting to spend all that time with Warren.

They spent the next hour showing each other their favorite stunt sequences online. Then Sam toggled them back to one of Warren's videos again. He read the profile name. "What's 'No Obstacles'? Why not do it under your real name?"

Warren got quiet again, then shrugged. "It's a reminder. To myself I guess."

Sam waited for him to explain.

Warren stared out the sliding glass doors, but it was like he was seeing inside himself instead. "Sometimes, it can seem like the path ahead is only obstacles. But there's almost always a way through."

"Very Bond philosophy," Sam said.

"I guess…"

"Wait!" Sam had the perfect example. "Have you seen the opening sequence from *Casino Royale*? The one with Daniel Craig? It's parkour—free-run—madness!"

And they were off, showing each other more of their favorite stunts, more moments when Bond figures out a way through, for hours. They had dessert, pulling the cellophane off the pyramid of sweets and tasting, trying different bites, and sharing. Sam thought the sharing was the best. Almost like kissing Warren, or imagining kissing him. He kept catching Warren's eye and then glancing away.

"Why do you do that?" Warren asked.

Busted.

"What?" Sam pretended he didn't know what Warren was talking about.

"It's okay." Warren put his hand on Sam's chin, gentle, strong, turning him until they were looking into each other's eyes. Warren held him there. Sam totally got, um, hard. Crazy hard. His breath got all short... And then Warren turned away!

Sam wanted to kiss him so much, but what if Warren wasn't into that? Or just not into it with Sam? If Sam made a wrong move, it could pop this amazing bubble he was floating in. He didn't want to risk that.

They played a game of chess—Warren had a set in his backpack and gave Sam a refresher on how the pieces moved. Midway through the game, Warren took a break to use the bathroom and spotted Sam's ukulele travel case on top of the dresser in the bedroom.

"You play the violin?"

"It's a ukulele."

"Play me something."

Sam chuckled. "Let me finish losing first." He'd lost track of time— it was dark out, and he didn't want to check his cell phone. Didn't want to bring reality into this. Every time Warren studied the board Sam just let his eyes drink him in, letting himself swim in the wonder of it all.

After checkmate, which Warren was really kind about, Sam got his ukulele and sat on the arm of the couch. Warren leaned back against the other end, watching Sam with those eyes. Sam liked how close

Warren was to him, even though he wanted him closer. But too close and he wouldn't be able to concentrate on playing.

Sam made sure the strings were tuned. He was all set to play the Bond theme song—it was flashy, and he'd worked really hard at nailing it, but now he didn't know... The energy of the moment felt different somehow. And he didn't want to rev into action in that Bond way. They were mellow. It was sweet, and a little awkward. And kind of amazing, being there with this guy who felt like a real-life James Bond. This guy who seemed to like him. Well, like the James version of him anyway.

So the first note Sam plucked wasn't Monty Norman's "James Bond Theme." It was "Hallelujah," the Jake Shimabukuro version. It was a little rough at the bridge, but Sam thought he did a decent job with it. The music calmed him. Centered him. Picking the notes, the tune came out, weaving around Sam, around them both, and it felt like magic. Maybe more magic than normal, with Warren right there. Listening. Hearing. Seeing.

Seeing him.

When Sam glanced up, Warren was relaxed and beaming, with this warmth coming from him,

Hallelujah...

Sam had to keep glancing down at the frets to make sure he got them right, *Hallelujah...*

The glow from Warren felt like the sun,

Hal-le-lu...

And Sam thought that maybe he was glowing too,

uu...

jah...

He let the final G linger in the air.

"Wow" was all Warren said. Sam was going to hold on to that *Wow* forever. Every time he needed to convince himself to practice.

And then Warren stood up. "It's nearly midnight."

Sam pulled the phone out of his pocket: 11:48 PM.

"We should both probably get some sleep—I'll go home," Warren said.

"No—stay!" Sam popped up, wanting to pull Warren back to the couch but afraid to go too far, so he just got really close. His voice was low, tender. "Stay, so we can do gifts on Christmas morning. For me. Please. Otherwise it won't feel like Christmas."

"Says the Jewish boy," Warren teased.

"Half-Jewish," Sam explained. "We do Chanukah and Christmas. Come on, stay."

Warren hesitated. "I don't have a gift for you..."

"We could *do* something," Sam said, getting excited. "Something small. Play me a song off the internet—a favorite song. Dance with me!"

"That's a gift?"

That's a fantasy. But Sam didn't say that. He just said "Yeah."

Warren was quiet, then said, "Okay, I'll take the couch. I don't want the cleaners to see the other bedroom was used."

Sam pushed down his disappointment. He'd hoped Warren would stay in the same bed with him... After all, it would cover a second person in the suite better than someone sleeping on the couch... But Warren was staying, and Sam wasn't going to argue.

Sam changed into an off-white Rag & Bone Classic Long Sleeve Henley T-shirt over boxers, trying to channel Craig-Bond in a sexy enough way to make Warren change his mind about joining him in the bed.

Warren didn't have a toothbrush, so he just used his finger and some of Sam's toothpaste. Sam thought that he should have gotten him a toothbrush as a gift! But that would have been weird, like he'd known in advance Warren would be staying over. Like he thought he was easy, or trashy, or didn't respect him.

"Good night, James," Warren said from the bedroom doorway, toggling the ceiling light off in the living room as he headed to the main room. The couch was made up with the top sheet from Sam's bed and a couple of extra pillows.

"Good night," Sam answered, turning to his own bed, which felt way too big for one. How was he going to tell him his real name was Samuel? The longer he waited, the weirder it was going to be.

He just didn't want to ruin this.

TUE 25 DEC

<u>One Good Thing</u>

It was cool, the plot stuff Warren brought up about <u>Goldfinger</u>. And funny — Goldfinger not wanting Connery-Bond to talk and just killing him outright would have made for a very short movie! And why such an elaborate way of killing him?

I always notice it with other movies, but Bond gets a pass. Cause he's sexy? Cause he's Bond.

Maybe the wild plot stuff is part of why I love the Bond films so much.

It's fun to have someone to talk about it with.

Warren is pretty amazing.

Bond would have slept with him. Well, not James Bond — 99.9% straight, with only that one moment in <u>Skyfall</u> of Daniel Craig joking — but maybe not joking — when he's tied down to that chair by Javier Bardem (of course the gay guy's the villain). It's a line Craig-Bond delivers perfectly:

"What makes you think this is my first time?"

So sexy. So magical penis swagger, and all he's doing is sitting there while Javier can't stop touching his neck, his face, his legs.

And of course the big reveal (not delivered like Bond thinks it's a big deal) that Javier's Raoul Silva wouldn't be the first guy Bond had sex with. Or maybe Craig-Bond is just playing with him. Playing with the gay audience too, I guess.

But if there were a James Gay... Ha! I should totally change my name.

Gay. James Gay.

Shit—I snorted and almost woke Warren up.

Laughing silently now. My secret identity. I've always wanted one of those.

Well, if I'm James Gay, I should have done the Bond thing and at least tried to sleep with Warren last night... But no. We haven't even kissed yet. And I didn't—don't—want to push my luck.

Because look right there, not 10 feet from where I'm sitting in the doorway to the bedroom:

Warren, splayed out on the couch.

Shirt off, sleeping in his boxer briefs.

Sheet pulled down off his chest—thank you, tropical heat!

Light from the bar spilling over his skin, training my eye to see, like some old Renaissance painting...

His jaw, so relaxed.

The curve of his shoulder.

The faint line of hair trailing between his pecs, over

tight ab muscles, and down to his belly button, and then lower, under the sheet where I can imagine…

Okay, Sam. Don't be the creepy guy staring at him while he's sleeping.

Shit, Solomon, you're the creepy guy staring at him while he's sleeping!

Look away.

Count 10 breaths. I should get some sleep.

One Good Thing

It's past 4 AM, and Warren was moaning in his sleep — a nightmare, I guess. I wasn't sure if I should wake him, and then, when I came to the doorway, he settled down again. It must have passed.

I got caught up in watching him breathe — in, out — like a meditation, his face soothing back down to calm, and I'm feeling that glow again. How did this amazing guy end up here?

Hey, technically it's Christmas morning. And Warren's like a gift, half unwrapped already.

And they say that half-Jewish boys aren't supposed to believe in Santa Claus!

0713

When the sun and Warren were finally up, Sam was practically bouncing on his feet, the one with all the extra energy now. He was so excited to give Warren his Christmas present. Warren sat up on the couch, all groggy and cute from sleep. Bed-head hair all messy on top. Absurdly hot.

"Merry Christmas!" Sam said. "And tonight, first night of Chanukah."

Warren scrubbed his face with a hand. "Merry. Chanukah. Yes."

"I want to surprise you." Sam shifted from foot to foot, the bag with Warren's gift hidden behind him. "Close your eyes?"

"Does that mean I can go back to sleep?" Warren asked, but there was that left side of his mouth smile again.

"Close your eyes," Sam told him.

As quietly as he could, Sam got the puka shell necklace out of its bag. He walked behind the couch and reached his arms down over Warren's head to fasten the necklace on him. Sam's fingertip brushed the skin of Warren's neck and it felt electric—

"FUCK NO!" Warren roared, tearing the necklace out of Sam's hand and flinging it across the room. It hit the wall with a *CRACK!*

Suddenly standing on the couch, Warren rounded on Sam with his fists raised and fury on his face... He was so angry!

Sam just stood there, eyes wide, staring up and not understanding any of it.

Warren froze.

Neither of them moved. Or said anything.

And then Warren ran into the bathroom.

What did I do?

13

NICO

Hands trembling, Nico locked the bathroom door behind him. He'd almost...

Fuck!

He turned the sink faucet on, cupping cold water in his hands and burying his face in it.

He wanted to fling himself into the ocean.

Or off a cliff.

Dammit, get yourself under control!

He liked this guy, and he could have almost just killed him! In that split second, he'd wanted to burn up the whole world.

Maybe Gold Wheels Preacher was right. Maybe he was violent. Dangerous. A criminal. Maybe he deserved to get locked up and forgotten, eating mush and hating himself.

Nico's neck burned with the memory of being zapped, and he rubbed at it, trying to get the feeling to go away. Bec was still imprisoned there. Guilt seared through him with its own kind of electricity. It was day 180 for Bec. *Merry Christmas*, he thought bitterly, hating himself for flirting. For having fun. For ruining everything.

There was a soft knock at the bathroom door. *James.*

"Warren? I'm sorry."

Nico didn't respond. Swallowed hard.

James kept talking. "I don't know what I did to upset you, but... I'm sorry. It was just a necklace. I... I guess you don't like it. I'm really sorry."

Nico paced the bathroom, but it just reminded him of being trapped in the Institute, in that cell.

His body wouldn't stop shaking. He needed to go for a run.

He forced himself to stand still.

"Warren..." There was such pain in James's voice.

He hated that James was using this fake name for him. That no one knew who he really was. Like he could just disappear and nobody would even care. Except Viceroy, who wouldn't get his money. He could die like Warren, the real Warren, and nobody... *Shit*. He was going to start crying.

"Please," James said. "Tell me what's going on."

Nico took a deep gasping breath. Then another. Maybe it would be okay to let one person past his defenses. He'd just told Shira he'd been having nightmares, but not what they were about. She was a friend, but he kept her at a distance. He kept everyone at a distance. And this guy was going to go home soon, so what was he risking? Maybe it would help to not feel so alone.

Maybe... he could try to be that brave.

He turned the lock, and pulled the door open slowly.

"Hey," Nico managed to say.

James stood there, biting his lower lip. "Hey." His hair was always this perfect swoop. He was this perfect guy, living this perfect life, and Nico felt so unworthy. Ashamed, he turned to the view out the balcony's sliding glass doors. But he didn't see the ocean. Only memories, inside.

"A long time ago—well, I guess not that long, actually—someone tried..." Nico's hand went to his neck, and even though he wasn't wearing a shirt, it felt like he was suffocating.

"To strangle you?" James's voice rose in alarm. "Oh my God. Is that what...?"

"I guess it was some sort of survival instinct that kicked in." Nico was grateful he didn't have to go into it.

"Oh my God. I would never!"

"I know. I'm sorry I overreacted."

"I had no idea!"

"I know."

"I wanted it to be a good thing." There were tears in James's eyes. One spilled out and Nico stepped forward and used his thumb to brush the tear away.

"We can still make it good," Nico told him.

"Sorry," James said. "I'm ridiculous. I don't mean to cry." He sniffed, lifting the edge of his shirt to wipe at his face.

"It just means your heart feels things—strong," Nico said. And as he said it, the words sunk in, as if he were hearing it from someone else. Someone wise. This guy really felt things. For Nico. And they barely knew each other.

He wanted to change that.

Nico walked over to where the necklace lay on the floor. Puka shells. A couple were chipped from hitting the wall, but it wasn't ruined. Usually tourists got the white ones, which made Nico think of bleached coral, or the bones of animals long dead. This necklace felt alive with grays and caramels, rusts and pinks, pearl and sand, every circle of shell slightly different in shape and color. It was actually nice. He wrapped it twice around his wrist and held the silver ends out to James. "How about I wear it as a bracelet?"

James's face lit up. He kept his fingertips away from Nico's skin as he twisted the silver ends of the clasp together. Almost like he was afraid to touch him. Nico felt bad about that. He wanted to make it up to him.

Clasp fastened, Nico tried it out, dipping his hand down and shaking it—the bracelet didn't slide off. "It fits." He showed James.

"Yeah. It looks really good," James said, eyes finding Nico's. "Warren, again, I'm sorry."

Nico shook his head. Put his hand gently behind James's neck—the muscles were so tight—and pulled the guy close. Till their foreheads bumped lightly together. He held them there until he could feel James relax, just a bit. "Thank you," Nico said, his voice soft.

"You're welcome," James whispered back.

"Do me a favor?"

"Sure," James whispered.

"Spend the day with me."

0939

With easy kicks of his swim fins, Nico led James through clear sapphire water over rocks and coral teeming with life. It was a day to not think about anything—just be. With this pretty cool guy. And see where things went.

Some fish were gray with black stripes and bright yellow tails. Schools of silver fish with black fins darted this way and that. Others paraded by solo, sporting three different shades of spotted blue—it was something Nico never got tired of.

About four yards below them a sea turtle swam along. Nico pointed, and James signaled he saw it too. They followed the turtle, flippers propelling them. After a bit, the turtle stopped to eat something off a rock, and they paused above it. Nico and James floated there, side-by-side, the warm water lapping at them, and without thinking about it, Nico took James's hand in his own.

James spluttered and raised his head above the water, coughing. He pulled off his mask and snorkel.

Nico raised his head too. Pulled the snorkel from his mouth. "You okay? I didn't mean to startle you."

"Yeah," James said. "Just swallowed some water."

They pedaled their legs while James caught his breath.

"It's beautiful," James said. "Like a real-world aquarium."

James reached out to take Nico's hand this time. Their fingers intertwined, and Nico could feel his heart speed up.

"Thanks for bringing me here," James said.

Nico pulled off his own mask and pushed closer. "It's my favorite place."

James didn't move away. Just stared into Nico's eyes.

No obstacles. Nico leaned in and kissed him. Salty. Sexy.

But then James started to laugh, breaking the kiss.

"What?" Nico asked. He hadn't meant it to be funny.

"Not the first kiss I imagined," James admitted.

Nico arched an eyebrow. "I hear these things get better with practice."

James leaned in and kissed Nico, longer this time. But James's knee, pedaling to keep his body upright, socked Nico in the stomach.

"Ow!" It hadn't really hurt, but now Nico was laughing too.

"I'm sorry!" James chuckled. "Maybe we need to practice on land?"

"We'll have to see about that," Nico teased. "Come on."

They spent the day on the beach, in the water. Brushing up against each other when they didn't need to. Floating along together. Playing in the waves.

Back at the Azul Turquesa, they took turns showering off. Had dinner. Played another game of chess, sitting so close on either side of the ottoman where they'd put the chessboard that every so often their knees brushed against each other, and neither of them moved away.

James played better this time, but Nico paused before saying *checkmate* out loud. Once he won he wouldn't have any more excuse to stay.

He should leave. Didn't he have more pride than just being some tourist's vacation fling? He'd done it a couple of times, and it got old. Fast.

But if he held himself apart and away from everyone, he'd always be alone. He was sick of being alone. He liked James. And he didn't want to go. Not yet. He let his knee drift into James's.

James pressed his leg back. "You've been staring at checkmate for two minutes."

Nico looked up at him, surprised he'd read the board so well. He wanted to hold him. Be held. But not as Warren. "Can I tell you something?"

"Sure." James's answer was light, but then he saw Nico's face was serious and he said it again, more sober. "Yeah. You can tell me anything."

"You can't tell anyone."

James's eyes flashed mischievously. "Now you're making it sound exciting."

Nico shook his head. "If you're just going to joke about it..."

"I'm sorry," James said quickly. He reached out a hand.

Nico stared at the calluses on his fingertips. From playing the ukulele? He kind of loved that James played such an unlikely, tiny instrument, creating music that got inside him and made him feel such big things... He took James's hand in his own. It felt warm. Strong.

James looked him in the eye. "I promise I won't tell anyone." And then he was silent. Waiting for Nico to speak.

Nico studied James's face. Could he trust him? He didn't really know that much about this guy. And James didn't know anything about him. That was always the problem, wasn't it? No one knew anything about who he really was. He never gave anyone the chance.

"I want you to call me Nico."

James seemed puzzled. "Not Warren?"

"Not when it's just the two of us."

"Nickname?" James asked.

Nico steeled himself for the risk. "It's my real name—but no one can know."

James's lips quirked. "You are *so* James Bond, you know?"

"No. Just Nico."

"Okay. Nico, if it's cool with you, I'm gonna kiss you." James leaned forward, toppling chess pieces to the floor, and delivered what he said he was going to.

"I was about to win that game," Nico protested, but his voice was playful.

"Hmm," James considered, keeping his lips just inches from Nico's. Nico could smell the chocolate on James's breath. And mint.

"There's more than one way to win," James said, knocking the board and remaining pieces completely out of their way. Then his lips were on Nico's again, and his hands pulled Nico onto the couch.

Nico kissed him back. Guard down. It felt like the most dangerous thing he'd done in a long time.

And the most thrilling.

14

SAM

SAM DIDN'T SAY ANYTHING ABOUT his own name. That would be too weird. Nico clearly had reasons for the alias—someone had tried to kill him! And Sam... well, being *James* was just a lark, wasn't it?

Part of him worried that he'd have to say something eventually, but the other part of him pushed it away.

Because they were kissing. And he didn't want to stop that for anything.

Chess pieces were rolling everywhere as Sam pulled Nico down to the couch, marveling at how Nico's lips were a completely different, darker color than his tanned face. Sam guessed that everyone's were different, but his own were more of a matching color. Nico's were a contrast, a complement—a target! The stubble that made Nico so sexy was pretty scratchy, but Sam liked it. Like flint, it kept sparking things inside him.

They sat up, and Sam yanked off Nico's V-neck T-shirt, not able to go fast enough. His hands wanted to be everywhere, but stilled as Nico took his turn.

Nico lifted Sam's favorite Craig-Bond in *Casino Royale* Sunspel Riviera Navy Blue Polo Shirt, taking his time. Slowly kissing each inch of exposed skin, up, and up, over his waist, his ribs, his chest, the dip at the base of his neck, his cheek, his ear, his forehead, and then Sam's shirt was off, his breath was lost, and their mouths found each other again.

Hungry for exactly this.

Sam thought about how tongues are amazing things.

He thought about that substance abuse assembly in school, and how they'd been lectured to about the dangers of pot and alcohol, both legal in some states for adults, as "dangerous gateway drugs" for their young minds.

And he thought about how kissing Nico was like a gateway drug. It made him want more.

And then Nico pressed his body full up against his and Sam stopped thinking.

WED 26 DEC

Nico had to work again, but Sam did both adventures he was leading that day, hang gliding and beach volleyball, and hung out near him as much as he could get away with. He told Nico about his parents and their ridiculous, embarrassing affairs, about Ari and Frida and how cool it was to have friends that always had his back, and a lot more about his favorite James Bond movies.

Nico didn't talk a lot about himself, but he seemed like he wanted to know all about Sam's life. The one thing Sam didn't tell him was that his name wasn't James... it just felt too awkward, and like it might burst this amazing bubble they were in.

They spent the night together in the turquoise suite, Nico on the couch again, but Sam wasn't going to complain—they were having so much fun. For someone who wasn't a big talker, Nico was quite the kisser. They were getting whole kissing sessions in. Sam had missed the first night of Chanukah, and he didn't have any actual candles to light. But this flame, in both of them, felt just right for night two.

FRI 28 DEC
0914

Sam slept in longer than he'd planned. Nico was already at work, and the plan was to meet in the lobby at 9:30 AM for the morning adventure: four-wheel ATVing. Sam washed his face, threw on a Connery-Bond outfit from *Thunderball*—white Jantzen shorts and a navy Fred Perry polo—and on his way to grab something quick from the breakfast buffet spotted the note slid under the suite door. It was from the resort manager, saying they needed to know if Sam was staying for a second week. He'd talk to Nico about it, but Sam wasn't ready to leave Sunday morning!

Some other tourist got the spot near Nico in the van, and Sam didn't get a chance to talk to him before the twelve of them were racing dirt tracks in a hilly area about a half hour from the hotel. It was an adrenaline rush.

Nothing handled like one of Zoltan's exotics, but Bond knew how to drive anything, and Sam could hold his own with a powerful motor. He purred to a stop on the highest rise, checking out the view of the bay while the other tourists zipped and zagged on the trails around him.

Nico raced his four-wheeler over a packed-earth ramp, soared through the air, and landed solid. The ATV under him tore up the slope and skidded to a sideways ice-hockey stop right next to Sam.

Finally, they'd get a private moment to talk. Nico pulled off his helmet. The moment was so Bond. So sexy.

"You're like a real-life James Bond, aren't you?" Sam said, feeling all warm and connected to him.

Nico's voice was sharp. "I'm not this fantasy person you've created, okay? I'm real."

And then Sam got angry. He hadn't even known he felt that way until the words came bursting out of him like hot lava. "How much of your *real* life have you let me see?" He yanked off his own helmet. "I told you everything about me, but every time I ask you *anything* about your family, your friends, your past, you dodge it. I don't even know where you live! I don't know where you grew up." He lowered his voice to a whisper. "If all I have that's real is a name, it's because you haven't told me anything else!"

They were both quiet then. A long, uncomfortable silence. And the guilt started welling up in Sam. Had he just blown up this whole thing?

Nico just sat there on his four-wheeler. Stony and unreadable. "How do I know anything you told me is real? Samuel."

Oh shit! Sam's stomach lurched, like a trap door had opened and he'd just fallen inside. *How did he know?* But then Sam realized: Nico worked for the hotel. Of course he'd be able to see Sam's name on the room registration. The name on his passport.

Sam fiddled with his helmet's chinstrap, long past time to come clean. "I'm sorry. You're right. My real name's not *James.*"

"I know," Nico said, putting his helmet back on and staring off to the horizon. "Were you ever going to be honest?"

"I'm telling you now. My real name's Sam. Samuel Jonas Solomon. Maybe being James was a way to be a better me. And then when you told me you weren't really—"

Nico shot him a look that stopped Sam from saying what he'd promised to keep secret.

"You can trust me." Sam resumed. "I'm still the same guy. And I still like you. A lot."

Silence.

What is he thinking?

Finally Nico said, "You know what, don't come this afternoon. I need some space." He pressed the throttle with his thumb and roared down the slope.

Nico didn't talk to Sam the rest of the morning.

All afternoon, Sam was in a funk. It felt like he'd failed some really important test. He replayed everything over and over, wishing he'd made different choices. Wishing he'd been honest with Nico right away. Been Sam and not pretended to be cooler than he was. But Nico wouldn't have paid *Sam* any attention, would he?

He knew it was too needy, but Sam parked himself on a lounge chair by the pool and stared at the Azul Adventures cabana, waiting for five o'clock, for Nico to get back from leading that afternoon's adventure—sea kayaking—so he could go up to him. Apologize. Make things right.

But at 5:10 PM it was another employee, the one who'd driven him from the airport, the one who'd hugged Nico that first afternoon— Shira?—who came back to sit behind the counter. Nico didn't show. Sam waited almost another hour before he gave up. Went back to his suite to write things out. Figure out what to do next.

<u>One Good Thing</u>

I meant it in the ~~best~~ way. I <u>love</u> Bond.

I never even got to ask if Nico wants me to stay another week. Does he hate me now? But I can't imagine going back to New York on Sunday—the day after tomorrow!

But if Nico doesn't want to see me again, how can
I stand being here?
But going back to New York means New Year's alone.
I was so sure Nico and I were on track to something
amazing. The same track.

Sam stopped writing. He'd heard someone outside the suite, in the hallway. They were gone by the time Sam got there, but there was a note slipped under the door. It was on hotel stationery:

Sam—
Thanks for the time.
We have a lot to talk about.
Dinner tonight. My place.
If you're in, I'll pick you up at 7.
If you're not, just don't answer.

It wasn't signed, but Sam knew it was from Nico.

There was no one to tell, so he strode over to his journal. He had his one good thing.

I'm in.

1900

Nico got one knock before Sam pulled the door open. He was ready. "Hey!"

"Hey, Sam." Nico's voice rumbled through him.

He'd called him *Sam*. For the first time. Sam liked how it sounded. *Tender. And maybe a bit nervous?*

Sam was too.

They walked from the hotel, Nico leading the way inland. Neither of them said much. In fifteen minutes they arrived at a run-down apartment building. Up the stairs to the fourth floor.

Nico unlocked the bright purple front door and waved Sam in.

It was pretty humble, but Sam didn't want to be snobby. He tried to make his voice sound impressed. "This whole place is yours?"

Nico shook his head. "I share it with a couple of other guys from Club Azul. But I have my own room."

Nico's room was small. Probably the size of Sam's mom's walk-in closet back home. Mattress with a bright quilt on the floor. Nothing on the walls. Cinder block and wood shelves that held a few work polo shirts and khaki shorts, a pair of jeans, and a stack of three neatly folded V-neck T-shirts on top.

Nothing tight around the neck, Sam noticed.

The other shelf had one bathing suit, board shorts style. Three books from the library—two in Spanish, one in English. A single pair of flip-flops.

The whole thing felt like Nico had just moved in. Or like he could shove it all in that green duffel bag and be gone in under a minute.

"They don't pay you that well, do they?" Sam said, then cringed as he realized how bratty that sounded.

"They do, actually." Nico shrugged. "But I've been saving up. Lawyers are expensive."

Sam didn't understand.

Nico gestured for Sam to sit, and since there was nowhere else, they both sat on the mattress. Nico left so much space between them, it made Sam wonder if he was still mad. But Sam wasn't getting that vibe. Nico's leg vibrated, and Sam fought the urge to put his hand on it, to tell him it was all going to be okay. He didn't know that. He didn't know anything.

"Are you in trouble? Can I help?" Sam asked.

"I don't think you can help." Nico seemed so sad it hurt Sam's heart. "But I love that you asked."

And then Nico talked. For hours. About being thrown out and foster care. About recycling and being on his own. About Dr. H's Institute and the electric collar and escaping. About the cruise ship and Warren's gift and getting to Mexico. About the crooked lawyer and not having any leverage. And Sam heard, under everything, the guilt of not being able to help all those other teens who couldn't escape like Nico had.

And by the end Sam was holding him as Nico cried. Huge, messy, heaving sobs. Tears and snot, and all Sam cared about was being there for him. Holding him close until the hurricane of emotions passed.

And then they lay there, together, for a long time.

Nico. Not Warren.

And Sam, not James.

SAT 29 DEC

One Good Thing

He opened his heart to me, and told me… God, what a terrible hand he's been dealt. He's this self-made guy. I'm kind of in awe of him.

Afterward, to lighten things up, we went bowling. (He's a terrible bowler. I beat him with a 102!) And then late-night Chinese food—in Mexico!

And then we went back to Nico's room.

And kissed. And... more.
Yeah!!!

Best Things Ever
Being naked with Nico!

Best Things Ever
And then, it must have been two in the morning, with just the stars and a quarter moon above us, we went out, down to the beach.

Best Things Ever
Skinny dipping in the ocean with Nico!

Best Things Ever
Later, back at his place, just before we fell asleep, I was holding him close, snuggled up against his crazy-amazing body, the side of my face pressed into his scratchy cheek, and I told him.

"Nico?"

"Sam?" he answered, and I could hear the full-on grin in his voice.

"I want to stay," I told him. "Tonight, and all next week too."

And then he said it: "I want you to stay."

Best Things Ever
How I feel right now.

One Good Thing
Nico!!!!!

One Good Thing

Nico's lips. Heck, his whole body. And yeah, his lips.

That spark between us — all he has to do is touch me (like his finger on the inside of my arm. Or his nose on my neck, just under my ear. Or his chest pressed into mine, God!) and it feels like every cell in me is fired up, on some new level I didn't even know was there.

Like I've leveled up in life. Clarity. Are colors brighter? Maybe. Life is.

<u>One</u> good thing? ~~Every~~ <u>second</u> with Nico is one good thing. He's the math wiz, and probably knows off the top of his head how many seconds are in a day.

86,400

I used the calculator on my phone.

I get to spend another day with Nico. And when he's busy, I'll be thinking about him. And when I'm dreaming, I'll be dreaming about him. And when we're together... level up!

So yeah, 86,400 Good Things about today.

One Good Thing

New Year's Eve with Nico, tonight!

2359

Sam and Nico were lying on stand-up paddleboards, just a few yards past the soft-breaking waves. Their legs rested on each other's boards so they wouldn't drift apart as the water lapped at them.

"Ten! Nine!" They heard the countdown coming from the crowd at the resort's outdoor bar. Nico reached out and took Sam's hand.

"Eight! Seven!"

Sam got goosebumps, spreading from where their fingers touched.

"Six! Five! Four!" The countdown felt like it was speeding up. Or maybe that was just Sam's heartbeat.

"Three!" A firework shot into the sky. "Two!" Two more fireworks arced orange paths directly over them.

BOOM! BOOM-BOOM!

"Happy New Year!" Shouts and music blasted from the shore.

A salty breeze blew the smoke back toward land, and in the clear night, the stars shimmered more intensely than Sam could remember seeing them. The fireworks had been neon, but the stars felt like the real show.

Nico leaned in close. "Happy New Year."

"Yeah," Sam breathed. "Think we can kiss without tipping over?" He couldn't wipe the mischievous grin off his face.

"It's just water," Nico said.

Sam rolled onto Nico's board to kiss him, toppling them, laughing, into the gentle sea.

They surfaced and held on to one of the boards, side-by-side. "You did that on purpose," Nico accused, eyes teasing as he swept Sam's wet hair back off his forehead.

Sam repeated the gesture, smoothing back Nico's shorter hair. "I bet your hair would look great longer," Sam said, and Nico got that sad faraway look again. It happened a lot.

"They buzzed it off, in the Institute." Nico stared at the board under their hands. "Bec's been in there for 186 days. And now it's a new year, and she's still trapped."

Sam put his hand on Nico's back. "There's nothing you can do right now."

Nico gave a sad smile.

Sam wanted to take Nico's sadness away. "We should start the New Year off with a proper kiss, don't you think?"

"Proper?"

And then Sam stopped talking. Because kissing Nico seemed more important.

SAT 5 JAN
1742

Sam found Nico past the tethered jet skis, at the end of the skinny pier. Nico's feet drumrolled against the gentle waves as they rolled in below him. Like he was barely holding himself back from running on top of the water.

He didn't look up as Sam sat next to him, close enough to touch Nico's hand. Sam noticed Nico was wearing the puka shell bracelet. He'd worn it every day since Sam gave it to him.

They sat there for a quiet minute. Sam watched the sun about to set on the horizon, heart racing at what he was about to do. *Bond takes risks. It's what makes him so badass. I want to be badass.*

"Our last night," Nico said, eyes on the rippling waves.

"It doesn't have to be." Sam pulled the envelope out of his back pocket and handed it over. It was a gamble, but Sam was feeling lucky. Nico made him feel lucky.

Nico gave him a *What did you do?* sideways glance and opened it. Scanned the first class plane ticket to New York. The seat next to Sam's. Made out to Warren Bennett.

Nico slipped the ticket back in the envelope. "You should have just let it be." He said it so softly, Sam pretended he hadn't heard him.

"I want to take you dancing," Sam said, studying Nico's profile, wishing he could figure out what he was thinking. "I want you to hang out in my room. I want to watch every single Bond movie with you in a crazy marathon. I want to take you out for sushi. I want you to meet my friends. I want… more. More days. More sunsets. More everything with you!"

Nico still didn't say anything. It made Sam nervous, putting his heart out like this. But this was his last chance, wasn't it? Tomorrow he'd be flying home. "Come with me to New York."

"What am I going to do in New York?"

"You can do school. Finish high school."

"Where would I live? How am I going to eat?" Nico kicked at the water under them. "You've got all these people taking care of you, all this money. I don't have anyone!"

Sam put his hand over Nico's. "You have me."

Nico released his hand from Sam's and scrubbed at his own face. Sam's hand felt so cold on its own.

"Go home, Sam. Fly home in your first class seat to your first class life and let this be what we both always knew it was—a vacation fling."

"Fuck you!"

Nico's mouth quirked up in a half smile that was more wistful than anything else. "Don't get mad at me for telling the truth."

"The truth?" Sam scoffed. "You wanna know the truth? I think you're scared. And you're glad I'm going home, because then you don't have to feel anything!"

Nico glanced around them, left, right. End of the pier meant he was trapped. He acted like he was trapped. "Go home."

"Don't say it if you don't mean it. Third time I walk away." Sam struggled to keep his voice even. "Don't push me away."

Sam felt tears rolling down his cheeks. *Fuck!*

Nico finally looked at him. His hand went up, maybe to wipe at a tear on Sam's face, but paused midair, and then lowered back to his side. "This has been great. Like some fantasy. But it was never meant to last."

"Why not?" Sam's voice cracked.

Hold it together, Solomon.

Nico sighed, then started listing the reasons. "There's a warrant out for my arrest, I'm being blackmailed, my friend's on day 191 in prison and I just left her there to rot, and you're some fancy prince in a castle living this charmed life…

"Put aside the money. Pretend I don't have it—I don't, actually, it's my family's money."

"Only someone with money could care so little about it."

"Nico. Come on! We have something really good here. You said so yourself. Let's keep it going. Come with me."

"You don't know what you're asking. Go home, Sam."

That was three. Sam swiped at his face, got up, and headed back to his room without turning back. He had to have *some* pride.

He needed to pack. And kick himself for caring so damn much. For feeling everything, so strong. He wished he could surgically take out all this sensitive shit inside him and just be strong and silent and more Bond, James Bond, and less Samuel Jonas Solomon.

One Good Thing

I ruined our last night together, wanting too much.
Pushing for too much.
And I got nothing.

Except four more acts of _The Tragedy of Romeo and Juliet_ to slog through.

Figures.

I'm a Solomon. Unlucky in love.

Like the star-cross'd lovers in Verona.

~~Like Dad and Mom.~~

Like Bond.

SUN 6 JAN

1134

ELEVATION 29,000 FEET PUEBLA MEXICO

<u>One Good Thing</u>

On the plane to Mexico City, and then home to New York.

The empty seat next to me is taunting me.

I want... no, I wish...

I thought this was different than with Kevin. Kevin was fun while it lasted but hurt like hell when I realized he just used me.

Somehow, this is so much worse.

I was so sure Nico and I were both in it, together.

Maybe what I need to do is prove to Nico that I'm here for him. That I can help. That we can change his life.

I need to get him some leverage. Over that lawyer? No, he's just a henchman. It's Dr. H who's the real villain. If I can eliminate Dr. H's hold over Nico, the lawyer loses his leverage too.

And if I can stop Dr. H, maybe Nico and me — I —
we — will have a chance.

I'll need Ari's help.

First thing, I need to figure out Dr. H's full name.

15

NICO

Sᴘᴏʀᴛs Rᴀᴅɪᴏ Gᴜʏ sʜᴏᴠᴇᴅ Nɪᴄᴏ into a barber chair that was bolted to the floor. Nico was back. Again.

The instant Sports Radio Guy's hands let go Nico kicked out at him hard—first step on his free-run to freedom. But Sports Radio Guy dodged the boot and lunged with his full weight to pin Nico down, smothering him in a press of tobacco and wintergreen. "You're not going anywhere," he snarled.

Nico struggled, but he wasn't a wrestler and the guy was too massive. He thought about head-butting him, but Music Radio Guy grabbed Nico's legs and quickly zip-tied them to parts of the chair.

Now Nico couldn't get away. Wouldn't be able to get to the remote that maybe was—or wasn't—in the van. It hadn't been much of a plan, he admitted to himself.

So Nico forced himself to go still, to wait for another chance. Cursing him, Sports Radio Guy yanked Nico's elbows apart and fixed them to the armrests, wrenching the plastic ties deeper into Nico's skin. Nico's left wrist started to seep blood. He couldn't stop his leg from shaking.

He needed to be running. He needed to be free.

Music Radio Guy slid behind Nico and he could feel cold metal fitting around his neck. There was a click. Nico tried to see it but it was too tight around his throat... but he could feel it. Like a choker necklace, with a box or something on the back. Chilled, like it had just come out of the freezer.

Nico jerked awake with a sob. It was all just too much.

He hugged himself in the dark of his room, knowing he wouldn't fall back asleep.

Too much.

MON 7 JAN
0837
CLUB AZUL HUATULCO MEXICO

Nico's cell buzzed in his pocket as he finished signing up two sisters from Chicago, both in their thirties, for the afternoon learn-to-surf adventure with Shira.

He checked. Another text from Sam. That made nine since he left for the airport yesterday. They hadn't spoken after they argued on the dock. After Nico had told Sam to go home.

It wasn't even 11 AM in New York. Maybe something was wrong?

Nico knew—he'd ended things like a jerk. Robbed them both of one last night together. One more chance to hold him. Be held.

And now he felt more alone than ever. With this fucking lawyer blackmailing him.

At least he still had a job.

The phone buzzed again in his hand.

Clean break, Nico reminded himself, and pocketed it without opening the text. He hadn't read any of them. He wanted to. Wanted to hear Sam's voice in them, but why torture himself? It wasn't like there was any kind of future for him and Sam, not when he couldn't even set foot in the United States again without being sent right back to Gold Wheels Preacher, an electric collar, and a tiny prison cell.

Sam was hot, but nobody was that hot, to risk everything for.

He caught himself fiddling with the puka shell bracelet on his left wrist. He should take it off. See if he could return it to the lobby store, get cash for it, even if a couple of the shells were chipped. But... the bracelet was a way to hold on to just a bit of that feeling. Of having someone care about him enough to buy it for him in the first place.

Even the texts, in a weird way, felt good.

Terrible-good, but good.

Someone cared.

Sam cared, about him.

Maybe he *should* text him back?

Nico tried to shake it off, and was surprised to see Beatriz and Shira walking up to him, short quick steps. Like they were trying not to run but needed to. Weird. He'd just started his shift, and Shira didn't need to be there until noon.

"Warren, Shira's going to fill in for you."

"Everything okay?" he asked. Had Sam called her? If he'd gotten him in trouble at work... *Shit.* They weren't supposed to "fraternize" with guests. Beatriz didn't have a lot of rules, but keeping Club Azul's staff and guests from fooling around together was a big one.

Shira gave him a worried glance—she didn't know what was going on either.

His boss checked around them. A couple of families with younger children were staking their claim to lounge chairs around the pool before heading in for breakfast.

Beatriz gave her short blazer a tug. "Let's walk." She led him away from the beach, on the little pedestrian path that cut across the lawn to the main road—the way he took on his way home.

They walked side-by-side, Nico not sure what was up. Nervous about what she was going to say.

When they reached the group of trees between the field and the road, Beatriz pulled an envelope out of her blazer and handed it to him. He peeked inside. Cash. Quite a bit of it. Mostly American. And his passport. Strike that—Warren's passport. From the Club Azul safe.

"What's going on?" Nico asked. "Are you firing me?"

Beatriz made a pained face. "I got a call this morning. They said that you stole this dead tourist's money and identity, that you're dangerous, violent, escaped from some teen rehabilitation program, and we should hold you until the police get here."

Nico's body went still while his mind raced. They'd found him. Was it that crook lawyer? Had he given Nico up? He didn't owe Raymond Viceroy any more money until his next paycheck! But this cash wasn't his paycheck.

Nico swallowed hard. "You believe all that?"

"That you're not Warren Bennett?" Beatriz shrugged. "It explains why you don't look anything like the photo, even with the spilled coffee on it. And you're the most youthful thirty-four-year-old I've ever met. But the rest? I wouldn't be getting you out of here if I believed any of that."

Getting you out of here. Nico's brain held on to those words. But he had to ask: "How did they find out?"

"They said when neither of you landed in Newark, they worked backwards. Mr. Solomon stayed here. I guess he bought you a plane ticket to go with him?"

"I didn't ask him to!"

Beatriz studied his face. "Warren Bennett's name was flagged. They called, demanding access to our records. I tried to stall them, but… they figured out you worked here anyway."

"How much time do I have?"

"I don't know." Her eyes flicked to the road. "They said they were on their way."

Nico thought of the cash he had stashed in the cinder block bookcase in his apartment: $187. All he had on him was flip-flops, board shorts, a Club Azul polo shirt, and a thin sweatshirt with a zippered pocket.

But there was all his money stashed in Viceroy's wood desk. Could he really rob a robber? "I need to get my stuff."

"The police are probably at your place already."

"Shit." He'd thought he'd have more time if this happened. It didn't make sense to get caught in town. And if he stole—even his own money back—then that made all of them right. He'd be a criminal. More of a criminal than they were already sure he was.

Nico ran a hand through his hair, trying to figure out his next move. He had to run but needed a direction. He needed a plan.

"I'm so sorry, Peter... the police said your real name is Peter, right?"

Nico shook his head. "The less you know, the less you can tell them."

Beatriz frowned. "I wouldn't tell them, but that makes sense." She gestured to the envelope in his hand. "It's $700. I'm sorry it's not more. I know you're in trouble, and I can't think how I can help except this. They say you're this terrible person, but in here"—she touched his chest, over his heart—"yo sé la verdad."

I know the truth.

Nico hugged her. "Thank you."

She pressed her arms tight around him. "When you straighten this out, know you'll always have a job here."

He remembered the first time he'd met her. With Warren. Parasailing. How free it had felt, watching everything from up above. Pulled by a boat across the blues of Huatulco's bays with the endless Pacific beyond... And suddenly Nico knew where he could run. *Not the town. The ocean!*

He zipped the envelope into his sweatshirt pocket and started running along the path back to the beach supply shed. Beatriz called, pointing inland, "You're not going that way?"

Nico turned. "They're going to expect that. I'll take a kayak, if that's okay?"

"Go," she agreed.

Nico gave her a grateful nod and sprinted to the supply shed. Grabbed his adventure backpack. He put the cash, passport, and his cell in the wetbag next to the first aid kit and Sharpie for labeling tourist bags, then shoved two full boxes of protein bars in the large compartment. Stripped off his shirt and sweatshirt and pulled on his dark blue long-sleeve rashguard from the dry line. Put on a large-brimmed straw hat.

Choosing his favorite blue sea kayak, Nico opened the hatch to the interior and dumped in a full case of twenty-four water bottles. Followed by the dozen tangerines from a small crate. Shoved his wetsuit, goggles, and snorkel in after it, along with a towel and his shirt, sweatshirt, and flip-flops. He jammed the backpack on top and sealed it all up, watertight.

Nico grabbed a life vest and dragged the kayak, with the double-sided paddle stuck under its crisscrossed bungee cord, down to the water's edge.

He paused. *His cell phone!* They were probably tracking him right now. And with GPS, they'd have him in an instant.

What was on it?

Chats with 321Boom and Power2People. But they were in the cloud, and he could log in anywhere.

Photos of tourists. *Who cared?*

A handful of photos of him and Sam. He hated losing those.

The texts!

He heard the sirens of the police car, fast bursts up and down a whistling scale.

He was out of time.

Nico lifted the hatch, opened the backpack, and snagged the Sharpie and his cell. He toggled to Sam's number and wrote it in neat black ink on his left forearm. Just in case he changed his mind and wanted to get back in touch... It was the only thing he couldn't replace.

And then Nico flung the phone twenty feet out into the waves. The salt water would kill it.

He pushed the backpack back into the Kayak's hull and resealed the hatch.

The police siren was louder now.

Nico took a breath, then charged the waves, pulling the kayak along with him. Then he was past them, water chest high. He hoisted himself into the seat and started paddling, hard.

The siren stopped, and in the sudden silence his breath and the paddle strokes seemed so loud. It meant the police were out of their car, walking to the hotel entrance. Would Beatriz meet them at reception? How long could she hold them off without revealing she knew where he'd gone?

Left, right, left, right, Nico pushed against the water, getting two hundred yards between him and the sand. The going got easier as the water darkened, waves not yet tripping on the raised shoreline. He headed to the outcropping of rocks at the base of the cliff just north of the Club Azul beach.

A paddle stroke from having the rocks completely block his view back, Nico paused, catching his breath. With the water an undulating indigo below, he looked, hoping to not see police. Maybe hoping Beatriz or Shira or someone else he knew would be there, standing in the shade of the palms, hand up in a goodbye. But the beach was clear, just some tourists with young kids, building sand castles.

He knew that meant Beatriz was covering for him. He had to disappear again. And no one would know. Or care.

Nico pushed past the rocks to be completely out of sight, and floated for a minute. He was far enough from land to not be identifiable to anyone onshore. They'd expect him to go to his apartment, and he hadn't. He hadn't even tried to get his money back from that crook Viceroy.

He'd left it all behind and gotten away, free and clear.

No obstacles.

He almost laughed. In his mind, it was *all* obstacles. Bec was on day 193. He'd need a new job to save up and pay a new lawyer who wasn't a crook, and come up with some strategy to free Bec and everyone else.

For now, he had a choice. Arc south. The future could be anything there. Guatemala, Costa Rica. There was all of South America to explore. To get lost in.

Or north. Back to the US. But how could he cross the border without being caught? Nico played through what Beatriz had told him. *Neither of them had landed in Newark.* What did that mean? Where was Sam?

The police had worked backwards. Tracing the ticket Sam had bought him under Warren's name back to Club Azul. Back to him. But that meant they could work forward too. That they knew Sam bought him the ticket. And Sam wasn't hiding his life. They'd know where he lived, in New York.

And it hit Nico, with a sickening certainty, that Gold Wheels Preacher would go after Sam.

Leverage.

To get to him.

So it was a trap! Wherever Sam was, he was heading into a trap.

And Nico had to warn him.

He cursed, almost wishing he still had his phone. But then the police would have already caught him.

He traced a wet finger under Sam's number on his arm, memorizing it.

Sam was in danger. This wasn't about how hot he was. And yes, he was hot. What mattered was that he was in trouble and didn't know it. And Nico was the only one who could save him.

He turned the kayak and dug his paddle into the water. Pushing north.

16

SAM

STILL NO TEXT BACK FROM Nico. Sam pocketed his phone and walked up to the library checkout desk. He kept on his blue-tinted silver frame Tom Ford Marko FT0144 sunglasses, his *Skyfall* glasses, because it made him feel more slick, more like Craig-Bond. The student reading a graphic novel behind the counter had dyed her hair into a rainbow. It made Sam like her instantly. But this wasn't about making friends. And if he imagined her with long brown hair, she was a match for the photo on the scanned work-study ID Ari had sent him.

"Excuse me," Sam said. "I'm looking for Vanessa Hergenreder." He used Dr. H's last name even though he knew that's not what his daughter went by.

Her head snapped up. "Who's asking?"

"Solomon. Sam Solomon." It didn't sound as good as when Bond said it. He kept going anyway. "A friend of mine's in trouble, and I'd like to ask you some questions about your dad."

"No." She returned to her book.

"Wait." This wasn't going the way Sam had planned it. Bond always got people to open up to him! "Why won't you talk to me?"

She didn't even raise her head. "I don't want him to know where I am."

"It wasn't that hard to find you."

She gave him a challenging look.

He walked her through it like it was a Bond movie plot. "Divorce records are public. The Point Foundation announced their scholarship winners with a press release. And the university's work-study schedule is on a shared Google doc. Vanessa Martin, Tisch Library, one to five, checkout desk, third floor." He spread his hands wide. At least he had her attention.

Vanessa crossed her arms. "What do you want?"

"You know he's running a prison, for Queer teens?"

"What do you think my home was like?"

"But you got out."

"I haven't spoken with my dad in years." She went back to her book.

Sam just stood there. He needed something. *Anything.* But she didn't want to help him. It was like they were adversaries instead of allies, but they were on the same side! How did Bond make allies? He usually slept with them. Pussy Galore. May Day. *Ha! That won't work here.*

Maybe the whole trying to be slick like James Bond thing wasn't helping. He took off his glasses and just spoke from the heart. "Okay, look, he's not a friend. He's… more. I really care about him. And your dad had him locked up. Shocked him with this electric collar. And then, once he got out, your dad lied to the police about him being a criminal. And now…" *Don't cry*, he ordered himself, swallowing past the lump in his throat. "I need to help him. I need something to stop your dad."

Vanessa put down her book. "Nothing's going to stop him. He's never going to change, or accept me. That's why we left."

"People change," Sam said, but he wasn't even sure he believed it.

"Not that much. Not enough."

"Is your mom still in touch with him?"

Vanessa made a wry face. "It wasn't a pretty divorce."

"Does he have a weakness?"

"You mean, like chocolate?"

"I was thinking allergies, but..." Sam shrugged. If she didn't give him something he could use, this whole detour to Boston was going to be a giant waste of time.

Vanessa scratched at a spot on the counter. "It's all about him, always. Like my liking other girls wasn't about me. It was about, what would people say about *him*? How would it affect his life? His reputation? That he had been too weak to mold me into the 'perfect' daughter." She scowled, but he could see the hurt in her eyes. "Like I'm some mindless piece of clay waiting for his *patriarchal molding*."

Sam felt bad that he was making Vanessa revisit this pain, but he pushed on. For Nico. "How do I stop him?"

"He's not some Jesus-powered superman."

Sam snorted. "Yeah."

"I mean, there's no kryptonite." Vanessa was quiet for a moment. "He's an upper-middle-class, white, straight, cis man, pissed off at everyone who isn't working toward making the world the way he's sure God wants it."

Sam tried to think about how any of that could be helpful. "That's it?"

"That's it." Vanessa picked up her graphic novel, pointedly done with Sam.

Dead end. At least he tried. He might as well head back to New York, regroup with Ari, figure out his next step.

"I won't tell him where you are," Sam said, and turned to head out.

"My dad's an asshole. We agree on that."

Sam turned back, but Vanessa kept her eyes on her book as she spoke. "Bottom line: He always has to be right. He wants to be right, more than he wants to be in a relationship. Any relationship. Except with God. And he and God don't argue, because God is smart enough to not talk back. Took me a long time to get that smart." She turned the page of her book, like she was already absorbed in it.

"Thanks," Sam said, but she didn't respond. It was all he was going to get from her.

Sam worked through what he'd learned as he left the library.

He was willing to give up any relationship. With his wife.

With Vanessa.

Because he has to be right.

And that focus on being right made him blind to other things—like his daughter wanting to be loved by him. Vanessa's pain, even all these years later, made that clear.

As he headed outside Sam put his Bond sunglasses back on, thinking that a blind spot wasn't much, but it was something.

One Good Thing

So the daughter wasn't the key to stopping Hergenreder.

Maybe Nico's not answering because I don't have anything concrete to tell him. I may like him, but it doesn't change the fact that his life's a mess.

Ari came up with a new lead, so I'm on another plane. Connecting through Phoenix. I'll crash at a hotel by the airport tonight and take the first flight out in the morning to Bakersfield. Connecting flights suck, but it's not like I can use the credit card to charter a plane from Zoltan. This isn't exactly an emergency I can explain to Dad and Mom — who are too busy living their best ~~lies~~ to even care about throwing their love away. Somebody has to be honest about how they feel. Care about holding on to something — someone — when it's great. When it's meant to be.

Isn't it?

Not if I can't prove it to Nico.

Not if I can't save him.

So that's what I have to do. I have to man up. Bond up? Save my guy.

And then, maybe, we'll have a chance.

The lead: Ari ran "Hergenreder" through some voice search tech and found an online wedding video, where the groom (so young — was he even 21?) thanked a Dr. Eugene Hergenreder.

I just watched it again.

They're doing toasts. The groom lifts his glass and looks off camera as he says the name: "And I want to thank Dr. Eugene Hergenreder, for giving me..." He pauses, nervous eyes darting to the young woman in the off-the-rack wedding gown next to him. "Sarah and me, the life I always dreamed of."

Why would he thank a monster?

Then there's a voice that says, "You did the work, Nelson. We're all really happy for you."

He doesn't sound like a monster. He sounds like a proud teacher. *Is that an act?*

Ari ran Nelson's face through some database and found an online profile for a Nelson Sutherland. The first six words describing him say it all: "Fantasy Footballer. Proud ex-gay. Husband."

Ex-gay? Bullshit.

That expression on Nelson's face? He's scared. Acting for the audience. His parents, school friends, Hergenreder, the online public.

What leverage did they use to make him "ex-gay?" Did they lock him up like they locked up Nico? Shock him, too? How did they break him?

My heart aches for Nico. For his friend Bee. For all those kids locked up just for being themselves.

Even for Nelson, this clueless pawn in Hergenreder's game.

So here's the new plan:

Get Nelson Sutherland to expose Hergenreder's reprogramming "Institute" for what it is. And with Hergenreder discredited, Nico will be safe. The rest of them will be freed as the whole thing gets closed down.

And while I'm out there, I'm going to case out Hergenreder's Institute. Bond always checks out the villain's headquarters — looking for where he can get an advantage. And I need some advantage!

Because if I can bring down Hergenreder — make that _when_ I bring down Hergenreder — then Nico and me (Frida would be all grammar queen and make me write "I" there, but to hell with the rules) can make things work.

I want things to work.

17

NICO

ONE TINY RECEPTION BAR. Nico finally had a phone again. He was standing in a parking lot just outside the night market. He entered the number from his forearm, digit by digit. He'd memorized it but kept checking anyway, not wanting to mess up this chance. His shoulders were exhausted. He was exhausted. But the police wouldn't be searching for him this far away. Not yet.

He pressed dial, but it just got him some high-pitched tone, a recording in Spanish that the call couldn't go through. He pressed the button to text, praying it would make it.

You can't go home. Dr. H will come for you. N.

He wished he had his old phone. Sam's texts from before. And a number Sam would recognize. Would he even open a text from some random international number?

Nico ripped into another protein bar. Lemon icing over dry cake wasn't his favorite, but it was better than Gold Wheels Preacher Institute mush. His foot bounced on the gravel under him, a fast packed-down crunching sound. He texted again.

Stay safe. On my way.

Two didn't make up for the ten he hadn't responded to. Hadn't even read. But it was a start.

He swallowed and took another huge bite as he logged into the vloggers lounge.

> **No Obstacles:** I need your help. I'm in trouble. No joke,
> life or death. Puerto Escondido, Mexico.
> **321Boom:** That's almost Guatemala! I'm in Arizona.
> **Power2People:** I'm even more north, in Bozeman,
> Montana.
> **321Boom:** Can you come here?
> **No Obstacles:** No.

He checked the map again on his phone. A straight shot north to the border would take him to...

> **No Obstacles:** Closest I can get is Reynosa, Mexico. It
> will take 22 hours—I can be there by midnight. Can
> you meet me?
> **321Boom:** Booking flight now.
> **Power2People:** In my van, GPS loaded. 27 hours.
> **321Boom:** I'll be there before you, get a motel room,
> and message you an address.
> **No Obstacles:** Bring your tools. Please. Both of you.
> We're going to need them.

An absurd burst of hope rose in his chest as Nico pocketed the phone. They were online friends he didn't really know at all, and yet... maybe they did know each other, on some level deeper than names, and faces, and the fake masks everyone wore in this world. At least, they knew Nico enough to care about him. Enough to meet him. Enough to try to help.

Nico popped the last third of the protein bar in his mouth and pocketed the wrapper. No leaving any clues behind.

He straddled the old motorcycle he'd swapped the kayak and a hundred dollars for. Put on the helmet. Dropped the visor in place. Started up the bike. The roar was good—it would keep him awake.

He pulled out of the parking lot, gravel spraying behind his tires until he hit the paved road. He wasn't going to stop to sleep.

18

SAM

TUE 8 JAN
1128
BAKERSFIELD CA

As the plane landed, Sam flipped the bracelet Ari had given him to make sure he couldn't be recorded. No camera would see him in California. But when he turned on his phone, there was still no text from Nico.

He tried calling again, but it just went to the prerecorded voicemail, so he didn't even get to hear Nico's voice. Sam didn't leave a message. That was too desperate. He'd already left a slew of texts, and Nico hadn't bothered responding.

There was another international text, another *Thanks for staying at Club Azul, please take our survey so we can rub salt in the wound because you're so much more into Nico that he is into you, because otherwise why isn't he even answering your texts?*

Sam wasn't going to read it. He hit delete.

And blocked the number.

It sucked being the one guy in the whole world who actually felt anything. Who cared.

At the airport curb, an Asian woman waved him over. She stood in front of an electric blue Ferrari 812 GTS Spider with a white racing stripe down the driver's side. "Linda Sue," she introduced herself, dropping the key into Sam's hand, "789 horsepower. Zoltan said you'd be kind to my baby."

"I promise." Sam thanked her, admiring the car's lines. It was perfect.

His phone app was already set with driving directions for the house where Nico had borrowed the bike. It was a point of pride for Nico that he had memorized the address—911 Jacaranda—and mailed them $872 in cash to pay them back the cost of that bike, new.

Sam had looked up *jacaranda*: they were these trees that bloomed purple flowers, pretty much like a Dr. Seuss illustration. And 911, well, heck, that was his birthday. Easy to memorize for him too. From everything Nico had told him, Hergenreder's Institute wouldn't be hard to find from there.

Getting behind the wheel felt oh so James Bond right. And on the open highway, shifting into fifth felt like how that lady had described meditating, the one time they'd tried to do it as a private family lesson back when he was in fifth grade.

"Don't try, just be, breathe." She inhaled. "Breathe, be just, try don't." She exhaled. "Don't try, just be, breathe." She inhaled.

The whole wonky syntax thing made Sam think of Yoda. He couldn't stop himself, and said in his best Yoda voice, "Meditating, I am." Which completely gave him the giggles.

The meditation teacher frowned as she exhaled. "Breathe, be just, try don't."

Trying to stop just made it funnier. His dad had cracked up then too. His mom wasn't far behind. And then, all three of them were laughing, and the meditation teacher lost track of where she was and had to start all over again. They hadn't meditated again, but it was a good memory to hold on to, of when they felt like a family.

Hardtop down and in fifth gear, with the V12 roaring behind him, shooting along CA 178 East at exactly fifty-five—cops with radar guns loved nabbing sports cars—was Sam's kind of meditation.

1311

KERNVILLE CA

Exactly 0.82 miles from the address he'd programmed, Sam crested the rise in the road and saw it. Hergenreder's Institute was two stone buildings on a hill with a construction crane on the far side. He turned onto one of the residential streets opposite and U-turned to park in the shade of a massive magnolia tree.

Sam tried to see the building with 007 eyes. Forty feet up, a row of windows glowed red in the shadows—prison cells, just like Nico had told him about. Seventy kids inside. Maybe sixty-nine, if they hadn't replaced Nico. Locked up just because they were Queer. Like Nico. Like him.

Sam set his phone to record video, propped it in the driver's window, and gunned the engine. Across the street and up the steep hill, he took it slow to not scrape the undercarriage. Crept past the Institute's driveway entrance, then up the hill. Left along an alley that had a chain-link fence with green privacy fabric blocking off the construction site—but the gate was open and he could see the construction office trailer and a fence with razor wire beyond. Left again, past a line of pickups and vans down the steep incline to the main road again.

He crossed back to the residential area where the Jacaranda house was and pulled off to the side. Sam checked the recording. He'd gotten what he needed and could study it later.

The idea of Nico being trapped in there was almost physically painful. And Bec and all those other teens were still locked up inside.

Sam shook it off. It was time to meet Nelson.

He roared back down the hill, leaving the Institute behind.

Sam parked outside the Target. He called up the image of Nelson on his phone, making sure he'd recognize him, and did his best magical penis swagger across the parking lot.

Entering the store, he took off his Bond aviators—no hiding behind sunglasses this time—and slid them into the neckline of his *No Time to Die* Craig-Bond blue Brunello Cucinelli Oxford button-down shirt. He'd had it tailored, and while he might not be as muscular as Bond, or Nico, at least Sam could work the muscles he did have. He scanned the aisles, checking everyone in a telltale red employee shirt. *No. No. No. No.* And then, by the quick-grab refrigerator shelves, something about the hunch of the shoulders of the guy stocking plastic tubs of lettuce caught Sam's eye.

He strode over.

His hunch about the hunch was right.

"Nelson?"

The guy raised his head, blinking in confusion. "Do I know you?"

"Instagram friends."

"Oh."

Sam could see him mentally running through his forty-eight followers, most of them from his church, trying to figure out who Sam was.

"I'm James," Sam said. The guy didn't need to know who Sam really was. "I was hoping we could talk…"

Nelson checked that no one was near them. "I'm kind of working… And I'm not supposed to be alone with another guy." He got really busy studying the dates stamped on the romaine lettuce containers.

"Any guy?" Sam knew he was being flirty. But this was for Nico.

Nelson blushed. Fidgeted with the ring on his left hand, fourth finger: wedding ring. Nelson checked again for someone to save him, but their section was empty. Just the two of them.

Sam turned on the charm. He'd been charmed by Kevin and Nico. Enough to know how it was done. Enough to do it. "I want to know how you pulled it off. How did you marry a girl, when what you want is…" Sam let his eyes travel down Nelson's face and neck to the unbuttoned V of his red polo. The white choker necklace set off alarms in his head. *It's what Nico freaked out about.* The same kind of necklace that had shocked him! And this guy wore it like it was just jewelry. Sam pushed the thought away. He had a job to do. He let his eyes slide down Nelson's chest. Made his voice flirty. "Something else."

"I don't know you." It was weak. Almost like Sam could feel Nelson's will crumbling under his gaze.

"You could." Sam tilted his head to the side and hooked a finger under his Craig-Bond *Quantum of Solace* black leather Prada belt with a silver buckle. Nelson's eyes went there, like the audience checking out Frida's Crank Shaft bulges. Sam waited for Nelson to look back up to his face. When he did, Sam gave him that half smile, lips a bit higher on one side. The look Nico had mastered. That had mastered Sam. Maybe it wasn't subtle, but then again, Bond wasn't a subtle guy.

Nelson's breaths got faster, and the pupils of his eyes dilated a bit, even under the store's bright LED lights. It was a bit of a thrill to know he could have this effect on the guy. And the store cameras wouldn't record him, just Nelson standing there, panting at a blur of color in the air.

"My parents want to send me to the same place you went," Sam said. "To get 'straightened out.' Does it really change you, or did you just shove it all down?" Sam reached out a finger and trailed it down the front of Nelson's shirt. "Down," he repeated. The guy was trembling, but he didn't stop Sam. He didn't back away. Sam stopped his finger at Nelson's leather belt. "Down."

Nelson licked his lower lip. "Maybe we could go somewhere... to... uh..." Nelson's words stalled.

"Talk?" Sam supplied, pulling his hand back a few inches but leaving it between them, hovering. Teasing.

"Uh huh!" Nelson swallowed.

A woman came over to the crate of bagged avocados behind them and Nelson said loudly, "Let me show you where that is."

Sam dropped his hand fast but kept his face smooth. Interested. Bond-slick.

He followed Nelson past pet food and detergent to an empty room by a side entrance. Nelson spoke as he closed the door behind them: "They're going to use this for curbside pickup, but they haven't—"

Nelson stopped talking as Sam moved in to stand way too close.

Sam's face was just inches from Nelson's, and he could tell Nelson wanted to him to kiss him. Nelson's breath was sour, like he'd just had a yogurt. Sam ignored it and reached past Nelson's waist to twist the lock in the doorknob.

"I can't believe I'm doing this," Nelson said, reaching out shaking hands to touch Sam's chest.

Sam traced his fingers along Nelson's arm. He'd be cute, in a nerdy kind of way, if he weren't so repressed.

Speeding up, Nelson pulled up Sam's shirt, touching Sam's bare skin underneath.

Maybe not so repressed after all.

Nelson lunged forward to kiss him.

Nico's face flashed into Sam's mind. Maybe he could do this without doing anything more. Nelson wanted him. Wanted this. And they both knew it. Which meant Sam had made his point.

Sam stepped back to avoid the kiss, letting Nelson's hands fall off him. "So, Hergenreder? The Institute? Good idea, or terrible?"

"Shit." Nelson covered his face. "Sarah would kill me if she knew I was here. So would Dr. H."

"I'm guessing it didn't change anything, about how you feel?"

Nelson's hands clenched into fists. "It changed what I do about it!"

"Doesn't seem it."

Nelson closed his eyes. He was so busted.

"Help me stop him," Sam said. "We can go public with it being a reprogramming institute. And that 'reprogramming' is bullshit. You're their star graduate. If you tell the truth, it will blow the whole thing apart. We can take Hergenreder down, free everyone else locked in there."

Nico's dream, and it was so close, Sam could almost taste it. The feeling of power was heady.

He reached out and touched Nelson on the cheek. "What do you think?" If it would seal the deal, maybe he *should* kiss him?

Nelson shuddered. "You're like some gay terrorist. You want me to blow up my whole life to live some sick lifestyle!"

Sam hated that *lifestyle* line. Standard-issue bigotry. Make it a choice, then blame people for not choosing better. He ran his hand down to Nelson's neck, skipping over the white metal necklace to press against Nelson's chest. Moved in closer. Their lips just inches apart, Sam said, "It's not a lifestyle, it's a life."

Nelson pulled away this time. "I'd lose everything. Sarah, my job, the church."

"Everything fake about your life?" Sam pointed out.

"NONE OF—" Nelson started shouting but stopped himself, shifting to an angry whisper. "None of that's fake!"

Sam gave him a *really?* look.

Nelson's eyes narrowed. "Did Dr. H send you, to test me?"

"No."

But in the silence that followed they both knew that if it had been a test, Nelson had failed it. Spectacularly.

And the humiliation of that was clear on Nelson's face.

"You need to leave."

"Nelson. Come on. We can still do this." Sam tried to appeal to Nelson's ego. "You can change everything. Be the hero—save everyone in Hergenreder's prison!"

Nelson let out a bitter laugh. "I don't know where you come from, but this is Lost Hills." He held up his wedding ring. "This already made me a hero."

There was nothing left to say after that.

Sam had failed.

One Good Thing

How come when James Bond flies all over the world following clues something always comes from it?

I do it, and two dead ends.

Shit.

I'm wiped. Got stuck in traffic from Lost Hills and a 48-minute drive became 2 hours and 14 minutes of bumper-to-bumper hell. Ferraris aren't built for traffic jams. They're built for the open road.

Like me.

Ha! Even I don't believe that.

Like Bond.

Like Nico?

Anyway, crashing at a hotel here in Bakersfield. It's not like there's any rush to get home before school starts. Maybe I'll take a day, drive to San Francisco. Go all A View to a Kill. It's just over a four-hour drive, if traffic behaves. I'll stay there overnight and fly home Thursday morning.

Nico still hasn't answered any of my texts.

Ari wasn't much help. "Oh, Baby. Cis-on-cis romance? Not my area of expertise. Frida's the advice queen. Run it by her."

Frida just said I should give Nico more time.

I almost feel guilty about flirting with Nelson. Bond would have slept with him — and I didn't! —but Nico's silence feels like somehow he knows. He knows that I almost kissed Nelson. That Nelson wanted more. That it so easily could have been more...

And the things I did. Touching Nelson. Letting him touch me. Would I have done that with another guy in front of Nico?

No!

I want Nico to know I'm into _him_, not someone else. Not anyone else.

It feels like I cheated on Nico, a little.

But I did it for him!

And, if I'm honest, there's another kind of guilt swirling in my stomach. I used Nelson, like Kevin used me.

I used being hot — okay, that's a crazy thought, but I guess some guys think I'm hot — I used it to try and get what I wanted.

Classic Bond. He uses sex to manipulate all the time.

Hell, he has sex with the Bond Girls in all these movies, and it's almost always to push them to do something they wouldn't have done before the seduction.

Classic magical penis move, like with Pussy Galore in Goldfinger.

Sex is a tool. Being sexy is a tool. That's where I learned it.

But I feel like shit.

Shit!

James Bond is a terrible role model.

19

NICO

WED 9 JAN
0047
REYNOSA MEXICO

THE MOTEL DOOR OPENED AFTER two knocks. A woman in her nineties stood there in a green sweater with a blue agate-slice necklace on a thin silver chain. Slight but not frail. The opposite, like she was made from the earth itself. The canyons of her face lit up on seeing him. "Well there surely are *no obstacles* for you!"

"Three two one—?" Nico started.

"Boom!" She pulled Nico into a tight hug. Like some grandmother he never had. "You call me Godeane."

His legs shook.

When she released him he sank onto the bed with its tucked-in orange comforter, wanting to tell her everything. At least he knew where to start. "I'm Nico."

0153

He'd caught them up over a late-night dinner of greens, mashed potatoes, and fried chicken that Godeane had waiting for him. Power2People—*Byron,*

219

Nico reminded himself—was on a live video chat on Godeane's tablet, still more than three hours from the nearest town on the Texas side, McAllen. With his own satellite booster, Byron had internet and full bars everywhere he went.

Godeane focused on Warren's passport in her hand, then on Nico's face. Studying him.

"I can make you look just like this photo, but it's not going to help if they've flagged the passport because he's deceased."

Nico didn't mean to wince.

She put a sympathetic hand on his arm. "I'm truly sorry."

Nico nodded. He didn't think he could talk about Warren dying. Not yet.

"It runs off a database, right?" Byron asked.

Nico and Godeane glanced at each other, then back to Byron on Godeane's tablet. He took a swig from a thermos. "Homeland Security runs off a database. The system is national. International, really. And it's all in the cloud."

Nico followed the thought. "So if they're running the passport control system off the cloud, they'll catch me."

"It just means we need to make sure they can't reach the cloud." Byron grinned.

"Power outage?" Godeane asked.

Byron pursed his mouth and took a quick glance at the camera. "You know that one antenna out of alignment can ruin an entire relay?"

0218

Nico slept while Godeane visited a twenty-four-hour thrift store, grabbing toast-colored corduroys and a green cowboy shirt with white piping. She tossed in a belt with a Texas-sized buckle.

She got back to the motel room and gazed down on Nico, fast asleep. Plugged in to charge, his phone was inches from his head. Like he didn't want to miss some important call. She shook her head with affection, then lay down silently on the other bed.

0722
2 MILES WEST MCALLEN TX

Byron's van, set off with orange safety cones, was parked near a utility pole at the side of a deserted road. The sun was coming up as Byron, in a reflective vest and hard hat, worked at the top of the pole, attaching a small circuit inside the junction box.

0923
REYNOSA MEXICO

A used car lot. Godeane waved thanks to a pleased saleswoman and drove off in a butter-yellow Mustang convertible.

1008
2 MILES WEST MCALLEN TX

An aerial view of the roof of the McAllen Customs and Immigration Control building.

The view zoomed in on a fenced-off area holding a seven-foot satellite dish.

Inside his van, Byron worked on the final line of computer code.

Back above the immigration building, a hummingbird buzzed down from the sky to land inside the fencing, two feet from the dish. The hummingbird's eye dilated like a camera shutter. A pinhole in its mechanical head opened to capture sound.

Byron watched the monitor mounted to the van wall, showing him the hummingbird drone's view. Waveform sound lines registered a slight mechanical whir at the base of the satellite dish, revealing it was moving.

Byron punched the air. "Yes!"

Nico toggled to the vloggers lounge as he slipped his way up the stairs of the foster house in Fresno.

He was back. Again.

321Boom and Power2People weren't online, so he messaged them.

No Obstacles: *Did a stunt I haven't seen in a movie— used a moving truck as a bridge between 2 roofs!*

Nico headed to Carlos and Donnie's room. He'd grab his mattress and drag it into the hallway where he slept. Settle in, maybe plan how he could video the truck bridge stunt with only one cell camera. The upside of electronics-free detention was that he'd gotten his homework out of the way.

He spotted a new 321Boom video, "Glamorous like Jon Snow."

No Obstacles: *Whoa, not a 1940s movie reference?*

With a chuckle at his own snark, Nico pushed the door open with his shoulder as he hit play, watching a teenage girl sitting there and the time lapse of 321Boom's hands transforming her with makeup and bits of silicone into Kit Harington, the actor that played Jon Snow in the Game of Thrones series.

Nico froze and his eyes left the screen—there were two guys in the room, but they weren't Carlos or Donnie. Security guards? Social services? They were big, muscled, standing in front of the bunk bed and staring at Nico.

Nico dropped his backpack by the sagging inflatable mattress propped against the wall. He noticed there was no yellow-pad note from Janice on top of the pile of his bedding on the floor.

"New placement?" Nico asked, trying not to care. Were they there to take him back to Mrs. Parker's? He knew the answer was no. That was just another burned bridge that had gone down in rainbow flames.

Nico glanced down at his phone, the makeover still speeding along, but all he could think was that the school probably called Janice again. These guys, and no copied-out Bible verse? It meant she'd given up on him. It wasn't like he liked Lincoln High anyway. Or this foster setup, sleeping in the hallway like some dangerous-to-the-other-guys animal. But this would be the eleventh time he'd been thrown out, into the government's no-one-cares-about-you recycling program. At sixteen, he knew it wasn't a record, but it still felt like shit.

Instead of answering him, the guys rushed Nico like a football play. One kneed him in the gut, making him drop his phone. It clattered to the floor. Nico grabbed at it to call for help, but the guy tackled him, slamming Nico's head against Donnie's Roswell Is Real alien poster on the wall. Pain shot through Nico's skull.

He was seeing spots of light and trying to swing at them, but they grabbed his arms. Forced his wrists together and zip-tied them like handcuffs. They threw him to the floor and Mexican Jesus stared down at Nico from Carlos's half-finished paper-taped-to-the-ceiling art of the rapture, buses crashing and cities on fire while the saved floated up to heaven. A knee and three hundred pounds behind it crushed into Nico's chest. The shorter guy wrenched Nico's arms over his head, then stood on them, sneakers digging the plastic cuff deep into Nico's wrists.

Nico kicked. Screamed. Bucked like hell to try to fight back... but it was all business to them. In seconds the shins above Nico's boot tops were zip-tied together. Then his knees.

Nico's fists trembled with rage and freak-out fury, and his phone was only two feet away on the scuffed floorboards, probably showing Jon Snow's double, but he couldn't move at all.

They hoisted Nico up, carrying him out like a thrashing, cursing, screaming-for-help rolled-up carpet. Janice, foster mom of nobody's year, just stood there in the living room, taking a long drag on her box mod e-cigarette. Staring. She blew out an endless cloud.

Nico stopped struggling when he saw she was in on it. Went still.

And all he could think was that you probably couldn't call it kidnapping if they gave you away.

Outside, the men shoved Nico into the back of a white van, windows painted over white. More zip ties locked him to a seat facing backward.

Where are they taking me?

The engine started and they pulled away.

Bouncing his hand on his leg made the too-tight zip tie on Nico's left wrist dig into skin that was already raw. He tried to tap his leg instead. Anxious energy surged around inside him with nowhere to go. He wondered if you could call it kidnapping if there was no one to pay any ransom.

They got on the freeway and picked up speed.

And it hit Nico that no one knew where he was. No one even cared.

Nico gasped awake, eyes wide. Godeane smiled down at him. She had been putting makeup on his face while he slept. "It's okay, Nico. You're okay. Go back to sleep."

And though he wouldn't have thought it possible, he did.

1015
REYNOSA MEXICO

Godeane worked her makeup as Nico slept flat on his back. New layers of skin. A false beard with bits of gray. Graying his hair at the temples to match.

Three hours later, Godeane woke Nico with a gentle shake. "Time to go, darling."

Nico blinked, sitting up. He rolled his shoulders, raising his arm—

"Don't touch your face," Godeane reminded him.

Nico dropped his hand.

"Clothes are hanging on the bathroom door."

He headed for the mirror over the bathroom sink.

Warren stared back at him.

He closed his jaw. "You're a magician."

"Do what you have to in there, and put on the outfit." Godeane sounded giddy. "The reveal is the best part!"

A few minutes later, Nico stepped out of the bathroom, transformation complete. He put his hands out in a *what do you think?* gesture.

Godeane studied her work. "Handsome."

Nico walked over to the full-length mirror on the inside of the closet door. He really did look like Warren, but healthy. "Warren would have loved this."

He took a selfie and texted it to Sam, even though he was pretty sure Sam wouldn't get it. Sam probably hated him. Had blocked his number. Forgotten all about him.

Nico sent the text anyway.

On my way to you. N.

1352

MCALLEN-HIDALGO INTERNATIONAL BRIDGE US/ MEXICO BORDER

The US border guard standing by their car flipped through Godeane's passport, stopping at the stamp showing where she'd entered Mexico. "You flew to Mexico but you're driving home in this? Is it a rental?"

Godeane leaned over Nico in the driver's seat to answer. "Do you know I had to take four connecting flights from Tuscon to meet my grandson at the General Lucio Blanco International Airport in Reynosa? Darling boy was on vacation and spotted this car. Knows I love a convertible. Anyway, Warren hates flying. Weak stomach."

She didn't give Nico a chance to speak, which was good. He wasn't sure he could sound like a thirty-four-year-old. And he was laser focused on not bouncing his leg, not tapping his hand, not revealing anything about how freaked out he was on the inside.

Godeane chatted on: "And this way, we get to go on a grandmother-grandson road trip together. We've got the bill of sale right here, "she opened the glove compartment, handing papers over. "We even have our customs form, all filled out."

"It's a stick?" The border guard leaned in, so close to his face Nico was sure the man would see his beard was fake.

"It's the four-speed automatic," Godeane admitted.

"Eh. Shame about that," the border guard said.

"Isn't she a beauty though?" Godeane ran her fingers along the dash.

"The color?" The border guard made a face. "But the lines..." he whistled in appreciation.

"Good bones," Godeane agreed. "The rest is just makeup."

Nico shot her a *don't push it* look, but she ignored it.

The border guard mused, "You can always paint it."

"There's an idea, Warren!" Godeane said, squeezing his arm.

The border guard tapped their forms and passports against his palm. "Internet's down. Again. I'll just make copies of these and we'll get you on your way." He went back into the booth for their lane.

Will the internet still be down? Will he figure it out?

Nico turned up the air-conditioning, trying not to sweat under all the makeup and fake parts of Warren's face on his. The beard was hard to get used to. He checked out his reflection in the rearview mirror. Drops of sweat in his hairline.

Chill, man.

If he floored it, they could break the little arm blocking the car and be off—but then they'd have cops chasing them and he'd never get to Sam. He'd be arrested and thrown right back in a prison cell under Gold Wheels Preacher's control. And he'd probably get Godeane arrested too.

He rubbed his fingers sideways on his corduroy pants, making it scratch. Back and forth. Back and forth.

Godeane put her hand on his to still him. "Trust. Byron is a professional."

A flash of iridescent wings as a hummingbird landed on top of the mechanical arm, eye dilating toward the guard booth.

The border guard walked over to their car, passing everything back to Godeane's outstretched hand. "Okay, we've done what we can. Drive safe." He used a clicker and before the metal arm lifted the hummingbird darted into the sky, leading the way. With the arm all the way up, they could go.

"What color do you think?" Godeane asked the border guard. "For the car."

Nico just wanted to floor it, but her hand was still on his. Telling him to wait.

The border guard took the car in, bumper to bumper. "I'm a fan of gold, but this is more..."

"Butter," Nico said.

"Yeah," the border guard agreed.

"Gold!" Godeane radiated charm. "Great idea. We'll kick it up a notch to gold. Thank you!" Godeane gave Nico's hand a quick pat.

Time to go.

"You two take care now." The border guard waved the next car up, as Nico eased down on the accelerator and they crossed into the US.

1549
US 281 NORTH 44 MILES WEST CORPUS CHRISTI TX

"I need to get to New York. To Sam," Nico said as soon as the waitress left with their order. They'd met up with Byron in a Denny's on the road north.

"They'll be watching ticket purchases for planes, trains, buses." Byron said. "Driving is really the only option. New York City is twenty-eight hours, if all we do is stop for gas."

"We can take turns," Nico said.

"We'll have to," Byron agreed.

"I'll drive the Mustang straight home and lock it in the garage," said Godeane. "They'll be searching for it."

"They'll track you," Nico protested.

"I'm ninety-two, darling. I can always play the..." She blinked, a distant, confused expression coming over her face. "*I did—what?*"

"Great, they'll think I took advantage of you."

Godeane laughed. "What do you think, Byron?" Sharp as ever, she put her arm around Nico's shoulder. "Do we make a cute couple?"

"Not like that." Nico shrugged her arm off, but not roughly. He sighed. "How am I ever going to get my life back?"

"One thing at a time, darling."

Nico nodded. "Sam." He turned to Byron, who was blowing on his coffee.

"They always make it so hot," Byron complained. "And adding ice just dilutes it." He blew on the steaming drink again, then put it down in frustration.

"How long do we have till they're back online?" Nico asked.

Byron stared at his mug, like he was willing it to cool down. "I buried the code to adjust for leap year every ten minutes. It started hours before you crossed. And it self-duplicates."

"Could I get a translation for my generation, please?" Godeane asked.

"I figure it will stall them for about twenty-four more hours. Then they'll run all the passports from the last day through." Byron took a cautious sip. "That's a manual process, could give us another hour. But once they're back in the cloud and the passport is uploaded it's only seconds..."

"For them to see a dead man reentered the country." Godeane followed the train of thought. "They'll find the identity theft alert on Warren Bennett... and call the police."

"And the police will tell Dr. H." Nico finished. "He'll know I'm coming for Sam."

"He'll have to get to New York too," Godeane pointed out.

Nico bit at the corner of his lip. "What if he's already there? What if he left for there as soon as he saw the ticket and figured out where Sam lives?"

Byron considered it. "Better expect a trap."

Nico checked his phone. Still no text from Sam. He set a countdown clock on his phone: 25 HRS 00 MIN 00 SEC. Hit START.

"If we're going to get there first, we need to make up three hours— four would be better." Nico called to their waitress behind the counter. "Excuse me? We'll need that order to go."

"Let's get you cleaned up first," Godeane told him.

1608

COUNTDOWN CLOCK: 24 HRS 46 MIN 13 SEC

Leaving the back of Byron's van, Nico looked like himself again. He'd kept the corduroys and borrowed one of Byron's T-shirts and a denim jacket.

Godeane wrapped Nico in another one of her hugs.

Byron placed the bag of food between the seats and stood by the driver's door, ready for them to go.

As Godeane held him, Nico told her, "No one's ever risked their own safety for me before. Thank you."

"Darling, don't you know?" She held him out to look at him, eyes shining bright. "That's what we do for people we love."

20

SAM

SAM DOWNSHIFTED THE FERRARI TO the Treasure Island exit, but it didn't feel like meditating. None of the drive had. He pulled off to the lookout point and got out, hitting lock on the key fob and making his way down the stack of boulders to the water's edge. He sat on one, propping his feet on a log that had long ago washed up on the island's shore. He pulled out his phone. Started a text to Nico: I miss you then forced himself to delete it, letter by letter.

He pocketed the phone and put his head in his hands for a long moment. Eyes wet, he raised his head to take in the skyscrapers and sprawl of San Francisco spread out across the water. The rest of the Bay Bridge was to his left, and north of the city the Golden Gate Bridge gleamed.

The climactic moment from *A View to a Kill*, with Moore-Bond and Zorin fighting it out seven hundred feet above the water on the main cable of the bridge flashed through his mind. Stacey screaming in fright just below them as they wrestled for the axe. So old-school sexist. And how annoying that Bond's love interests were always these women who were amazing and capable... until they were forced to slip around in heels to get out of the way while the "men" settled things. And after Zorin's plunge to his death, of course it's Bond who axes the mooring rope, jerking Zorin's Nazi father figure back into the airship's passenger car with the lit sticks of dynamite, causing the final explosion that takes out all the bad guys.

Bond for the win.

Stacey for… well, the in-the-shower love scene just before the end credits roll.

Like Bond couldn't deal with an actual equal. Didn't *want* an equal. Sam did. More than anything.

1347

MUSEUM OF MODERN ART SAN FRANCISCO CA

Sam walked out into the rooftop sculpture garden. San Francisco was freezing, and he zipped up his dark blue Tom Ford knitted-sleeve bomber jacket, like Craig-Bond wore in *Spectre*.

He made a slow circle around the statue of a young man. It was exaggerated in size, two feet taller than Sam, and nude. He read the museum label:

> Wilhelm Lehmbruck
> German, 1881–1919
> **Standing Youth**
> 1913

Sam felt rooted there, staring at a guy who could have been his age, from the past. Cast in stone.

Stone boys don't feel, he told himself. *But the real boy who posed for that felt things.* Sam stared at the hand, raised like the guy was about to say something. About to spring into life. Like Nico, always on the edge of jumping into action. He loved that about him.

Sam turned away. It didn't help that everything reminded him of the guy he'd lost.

ONLINE VIDEO, uploaded 1710
PLOT HOLES—Episode 1—Earth 2.0

Sam's finger moved back from turning on selfie mode. Modern hotel wallpaper behind him, he slouched in a chair, in a white Henley T-shirt and gray jeans, as he spoke to the camera.

> SAM
>
> Hey, I'm Sam. This is my new video series—calling it *Plot Holes*. Just watched *Earth 2.0*, it's in theaters, and, uh, I saw it on demand. Anyway, yeah. The plot?

He sighed, then reached over to grab his ukulele. Strummed a few chords, the music helping him focus. Sitting up with more energy, Sam picked at the strings as he ran it down.

> SAM
>
> Okay, making the mission to find, and then terraform, a hostile-to-humanity other planet, while not explaining why we can't terraform the getting-more-hostile-to-humanity Earth we're already on, is a logic thread that, once you pull it, unravels the whole movie. Like the sweater my savta tried to knit me last year—and let's just say chess is more her thing. No offense, Savta.

Not that you'll be watching this. Not that anyone will. It's just... a friend does these videos that are so cool, and I thought this... Well, I thought it would make me feel kind of closer to him.

His hand stilled on the ukulele as he closed his eyes. Took a breath. Opened them again.

SAM

Yeah. This is stupid.

Sam stood, bonking his ukulele against the chair holding his cell phone and knocking it to the carpet. Lens blocked, the phone recorded only the dissonant echo until he turned the camera off.

1838
CASTRO SAN FRANCISCO CA

Sam walked slowly by the Castro Theatre. His favorite Craig-Bond baseball cap from *No Time to Die* didn't make him feel any better, or any more Bond.

An older Gay couple in animated conversation, one with his arm around the other, strolled through the neon light toward him. Sam turned to watch them as they passed, and stood there staring after them until they disappeared around a corner.

1852
LGBTQ+ HISTORY MUSEUM CASTRO SAN FRANCISCO CA

Sam paused at the photo labeled TREASURE ISLAND NAVAL BASE to read the caption:

> During World War II, men in the US Armed Forces who were caught being Gay were locked up and experimented on in this military psychiatric prison.

Pretty sad history, Sam thought. *We've got to make Hergenreder's Institute history too.*

1923
TELEGRAPH HILL SAN FRANCISCO CA

The high-end Japanese restaurant was famous for its amazing view. But eating alone at his table for two, Sam's eyes kept going to the empty chair opposite him.

<u>One Good Thing</u>

A lonely day. I don't think I spoke with anyone, except for doing the video. Vlog. I uploaded it, but it's not like there's any point. Nico's not going to see it.

He's not going to text me back.

I'm not going to get him back, not unless I can pull off something Bond-level brilliant. Neutralize Hergenreder as a threat, and prove to Nico I'm the guy for him. That we can make it work. That we can be a team, neither of us needing to slip around in heels. That we can fight side-by-side.

It's past 2 AM, which sucks because I have to be up early for the flight home. But the day's not technically over until I go to sleep! And I still don't have my one good thing.

I guess... I tried? It didn't do anything, but I _tried_ to get something on Hergenreder.

Tried to figure out what motivates him.

Tried to find some leverage to get the upper hand, to free Nico and all those other kids.

What would Bond do?

- Race Zorin in a rigged steeplechase.
- Make love to kick-ass Grace Jones to cover his snooping. She's so amazing and he's like, _Well, I'll do it for God and country..._ May Day was so much more an equal than Stacey. Focus, Sam.
- Break into Zorin's office to copy the check Zorin had just written Stacey. To figure out who she was and follow the money.

Follow the money...

FOLLOW THE MONEY!

21

NICO

"And they shall come from the east, and from the west, and from the north, and from the south, and shall sit down in the kingdom of God. Luke 13:29." Gold Wheels Preacher and Nico were crossing the Institute courtyard.

Nico was back. Again.

Gold Wheels Preacher gestured grandly for Nico to take it all in: "No doors. No bars on the windows. No giant walls."

Nico wasn't impressed. "It's still a prison."

"Given your history of violence, Number Seventy, wouldn't any rational person say you deserve prison?"

"No! And I'm not violent!"

Gold Wheels Preacher scoffed. "Four fights in eleven days?"

"I'm not the guy throwing the first punch!" Being Gay hadn't exactly been a plus at Lincoln High. And somehow the whole student body, the teachers, everyone knew before he even set foot on campus. The two ideas clicked together, and Nico realized that Gold Wheels Preacher knew too. If they couldn't officially kidnap him and lock him up for being Gay, it meant they had to come up with another reason. So they decided he was violent.

The thought made Nico want to punch him.

"*Newborns will scratch themselves bloody if they're not properly swaddled, arms tucked safely against their bodies. They don't even realize the things scratching them are their own fingernails. They're just not ready for that kind of freedom.*" Gold Wheels Preacher headed to the building due west, and Nico kept pace, trying to figure out if there was a way to get the tablet from him and control the electroshock collar before he could get zapped again. "*And that's what we're doing here at the Institute.*"

"*You're swaddling me?*" Nico didn't even try to keep the mocking tone out of his voice as he cradled his left wrist. It wasn't bleeding anymore but throbbed like hell.

"*We remove all distractions.*" Gold Wheels Preacher led them into the stone building. There was a guardroom on the landing, and beyond that two short staircases going up and down. The door was open, and the guard took his feet off the desk fast.

"*Dr. H!*"

"*How are things, Brian?*"

"*Living the dream,*" the guard said, but not like he meant it. "*Hey, do you think my cell will work in the new building?*"

Nico studied the screens in front of the guard while the two men spoke. One was a grid of faces, the other security camera shots. He focused on those.

"*They don't build them like this anymore, that's for sure.*" Gold Wheels Preacher slapped the stone wall. "*But honestly, most of it will be underground. That's why we have landlines.*"

"*Landlines don't have internet. In here, even in the cafeteria, it's a total dead zone,*" the guard groused. "*Maybe we can get Wi-Fi?*"

"*Your job doesn't have much need for the internet though, does it?*" Gold Wheels Preacher used two fingers to point to the monitors on the guard's desk. "*That ye may attend upon the Lord without distraction. Corinthians 7:35.*"

Sheepish, the guard focused where he'd been told.

Nico took inventory of the views: multiple hallways; a large cafeteria; and only two exterior camera views, one of the courtyard they'd just walked through and the other of some bushes and the edge of a metal garage door. So there probably isn't a remote in the van after all. The guard sees who drives up and opens the gate from here. He'd need a different way out.

Gold Wheels Preacher continued lecturing the guard: "Security protocols require this door to be shut at all times, for your own protection. You know that, Brian. Don't make me tell you again." He shut the door. Through the chicken-wire-glass window, Nico thought the guard looked like a prisoner himself.

Byron's van hit a pothole and Nico startled awake.

Nico thought about how in some ways, even though he'd escaped, he still felt like a prisoner.

THU 1Ø JAN
Ø612
I-59 NORTH AL
COUNTDOWN CLOCK: 1Ø HRS 42 MIN 33 SEC

Whoa. He'd slept fourteen hours. That meant Bec was on day 196. And Squirrel Boy and all the others were still trapped there too... But he had to save Sam first.

Nico checked—nothing from Sam. From his spot on the beanbag squeezed between heavy-duty computer racks in the back, he stared at the two shelves holding wire bins with... birds inside? Four pigeons. A pair of hummingbirds.

"What's with the dead birds?" Nico asked.

Byron kept his eyes on the interstate. "My drones. And their models."

"You made them?" Nico was impressed. He stood to get a better look. Even up close, it was hard to tell which were mechanical and which were stuffed.

"I can't just walk around testing random electrical plugs. The birds do it for me."

"How?"

"Pigeons, mainly. One's a decoy, strutting and flying around the tester, keeping people away. The tester backs its tail into electrical sockets out in public. Readout on the controller tells me if it's live."

Nico remembered how Power2People's videos zoomed in from a thousand feet up to photos that stepped closer and closer to the live plugs. "Which one takes the pictures?"

"Tester's programmed after every live test to get two and then five feet away. Camera's in its butt." Byron chuckled. "No one's going to look too close there!"

Nico snorted at the truth of that. "And the hummingbird?"

Byron sighed in satisfaction. "That beauty's my eyes and ears. It does the swooping-down-from-high videos. It's how I knew you and 321Boom got through the border. It even has a panic mode to dive-bomb folks in a ten-foot radius to help me get away. Haven't had to use it yet, but good to have."

"That's... amazing." Nico made his way to the passenger seat and plopped down. The two-lane separated highway didn't have any lights, and clouds blocked out the sky as Byron sped them north.

"I'm trying to figure out my next bird," Byron said. "It has to blend in, so no one pays it too much mind. And it has to be useful. Any ideas?"

Nico thought back to the moment when he most wished he had some help. Back when Gold Wheels Preacher had him in that chair. Before Sports Radio Guy and Music Radio Guy put that fucking collar on him. If Byron had been there to help him get away... A dive-bombing hummingbird would have helped, but it wouldn't have taken his captors out. "What about a bee?" Nico suggested.

"Hmm. What could something that small do?"

"Maybe knock someone out with a tranquilizer dart, without anyone knowing who did it."

Nico imagined Gold Wheels Preacher and the guys that had abducted him from the last foster home unconscious on the floor of that intake room, and his past self just walking out the open garage door. Free. Three drone bees flying over his shoulder like in some Disney movie. But that would have left Bec, and Squirrel Boy, and all the rest of them trapped in Gold Wheels Preacher's Institute. And Nico wouldn't have even known they were there.

He still hadn't done anything to help them. But he had to save Sam first!

One thing at a time. Like Godeane said.

Byron considered it. "There's no science reason I couldn't go that small. Have to hold enough tranquilizer, so maybe more than one... Folks sometimes get stung by multiple bees, right? I'll have to do some calculations."

Nico noticed the time to destination on the dash: 13 HRS 51 MIN. He checked the countdown clock on his phone: 10 HRS 39 MIN 57 SEC. They were still three hours behind! "You were supposed to wake me!"

"You're exhausted," Byron pointed out.

"I'm fine. Let me drive—I can go faster."

"A Black man doesn't speed in Alabama," Byron agreed. "Wake up all the way first. Eat something. You can take over when we get to Tennessee."

Nico couldn't argue about being hungry. He opened the takeout bag. "As soon as I'm done, I'll drive. We need to make up that time!"

THU 10 JAN
1103
I-81 NORTH 60 MILES NE KNOXVILLE TN
COUNTDOWN CLOCK: 06 HRS 52 MIN 11 SEC
TIME TO DESTINATION: 09 HRS 42 MIN

They weren't making up enough time.

Nico was driving, and he allowed himself a swig of Red Bull each time the odometer clocked another five miles. Thinking how ridiculous it was that he fought with that idiot Clark about something so stupid. The day he got kidnapped and taken to Gold Wheels Preacher's Institute—a lifetime ago. But it was never about the energy drink. It was a pissing contest because Clark couldn't deal with Nico being Gay.

And Nico couldn't shake the idea that this thing with Gold Wheels Preacher was a weird extension of that. Another pissing contest because he was Gay. But really, wasn't there something pretty Gay about holding your dick next to another guy holding *their* dick to see who could piss the farthest? Nico snorted at the thought.

He wished Sam would text him back. Call him. In Byron's van, his phone had full bars, full internet. But outside Sam's voicemail greeting, a brassy musical sting—*Like from one of the Bond movies he loves so much*—followed by just "You know what to do," Sam was radio silent.

Nico had even tried calling from Byron's phone, but again the call went right to voicemail. So he'd texted:

Sam, it's N., using a friend's phone. Don't go home. Dr.
H is after you. On my way.

But still nothing.

And they hadn't been able to grab the GPS signal from Sam's phone to figure out where he was, which Byron explained probably meant it was turned off.

Nico eased off the accelerator when he saw he was going eighty-two. They needed to make up time, but twelve miles over the speed limit was too risky. *Being white, you can get away with nine miles over,* Byron had told him. *I need to keep it two miles under.* That eleven-mile-an-hour spread was why Nico was trying to do all the rest of the driving: eleven miles an hour faster meant they could shave off one hour twenty-one minutes from Byron's time for the 665 miles remaining. Which could be the difference between saving Sam... or being too late.

Nico checked the time gap between the countdown clock and the time to destination: two hours fifty minutes. Minus one hour twenty-one minutes, and even with him driving, Gold Wheels Preacher would still have a one-hour-twenty-nine-minute lead—if he wasn't already at Sam's apartment holding him hostage. He wanted to be pissed at Byron for letting him sleep too long earlier, but it was out of kindness, and Nico couldn't be mad. He just hoped it wouldn't cost him everything. That it wouldn't cost Sam more than even *he* could afford.

The asphalt rolled under their headlights, but a bank of clouds hung heavy and slow above. There was no real traffic to pass, and only the occasional truck on the other side of the dark embankment to the west. Everything reminded Nico that they weren't going fast enough. His fingers drummed the steering wheel. Not a melody, just movement. Just something that felt fast, that he could control. He watched the odometer tick past nine to zero and took another sugary cough-syrup sip so he could push through. He shook off the shudder that always came next.

Byron called up from his beanbag workstation, "I did a dark web alert on Warren Bennett. Found his sister."

"Geena," Nico supplied.

"She's presenting at some teacher conference, later today. You might want to drop in and see what she's saying."

Nico shook his head. "We can't detour."

"But we can multitask…" Byron typed fast on his wireless keyboard. "All we need is an audio patch, full feed, untraceable. Oh! " He laughed. "They just put in LAN lines? I won't even need to send a bird."

1659
I-81 NORTH 4 MILES NE CARLISLE PA
COUNTDOWN CLOCK: 00 HRS 56 MIN 49 SEC
TIME TO DESTINATION: 02 HRS 32 MIN

Nico felt panicky about the time, but Byron convinced him five minutes wouldn't matter. And Nico felt he owed it to Warren, in a way he couldn't really explain.

The video feed playing on the van's wall monitor was branded THE PITTSBURGH AIRPORT HOTEL & CONFERENCE CENTER. Pittsburgh was three hours west as Byron drove them north.

Nico's foot tapped the rubberized van floor while his leg packed down the beanbag filling, creating a dual rhythm as fast paced as his pulse. On the screen, he counted fifteen people scattered around a raked session room that could seat a hundred, and in the half circle at front was Geena. She stood at her laptop, all business in a tweed skirt suit. It made him think of Beatriz, overdressed for the beach. He missed Beatriz, and Shira, and the life he had worked so hard to build there. He hoped Beatriz hadn't gotten into too much trouble with the police because of him.

Geena pressed a key, and the slide projecting behind her inset in the monitor:

Identity Theft
What you, your students, and their parents need to know
(If it happened to my brother, it could happen to you.)

"Holy shit. It's about me?" Nico hadn't expected that.

"Probably good to know what she's saying about you." Byron put in a wireless earbud, then pointed over his shoulder. "The headset's muted, but press the button and they'll all hear you."

Nico snagged the wireless headphones from their hook under the monitor and put them on.

Geena was speaking. "Thank you all for coming to this session. They've asked us to start on time, so..." She eyed the many empty chairs, then focused on the people in front of her. "That's the respectful thing to do. I respect you."

She pressed a key, and a photo of Nico and Warren filled the screen behind her.

Nico leaned forward to take in the inset image of him and his friend. It was the selfie he'd taken on his birthday. Warren in his wheelchair flashing a peace sign, Nico leaning in, and the mysterious ruins of Machu Picchu spread out behind them. He hadn't seen the picture since he took it. And he hadn't seen Warren since that restaurant in Cuzco... just an obituary photo online that didn't really look like him at all.

He felt a pang in his chest.

"This was my brother, Warren Gilbert Bennett." A red arrow pointed to Warren.

Another press of a key and a red circle appeared around Nico's own face. "And this, is the face of a criminal."

A stout woman in the front row put her hand up and called out, "If we're calling them 'students who engage in bullying behavior,' shouldn't we call that boy—who can't be much out of high school—a 'young man who engaged in criminal behavior'?"

Geena's fury was instantaneous. "You have no idea the lengths he went to! The deception! The sheer scale of larceny! And now Warren's DEAD!"

The room went silent. Geena pressed a palm to her forehead.

Nico unmuted his headset. "I miss him too, Geena."

Her head jerked up, left, right, trying to find Nico in the room.

There was a low mumble of concern from the audience.

Geena's voice was a growl. "Peter?"

"I don't go by Peter," Nico said.

"Oh my goodness!" one of the teachers cried out. Most of them held their phones up, recording Geena, and Nico's voice. Murmurs. Whispers. But Byron had assured him this was untraceable.

Geena stepped to the center of the floor. "Peter Josefs, I don't know where you're hiding, but why don't you come out? Turn yourself in."

She leaned toward the handful of people in the first row and whispered, loud enough for the audio feed to pick it up, "Someone call the police!" Then Geena walked slowly along the curve of seats, eyes searching for him. "The police know all about you. I know all about you. I've spoken with Dr. H."

That surprised him.

She was almost prowling. "He told me how you attacked his guards. How you're violent. We know you're a pathological liar. And a thief. Who knows what other crimes you've committed? You need professional help. Dr. H is trying—"

"He's not helping anyone!" Nico cut her off. "But I'm not here to talk about him. I want to tell you about Warren."

Her face flushed and the anger was back. "You have no right to speak about my brother!"

"Geena." Nico kept his voice calm and clear. "He gave me his passport. He signed the traveler's checks. He was trying to help me."

"Lies!"

"How else did I get them signed?"

"You forged them!"

"Didn't he tell you?"

"We didn't know you'd stolen everything!" Her voice was bitter. "We didn't discover any of it was missing until Rio. When we got off the ship.

And it was gone. His passport, all those traveler's checks. His whole identity!"

So Warren had kept his secret. Given him that extra time. A wave of gratitude surged inside him. But something didn't make sense. Once Geena discovered Warren's passport and the money were missing, Warren would have told her. He wouldn't have wanted Nico to be blamed for it.

"Didn't he explain?"

"He died in his cabin. The last night of the cruise."

Nico's eyes filled with tears. "Oh. God." He imagined her finding Warren gone, just the shell of his body left behind in the bed. His soul somewhere else. And Nico realized how horrible it must have been for her. "I'm so sorry."

She swiped at a tear. "Quite convenient that the only person who can exonerate you is dead, isn't it?"

Nico ached. "Your brother was kind to me."

"You're not allowed to be sad!"

"I cared about him too."

"You stole his identity!" She leaned against the presenter table for support.

"It was a gift, but I don't need it anymore," Nico said. "And I'll pay you back the money. The whole $1,500. I've been saving up, but it's taking time."

"You don't get to be the good guy!" She was crying openly now.

"I am who I am, Geena," Nico said. "And for what it's worth, Warren was one hell of a good guy."

He pressed mute and pulled off the headset. Stood and walked the two feet to where Byron was driving.

"Can you turn this off? I'll take over driving."

"Sure thing." Byron signaled to change lanes, and took out his own earbud.

"Any chance it recorded?" Nico asked.

"I record everything." Byron eased them to a stop in the emergency lane. Unbuckled so they could switch places.

"Can you pull out a photo, from the video? I want to put it on my phone."

"Sure thing." Byron wrapped his arms around Nico and slapped his back twice. Nico stood very still.

Byron pulled back.

Nico stared at the green sneakers Godeane had gotten him at the thrift store. They were nice. A lot more comfortable than the cowboy boots that had been part of his Warren outfit. "What was that for?"

"Sometimes, words aren't enough," Byron's voice rasped. "But you need to feel, you need to *know*, that you're not alone."

Nico nodded.

He grabbed Byron and hugged him back.

After a long moment, Nico pulled away. He got them back on the interstate, easing the van faster and faster till they were right at seventy-nine miles per hour.

Countdown Clock: 00 hrs 52 min 03 sec

Time to Destination: 02 hrs 27 min

He needed to get to Sam.

1908

I-78 EAST 7 MILES SOUTH ALLENTOWN PA

Countdown Clock: -01 hrs 12 min 14 sec

Time to Destination: 01 hrs 41 min

Dr. H for sure knew Nico was on his way.

Traffic was down to one lane. Byron was driving, because while the speed limit sign said 70, the cars ahead of them weren't even going forty miles an hour.

"We're falling even more behind!" Nico couldn't sit and started pacing the few feet in the back.

"Construction, accidents, just too many cars and trucks on roads that were designed for a different time. The Northeast is a mess. Loads of free electricity though." Byron glanced at the dash. "We're going to need to stop for gas."

"Fuck!"

Byron glanced at Nico in the rearview mirror. "So when we get there, what's your plan?"

"Get Sam out, and safe."

"You think Dr. H is already there?"

"I hope not."

"But if he is?"

"You got a gun?"

"You ever watch the news? I'm not going to have a gun!"

"That tranquilizer bee drone would be helpful right around now."

"I still need to design and build that."

Nico made a face. "I don't know, I'll... improvise."

Byron shook his head. "Not much of a *knight in shining armor* rescue moment if all that's going to happen is that asshole traps you again."

"I won't let that happen."

"Nico, you have to be realistic."

"I'm not going to let anything happen to Sam!"

They were both silent as Byron pulled into a service station.

Nico thought furiously. "What about, if Dr. H is there, and he has Sam, we use the hummingbird to video him? Then we'll have proof. And we can take that to the media. Bring him down for kidnapping."

"Now that's starting to sound like a plan," Byron agreed.

"Fucking traffic!" Nico felt like his whole body was about to explode. His leg jackhammered the floormat on the passenger side.

Byron was still driving. They were half a mile into the tunnel and literally weren't moving.

Nico watched the TIME TO DESTINATION tick up to 32 MIN. "We should have been there already! It's been hours that Dr. H knows!"

"Probably an accident ahead." Byron pointed to the wire bins in back. "Practice the hummingbird. Find out what's going on."

Inside the wire basket, Nico saw that one of the hummingbirds rested on a charging pad. He gently picked up the drone and its handheld controller. It was like a video game—one side of the screen controlled the motion, the other showed him the hummingbird eye-camera view.

The moment he turned the controller on, the drone's wings started moving in a blur. He lowered the window, then shot the hummingbird drone out and east.

Byron watched the controller screen. "Keep her high."

The hummingbird drone zoomed ahead, showing them traffic stuck in both directions. Frustrated drivers. Nico counted... Fifteen cars up, a minivan with eyelash appliques over the headlights and a dad soothing a crying baby. Thirty cars up, a woman in a business suit cursed into her cell phone. Forty-five cars up, a woman in overalls was in the flatbed of her pickup, fastening the straps on a mud-covered dirt bike. Seventy-eight cars ahead, they saw it.

It was a head-on collision: the hood of a mint-green Corvette pyramided up against a white Audi SUV whose front left corner was smashed in. The tire was flat and splayed out, revealing the axle had snapped. The cars blocked both lanes.

They weren't getting out that way anytime soon. Nico turned the hummingbird around. "We should be able to back out. We're only a half mile from the entrance."

Byron seemed dubious. "There's a reason it's stopped both ways."

Nico piloted the hummingbird back, past the dirt bike, angry businesswoman, minivan with eyelashes, and the two of them in Byron's van.

A hundred and eight cars behind them, an RV in their lane had tried to turn around. Now it was stuck, perpendicular to the tunnel. People were out of their cars, screaming at the driver, who was trying to move it but had jammed himself in tight. Someone had climbed onto the maintenance catwalk to get a better view. She shook her head, tossing her hands in the air, not able to see how the RV could get out.

"That's a clusterfuck," Byron said over Nico's shoulder.

Nico's head spun. "What are we going to do?"

"Give it a minute? They're going to have to clear one of those." Byron paused. "You don't know he's in trouble."

COUNTDOWN CLOCK: -03 HRS 28 MIN 47 SEC

TIME TO DESTINATION: 00 HRS 41 MIN

Nico's hands shook as he flew the hummingbird back to them. He could feel it, a nervous thrumming under his skin.

Byron was wrong. Sam was in danger.

22

SAM

SAM WAVED HI TO RAUL in the lobby and headed upstairs. Even after traveling first class, he felt grimy—maybe it was the off-brand sweatpants? At least when he dressed up Bond-level dapper, he felt better. Bond probably never traveled in sweatpants, T-shirt, and hoodie. Anyway, he'd get the mail later. Not like there was ever any physical mail for him.

He unlocked the apartment door and lifted his roller bag with his ukulele gig bag on top. He'd rolled it across the silk carpet once, and his mom had flipped out. Professionals cleaned it three times, but she still swore she could see the tracks. They ended up getting all-new carpet, which he had to pay half of out of his bar mitzvah money. He didn't need to live through that again. And he wanted the place to look good when they got home, whenever that was going to be.

Maybe he'd fly out to meet them. He didn't like the idea of getting on another plane, but just seeing his parents would be—*No*. Sam remembered he was pissed at them. They were cheating on each other—but if they knew about it, was it still cheating? He reached the marble kitchen floor and paused to put down the bag and switch hands. It was *lying*, at least to him.

Something cold pressed into the base of his neck, and the hairs all over his body stood up in alarm.

"No sudden movements." A man's voice.

It was a robbery? It was a gun!

Holy fuck!

James Bond was always so cool—how was he cool, when all Sam wanted to do was scream, cry, pee himself?

He tried counting breaths. In, one, two. Out, two, one.

Yoda. His last freaking thought on earth was going to be about that stupid meditation lesson.

The gun left his skin, and the man circled him, waving the pistol to show he wanted Sam to walk farther into the kitchen. *Gunmetal is a weird color.* His dad's color obsession popped up in Sam's silent freak-out as he stared at the weapon that could end his life. He'd never actually seen one in real life before. *Not gray, and not blue, and oh fuck.*

"Take a seat," the guy with the gun said.

Sam moved slowly to one of the leather stools. He avoided looking directly at the guy. So he couldn't identify him. So the guy wouldn't hurt him. "We don't have a lot of jewels and cash. But take what you want. I haven't seen your face, so they won't catch you because of me."

The man scoffed. "I'm not here to rob you! You can look at me, I won't hurt you."

Bond would have quipped about the gun not exactly selling that point, but Sam stayed quiet. He risked a glance. The guy seemed familiar somehow. Long silver-streaked hair. Thin nose. He'd just seen that same nose. Where?

The man gestured with the gun. "Hand over your cell phone so we're not disturbed while we wait."

"Wait?" Sam ran through faces in his mind.

"Peter Josefs crossed the border just over thirty hours ago. He should be here soon."

Vanessa. This was her dad. "You're Hergenreder!"

"*Dr.* Hergenreder, please. If you've done your homework, you should know that much. Or Dr. H, if that's easier for you."

"Isn't Preparation H a hemorrhoid thing?"

Hergenreder's lips thinned out.

Not much of a quip, but Sam needed Hergenreder to be sloppy. Distractable. His mind raced to put the pieces together. *Peter. He means Nico.* Nico was on his way... And Hergenreder was here to get him. It was a trap, and Sam was the bait.

He thought of Connery-Bond, strapped to the laser table with Goldfinger. He needed to keep Hergenreder talking. Buy some time. Figure out how to get the upper hand. How to live past the end credits.

"How did you get in?" Sam asked.

"My father was a locksmith." Hergenreder pointed to a small leather tool bag sitting under the built-in espresso machine.

"How'd you get past Raul?"

"There was an *unfortunate* fire in your building's trash bin this evening. There will be a notice distributed, but they believe it was just someone being careless with tossing cooking oil, and someone else a smoking candle, down the chute."

Hergenreder held the gun higher. "My turn. How about you pass me your phone. And unlock the screen."

Sam considered if this was his chance to call 9-1-1. But he couldn't see a way to do it without risking getting shot. He took his phone from his pocket, let it see his face to unlock, and slid it across the counter.

Hergenreder pulled the phone to him, finger swiping the screen. Sam's eyes went to the color wheel of spices on the kitchen island between them. If he was at six o'clock, cayenne pepper was at five.

"Oh, I thought so!" Hergenreder said. "Someone's been trying to reach you."

"What?" Sam looked up.

"Deleted calls. Blocked numbers. All these voicemails in your security folder." Hergenreder made a *tsk* sound "It's like you don't care."

Blocked number? Nico had been trying to reach him?

Hergenreder scoffed. "Number Seventy knew the police were tracking his old phone. After you bought him a plane ticket under a dead man's name. Thanks for that. Like a big Times Square billboard pointing the way to our problem teen."

Sam's stomach dropped. *Oh no.* He'd done this? Nico was in danger because of *him*?

The more horrified Sam felt, the more delighted Hergenreder seemed. "Let's call him, shall we? I've been camped out for hours waiting for you two. A little entertainment would be nice."

Hergenreder hit *dial.* Pressed *speaker phone.*

It barely rang before Nico's voice said, "Hello?"

Sam wanted to shout to him, but Hergenreder put a finger to his lips while his other hand leveled the gun at Sam.

He could have reached Nico this whole time?

"Hello, Number Seventy." Hergenreder's voice dripped satisfaction.

"How did you—holy crap! *SAM!*" Nico's voice was tinny from the speakerphone, and stressed out, but it was *him.* "Sam, are you there? We're stuck in the tunnel, but I'm on my way!"

Sam could hear in his voice that Nico cared—about him!—and his whole body broke out in goosebumps. *Nico!* He had to get out of this. Had to stop Hergenreder.

"Your very..." Hergenreder waved Sam's phone about. "Sad Jewish friend and I are just getting acquainted. I'll rest in the Lord and wait patiently for him, Psalm 37:7, but not for you, Number Seventy. Not anymore. You have one hour. If you don't show, then Samuel here will take your place."

Hergenreder showed his teeth. "For souls aren't saved with a light touch. Isaiah 13:9," His voice grew like he was giving a sermon to a stadium. "Behold, the day of the Lord cometh, cruel both with wrath and fierce anger, to lay the land desolate: and he shall destroy the sinners thereof out of it!"

Hergenreder lifted Sam's phone high... and smashed it to the marble floor.

NICO

2121

HOLLAND TUNNEL NJ / NY

Nico didn't pause. The second the line went dead, he tucked the hummingbird and its controller into the pockets of his borrowed denim jacket and leaped out of the van. He sprinted between the cars toward Manhattan. Forty-five cars up, he saw the woman with the pickup and dirt bike.

He rapped on her window. She turned but didn't open it.

He held up a wad of cash, everything he had, plus what Byron could spare: "$1,023. For your bike. And the helmet."

She rolled down her window. "It's worth a lot more than that."

"Call it a rental! Please!"

A minute later, Nico was revving the dirt bike's engine to speed down the catwalk, passing jammed traffic on the tunnel roadway below him.

"Go!" Punching the air, Byron stood on the driver's door frame, shouting his encouragement.

The engine roaring under him, Nico didn't hear it. He was focused on only one thing: saving Sam.

SAM

2121

UPPER EAST SIDE MANHATTAN NY

Hergenreder ground the heel of his dress shoe into the shards of Sam's phone. Watching Sam. Hoping for a reaction. Sam wasn't going to give him the satisfaction.

"Sam? What the hell is going on?" Ari appeared in the kitchen entrance, dropping the black takeout bag from Kurosaka that matched their black octopus tiny hat.

Hergenreder whirled with the gun, surprised at someone coming in so soon, surprised at the voice he didn't expect, and it was the split-second Sam needed.

Ari threw both hands in the air and screamed, a noise that started high and then became a roar, like a video game warrior about to charge.

Sam grabbed the cayenne, twisted the top open and yelled as loud as he could, *"FUCK YOU!"*

Hergenreder spun back and Sam flung the rust-colored powder in his face. Got him full in the eyes.

Howling, Hergenreder dropped the gun. Sam ran around the island and kicked it across the marble to Ari.

With the loose hem of their shirt, Ari picked up the gun like it was a dead animal, and darted down the hall.

Hergenreder clawed at his own face. Snot and tears streamed down his cheeks, all red cayenne and rash. He thrashed his fists around, trying to hit Sam, but he was blinded and the punches were easy to dodge.

Retching and stumbling, Hergenreder started feeling his way along the counter, and Sam could tell he was going for the sink—but if he let him rinse out his eyes he'd be able to see again, and they'd lose their advantage. Sam had to restrain him.

Circling behind, Sam grabbed Hergenreder's blazer by the back collar and yanked it down over his shoulders and chest to trap his arms. Something white fell out of a jacket pocket as he twisted on Sam, spitting and cursing. Hergenreder got one arm free and Sam was fighting him when Ari came back in.

"A little help!" Sam shouted.

Ari's eyes darted around the kitchen, landing on the pot rack over the sink. They grabbed the heavy copper skillet like a tennis racket, and with a two-handed backhand whacked Hergenreder on the side of the head. Nearly clocked Sam too.

Hergenreder went down.

Suddenly everything was silent.

Except Sam's breath, which he struggled to catch.

Ari gripped the pan's handle so hard their knuckles on both hands were white. "Did I kill him?" They sounded scared.

Sam checked. "No. He's still breathing. But he's out."

"Who?" Ari pointed the pan at the body.

"Hergenreder." Sam picked up the half circle of metal with the attached rectangular box that had fallen from Hergenreder's pocket. If you pulled the two sides apart at the hinge, it would make a white— suddenly, Sam knew what it was: the necklace with the electric charge Nico had told him about. The same kind he'd seen on Nelson. He dropped it on the counter, not wanting to touch it. "It was all a trap for Nico. I was the bait."

"Oh, poor baby." Ari put the pan down and came over to give Sam a hug.

"I'm not a baby." Sam bristled, but leaned into his friend's shoulder, keeping one eye on Hergenreder, who was out cold.

"No, you're not." Ari pulled back and crossed his arms to appraise Sam. "You're *Mr. Man*. Taking out the bad guy."

"You going to snap or something?" Sam asked wryly.

"Will it make you feel better?"

"You lost your hat," Sam pointed out.

"Did I?" Ari put a hand to their polished head.

"You were fierce," Sam said.

"Yes, we were," Ari agreed.

They hugged again.

"Where's the gun?" Sam asked.

"Trash chute." Ari used an octopus-print slipper to poke at Hergenreder's limp body on the kitchen floor. "What do we do with this one?"

There were two rolls of duct tape in Hergenreder's father's tool bag. Disposable gloves too.

Both of them wearing the gloves, Sam wiped down one of the Philippe Starck Ghost dining chairs so there would be no fingerprints. Together they lifted Hergenreder to the chair and duct-taped him to it. They used more tape over his mouth so he'd stay quiet once he came to. And one more stretch of tape covering his eyes.

Once he was completely trussed, they both stood back.

"Let him be scared for once," Sam said.

One Good Thing

My hand's still shaking. All that adrenaline. Fight or flight or freeze.

Damn, I'm glad I fought.

Nico will be here soon. Ari's trying to see if they

can get Nico's phone number off my smashed cell. So I can call him, let him know I'm okay. Raul knows to let him right up.

I texted Frida to come. But now I don't know what to do with myself. Writing kind of helps, even if it's just to sort through the jumble of everything in my head.

I shouldn't feel guilty, about Hergenreder.

James Bond wouldn't flinch at how much it was to going to hurt the guy to take super-sticky duct tape off his eyelids. Even Lazenby-Bond would have dropped him out the window with a funny quip, and Hergenreder would be splattered on Eighty-Seventh Street.

After everything he did to Nico, and threatening me with a gun, why should I care about him? I don't. Hergenreder is an evil jerk. It's just... movies are one thing. But in life — right in front of you — it's different. Pain someone else feels because you threw cayenne in his eyes — it's like there's a cost to it.

Maybe it's to your humanity. <u>My</u> humanity.

And if I killed him, I'd be thinking about Hergenreder the rest of my life, having that haunt me.

Even though I know what he did to Nico is going to haunt Nico forever. All those nightmares he has... And there should be some payback for that!

I shouldn't care about the scum. <u>I don't!</u>

Maybe... maybe I care about me. And how killing someone else — even someone as despicable as Hergenreder — would change me.

Maybe I'm not cut out for this Bond thing after all. I don't want a license to kill.

23

NICO

NICO DROPPED THE DIRT BIKE on the sidewalk and tore into the building.

The doorman moved from his alcove toward him. "You can't leave that there."

"You've got to help me!" Nico tried not to sound desperate, but he was. "Sam Solomon! Apartment 42C!"

The doorman's whole attitude changed. He quickly waved Nico to the elevators. "They're expecting you. Go, I'll take care of the bike."

2141

Body vibrating with anxious energy, Nico slipped off the elevator, telling himself to be ready for a trap. At the end of the hallway, Sam's family's apartment door was open, swung in five inches.

Not a good sign.

He hung back, pulled out the hummingbird and controller. Flew it down twenty feet to apartment C. There was a sticky note posted on the door. Nico hovered the drone to read it:

N —
Safe to enter.
Keep quiet.
S.

Was it a trick?

It seemed like Sam's handwriting, but did he write it with a gun to his head? An electroshock collar around his neck? The thought of Sam being so vulnerable made Nico want to charge in, guns blazing, but he didn't have any guns. Which meant he had to be smarter than Gold Wheels Preacher.

He piloted the hummingbird inside, floating to show the view down the hallway east, then west. There was more light from the west, and a bright red stain on the hard white flooring beyond.

Oh no!

Nico's heart lurched, and he lowered the hummingbird to just an inch above the carpet, flying it fast down the hallway and pausing at the corner where the carpet ended.

It didn't seem like blood—it was powdery. He tilted the hummingbird eye-camera up, getting a glimpse of a wall oven and cabinets but then just streaks of colors, like someone had melted the video into hot wax and everything just ran together. Like the candles at the restaurant in Cuzco, where he'd said goodbye to Warren...

He needed the screen to focus. Sam needed *him* to focus.

No obstacles.

Nico selected Panic Mode on the hummingbird controller, and when the screen prompted for a center location, he guessed about ten feet into the kitchen, where the smear of colors started. He set the timer to twenty seconds.

Counting down, he buttoned the controller into a denim jacket pocket and padded softly down the corridor. Two feet before the corner he pressed into both sides of the hallway, walking hands and feet up to just under the ten-foot ceiling height. Like James Bond did in Goldfinger's prison cell, just before he dropped down on the guard. *No one ever looks up. Especially with a hummingbird dive-bombing them in loops.*

At twenty seconds, the drone launched into action.

Nico heard the voices.

"Hello! What are you?" Someone else. Not Gold Wheels Preacher, and not Sam.

"Whoa!" *Sam.*

Which meant he was okay. Nico peered around the corner.

Sam was sitting at the closest counter stool, his friend Ari next to him. Nico remembered them from the photos Sam had shown him, pretty distinctive with their bald head and tiny hat that was like a fabric sculpture of an octopus, batting at the hummingbird drone with a frying pan.

"Don't hurt it!" Sam cried out.

"What if it hurts us?" Ari argued.

No Gold Wheels Preacher that Nico could see. But maybe he was around the corner, holding a gun on them, just waiting for Nico to walk in...

Sam must have sensed Nico was there, because he looked up—*no one ever looks up*—and their eyes met. Sam's face opened like a flower to rain. He ran to Nico, a finger to his lips.

What did that mean?

Nico dropped to his feet and Sam crashed into him, hugging him hard.

"You okay?" Nico whispered. He held Sam's face. His arms. His chest. Like he couldn't stop checking that Sam was really okay.

"Yeah," Sam told him.

Nico kept his voice low, but it came out a growl. "Where's Dr. H?"

Finger still warning him to be silent, Sam pulled him through the kitchen to the living room. The shades were down, and Gold Wheels Preacher was duct-taped to a ridiculous plastic chair that wouldn't hold anyone for long. He slumped like he was knocked out, but with his eyes and mouth taped it was hard to be sure.

Sam pulled him back down the corridor. Moved in close to whisper, "I don't want Hergenreder to know you're here."

Hergenreder. Dr. H. It registered that Sam knew who he was. How did Sam know who he was?

"I... came to save you," Nico told him, feeling like an idiot.

"I've been trying to save you." Sam's smile was shy. "And this time, I kind of saved myself. With some help." He tilted his head to Ari, who was right there, hovering a few feet from them in the hallway.

Nico turned to them. "Thank you."

Ari just stared at Nico. "You the reason this madman was after Sam?"

"He wasn't after Sam," Nico corrected them.

"He had him at gunpoint!"

Sam put his hands on both of their arms, to stop them. Nico and Ari fell silent.

Sam's finger brushed a puka shell on Nico's wrist. "You're still wearing the bracelet!"

Nico stared into his deep brown eyes, wanting Sam to know how he felt. "I haven't taken it off." And suddenly, their whole fight seemed crazy. "I've fucking made a mess of this," Nico said.

"I'm sorry." Sam said it at almost the same time. He sniffed. "I shouldn't have bought you the plane ticket. That unraveled everything. Hergenreder told me it's how he found you."

Nico swiped at a tear on his own cheek. "I'm sorry too. I was such a jerk!"

Sam noticed. "Hey, you okay?" He cupped the side of Nico's face.

Nico could feel the pull between them, like gravity. Their own gravity.

"I was worried about you." Nico's voice felt like it was going to crack.

Sam kissed him. And the instant before Nico closed his eyes to really kiss Sam back, he saw Ari turn away.

2220

"You're not coming with me!" Nico said it again, trying to get Ari or Frida or Byron to back him up. After checking that Hergenreder was still unconscious and not going anywhere, they'd gathered around the zebra rug in Sam's bedroom to plan their next steps. For Nico, that meant saving Bec and Squirrel Boy and everyone else in the Institute.

Sam pointed to his fancy stainless steel blue-faced watch. "I'm your ride. Zoltan has a plane set to go from Teterboro anytime after eleven."

Nico wouldn't put him in danger again. "I'll drive." Byron would do that with him, wouldn't he?

Byron avoided his gaze.

Okay. "I'll take the dirt bike."

"Across the whole country?" Sam said. "It will take you too long. Hergenreder might be free by then, and we'll lose this chance."

He was right. *Damn it.* Nico stared at his own leg, bouncing against the dark wood floor of Sam's bedroom that was more like some magazine-cover lounge, all silver and glass, with black walls and a shiny fur chair that was like a rich person's beanbag. He didn't even see a bed. Sam was so full of mysteries, and Nico wanted time to solve every one of them. "I don't want anything to happen to you!"

"Shut up," Sam said tenderly. "It already did."

Nico ran a hand through his own hair, distressed. "I feel terrible about that. If I hadn't—"

"Hey." Sam crossed the zebra and put a finger to Nico's lips to stop him. "I meant, what happened was, I fell for you. We're going to do this together. Got it?"

To answer, Nico pulled him close, and they kissed. It was hot. Grateful. Full of desire. And Nico's heart cautiously, cautiously... opening.

2227

Sam swung open an over-sink vanity in his parents' bathroom. Nico watched him grab the can of shaving cream. Twist the bottom. And pull out a wad of cash that would pay Geena back and then some. He split the cash with Nico and pocketed the credit card.

How did this guy, from another world, care anything about him? Nico was afraid to ask it out loud.

2232

"We're one short, and there isn't time to make another," Ari said. Four bracelets sat on the modern glass coffee table next to Sam's fur beanbag. Ari had explained how the black stone bracelet Sam wore prevented cameras from seeing him. That was why the hummingbird eye-camera had just seen that wash of colors.

If the five of them were going to pull this off, they needed them.

Nico snagged the bracelets and handed them out. One to Sam, one to Ari, another to Frida, and the last to Byron.

"I don't need one," Nico said. "I want Hergenreder to know it was me."

2254

They were ready. Nico watched from the door to the art restoration studio in Sam's apartment. Ari used a power drill to put the final screw into the five-foot-square wooden crate with Hergenreder inside. Byron adjusted some electronics. Nico wasn't surprised the two had hit it off.

Sam had changed into a gray suit with a light blue shirt. Silver mesh ukulele backpack on his shoulder, he turned to Frida one more time.

"You sure you're set?" Sam asked.

"We've got this," Frida told him.

"Be safe." Sam glanced past her, to where Byron and Ari were deep in conversation. "All of you."

"I'll tell them." Frida pinned Nico with a dead-serious expression. "You take care of him."

"Yes, ma'am," Nico told her, and put his hand on Sam's shoulder. "Better than I'll take care of myself."

Sam turned his head so they were just inches apart. "And I'll take care of you."

With Sam looking at him like that, Nico felt like he could take on anything.

"Get out of here. You'll miss your plane." Frida was happy for Sam, Nico could tell.

"You can't miss a private jet," Sam reminded her.

Laughing, she pushed them to the front door. "Go save the world, or at least part of it!"

Sam's grin was epic.

And Nico realized: that was exactly what they were going to try to do.

24

SAM

"I THOUGHT THE HOTEL SLIPPERS were made in California. Thanks, Savta."

"You have a good heart, Samika. But neither of these gifts you want are even for you!"

Sam was just finishing up the call with his grandmother when his phone buzzed with a text from Ari: News. He headed to the front, where he'd left Nico doing research, and tried to wrap up the conversation.

"They are, and I'm grateful," Sam insisted, dropping into the plush leather seat next to Nico. Private jet, with his cell fully functioning, was such a Bond way to travel. He hoped his parents wouldn't freak out too much about his using the *emergency* emergency credit card.

"You know, it makes your Savta's heart happy when she can do something for *you*. Her grandchild."

"This is what I want. Trust me."

"I don't understand, but I do trust you. *And* love you."

"I love you too. We'll talk soon." Sam ended the call and hit some buttons on his armrest. The flat-screen TV in front of them flicked on. "It's hit the news."

Next to him, Nico paused the same lock-picking video Sam had studied earlier. "That was fast."

"News is 24/7, but not a lot usually happens at 2:30 AM in Manhattan, so they're all over it," Sam said.

A female reporter with a British accent stood in the famous intersection of streets, the risers for TKTS behind her. "We're in Times Square, where a growing number of social media reports have shown a bizarre pop-up... honestly, we're not sure what to call it. Protest? Performance art?"

The camera swiveled to show a sixteen-foot area squared off with red boxing-ring ropes. A wooden crate sat in the middle, with a man blindfolded, gagged, and duct-taped to a clear plastic chair on top. Hergenreder.

Inside the wide-open collar of his black dress shirt a white band circled his neck. Sam knew that necklace. The one Hergenreder had brought for Nico.

Perfect.

Ari, Frida, and Byron had done their job, spectacularly.

The reporter walked into the frame, pointing. "While at first glance it might appear a Houdini-style escape artist trying to get publicity, words burned into the four sides of the crate tell a different story."

The images inset on screen as the reporter read the words out loud.

"Side one: 'They shaved my head. Shocked me with electricity. Locked me up. Just because I'm Gay.'"

"Side two: 'This is Eugene Hergenreder. He's running a prison for Queer teens in Kernville, California.'"

"Side Three: '$47,421 per locked-up teen a year. Times seventy teens. Equals $3,319,470.'"

"And the final side is a warning: 'Don't get too close, or he'll get a taste of his own medicine.'"

The image returned to the reporter. A larger crowd had gathered, ringing the ropes, with dozens of cell phones out, recording Hergenreder, the reporter, the camera operator, and taking selfies.

"It's unclear if anyone has yet crossed the ropes. Wait…" The reporter spotted movement out of the corner of her eye. Motioned her head for the camera to follow the tourist in the cherry-red raincoat duck under the ropes and start toward the crate.

Hergenreder's body suddenly arched in pain. People screamed. Hergenreder was sweating, twitching uncontrollably. Stunned, the tourist stopped in their tracks, then darted back outside the ropes. As soon as they cleared the ring, Hergenreder stopped shaking.

The camera zoomed in on Hergenreder, a wet streak coursing down the inside of his jeans leg.

"Bloody hell," the reporter breathed into her mic.

Nico's eyes were locked on the screen, but his foot was tapping madly against the floor.

Sam put his hand on Nico's leg, trying to send comforting vibes to him. He forced himself to keep watching, to not turn away. Hergenreder did that to Nico. To all of them. Sam wasn't going to feel bad about it. Bond wouldn't feel bad about it. Connery-Bond didn't feel bad about Largo getting zapped from losing the video game in *Never Say Never Again*. He'd already been zapped. And he knew that Largo needed to be stopped.

Hergenreder needed to be stopped too. And at least they weren't using a harpoon. They hadn't even shaved his head.

The reporter gathered her composure. "Apparently, someone has rigged this up to administer some sort of electric shock to whoever it is in that chair, allegedly a Eugene Hergenreder." She turned back to the camera. "Many questions remain. If the warning is true, is the rest of it as well? 'His own medicine'—did he do this to seventy young LGBTQAI2+ people? Lock them up? Shock them? There's so much we don't know, but we'll be right here as the story unfolds. Back to you, Chimamanda."

Nico squeezed Sam's hand on his leg and pressed mute as the program went back to the studio anchor. "Clock's ticking. Let's check out the footage you took of the Institute again."

He was right. They needed to focus. They'd land in an hour and twenty minutes, just after 1:00 AM in California. "We need to get our final supply list to Linda Sue." Sam told him. "And there's more videos to watch so I can learn what the hell I'm supposed to do."

"Matrix style." Nico couldn't stop the half smile at giving Sam a movie reference that wasn't James Bond.

"Yeah," Sam agreed. But all he could think was *That smile.*

Five minutes before landing, Sam pulled out the Montegrappa James Bond 007 Spymaster Duo rollerball pen and his journal.

<u>One Good Thing</u>
Nico and me? We're in this together.

25

NICO

*No one expects you to break **into** a prison. Which comes in handy when you actually need to.* There was no barbed wire blocking the construction site from the outside—just a padlocked chain holding a swinging section of fence across the alley truck entrance. Linda Sue had gotten everything they'd asked for. They were both in the all-black outfits Sam had gotten them, and with Sam at his side, Nico pulled the two-foot-long bolt cutters off his toolbelt. With a massive snip, he let them in.

It had been four months since Nico had been there, and the security lights just made the hole for the new building seem deeper. Off to the side was a ten-foot-tall berm of dirt, forty feet long. Next to it stood a yellow front loader with its five-foot-tall tires and giant metal bucket.

Nico had studied the footage from Sam's phone frame by frame, spotting a new security camera mounted to the top of the construction office trailer, aimed at the courtyard.

Sam went first, wearing Ari's bracelet that let him walk right up to the camera as just a blur of color and shadows. He wrenched the lens up so it pointed at the night sky. Then he pulled out two thin metal tools from Gold Wheels Preacher's father's locksmith bag and started on the lock to the construction office door.

Backpack heavy on his shoulders, Nico headed past the construction utility pole, a four-inch-square post sticking twelve feet up from the ground. Two cords draped to it from the alley and then over the chain-link fence topped with barbed wire to attach to the cafeteria building. One was four feet higher than the other, wrapped with metal wire, and attached to the roof. Electricity.

The plain black cord was lower, actually resting on the barbed wire before it slumped to a junction box on the stone wall. With the bolt cutters it was within easy reach. *Snip.* With no landline and no cell reception, no one in the guardrooms would be calling for help. Nico headed back to Sam, who was still working on the lock.

He was about to tell Sam they should just break the little glass window so they could reach in and unlock it from the inside when Sam let out a low "Yeah!" and twisted the doorknob open. *He's a quick study.*

Sam gestured Nico in first.

Nico used his phone light to scan the trailer. A little rack by the door held a row of four keys. Their video homework paid off again, and Nico snagged the one they needed—it had an orange plastic spiraled wristband attached. He tossed it to Sam, who caught it in midair.

At the chain-link facing the courtyard, Sam grabbed the fourteen-inch bolt cutters from his own toolbelt and clipped the thick wire six feet up, moving down. Nico began at the ground directly below Sam, cutting his way up. Together they worked to make a vertical slice in the fence. In minutes they met in the middle, Nico's last snip completing the line. Sam hauled back on the north side of the fence, making a gap big enough to get through.

Nico hesitated. Across the courtyard, the columns with their red lights felt menacing—even without a collar that could zap him. He pulled at the neckline of his thermal shirt. It was a V-neck, but still. Part of him couldn't believe he was going back inside a prison he'd done everything to leave. But a larger part of him knew it was what he had to do. He met Sam's eyes.

Sam whispered, "You got this."

Nico grabbed the back of Sam's head and kissed him, trying to put everything he couldn't put in words into that second of their lips pressed against each other.

He pulled away, and without glancing back, Nico grabbed the locksmith bag and slipped through the fencing. He ran the twenty feet to the building, then stayed tight and low against the south glass wall until he reached the cafeteria door. The security camera was mounted right above it. Up on his tiptoes, Nico swung the bolt cutters to knock the lens up to the sky.

Whack! Sam's trick worked on the first try.

Nico tried the thumb latch on the cafeteria door and gave it a gentle pull. It swung toward him. He wouldn't need the tools after all. Even after his escape, Gold Wheels Preacher still had bozos running his security.

Inside, Nico stuck to the shadows along the south, east, and then north walls, staying low when he crossed under the guardroom window. He made it to the guardroom door, and a quick glance inside showed him Living the Dream Guy sleeping in the chair. Or maybe he wasn't sleeping, just listening to something on his headphones with his eyes closed. He wasn't the worst of them.

Nico pulled out the industrial quick-set glue that was supposed to be like cement. And the little box of baking soda that would make it set almost instantly. He jammed the tip of the glue tube into the door lock and squeezed. Then, like using up a whole tube of toothpaste at once, he pushed the rest of the glue into the doorjamb—right where the bolt would be. He dipped a paper straw into the baking soda box, and with a quick puff of air like it was a blow-dart, blew powder into the lock. Another four puffs and baking soda coated all the glistening glue in the doorjamb, hardening it and trapping Living the Dream Guy inside.

0204

When Nico was in position, he texted Sam a thumbs-up.

SAM

0204

Orange coil dangling from the key in the ignition, Sam started up the front loader. It was damn noisy, and he worried about the neighbors... but he only needed to go fifteen yards. He barely fit in the seat because of his overstuffed backpack, but it didn't matter. He drove straight for the temporary power pole.

Sam pulled the control lever toward him to lift the huge metal bucket. It groaned up to eye level, another sound that could give them away, but there was no time to worry about it. He was wearing rubber soles. The front loader had giant rubber wheels that rolled forward under his touch. *I hope this works...*

Sam stood so no other part of him was touching the machine. He felt like freaking James Bond operating the Caterpillar 320D L hydraulic excavator on the moving train in the opening sequence of *Skyfall*. Daniel Craig was such a badass, and in this instant, Sam felt badass too.

He gunned the accelerator.

CRACK!

The metal claw snapped the post like a toothpick, rocking Sam up and then down as he plowed over it and hit the brake. The two ends of the electrical wire whipped, sparking lightning as they fell to the ground around him, flopping and then lying still like a beaten piñata.

Like the one at that beachside birthday party he'd seen for some kid at Club Azul.

Sam shut off the engine.

Everything was quiet again. He scanned the courtyard.

Darkness. The security lights were out. The red barrier lights were out. Everything was out across the whole Institute. He smirked. His and Nico's own little blackout.

NICO

0205

Outside the guardroom by the stairwell, just down the hall from where he had been locked up, Nico watched Sports Radio Guy through the chicken-wire glass. In the locksmith bag by Nico's feet was a second tube of industrial-strength glue and the rest of the baking soda, untouched. Instead, he gripped a taser so tight his hand shook.

Sports Radio Guy was watching a TV show he'd downloaded to his phone as the lights went out.

"Fucking construction," Sports Radio Guy said in the darkness.

It took about ten seconds before the emergency generator kicked in and the lights flickered back on. Nico watched Sports Radio Guy check the row of red lights on one monitor, then the security camera feeds on the other.

Sports Radio Guy frowned at two security camera views that showed nearly black. He flicked the screen with his finger. "Did they go out?" The lights of a plane miles up crossed one, revealing it was the night sky. As he watched, a blur of color crossed in front of the camera for the upstairs hallway between the cells, and then *that* camera was staring at the ceiling.

"What the…? Dr. H isn't going to like this."

He opened the door to go check and Nico was standing in front of him, holding the taser.

"You?" Sports Radio Guy said.

Before Sports Radio Guy could do anything else, Nico jabbed the taser into his gut and zapped him. He crumpled to the floor, unconscious.

"Me," Nico said.

Sam stood at the top of the stairs, watching. He'd slipped down the corridor to meet Nico where they'd planned.

Nico gave him a defiant look. It was a part of the plan he *hadn't* told Sam about. "I wish I could say that didn't feel good. But this scum… he dragged me here with this other guy like I was trash…"

Sam came down to Nico. Squeezed his upper arm. "It's okay. This way we don't have to find the backup generator."

"Turn off cell sixty-nine first," Nico said, then jogged down the hallway that glowed red from all the barrier lights. No one seemed awake.

Bec was lying on her cot under a threadbare blanket, facing the stone wall.

One hundred ninety-seven days.

Nico walked in past the red lights—they couldn't hurt him, not anymore.

When he was a foot away, he spoke, keeping his voice low. "I didn't forget."

Bec startled, whipping around, fists up. He noticed her leg was healed.

When she saw it was him, she lowered her clenched hands, but her eyes stayed wide. Her hair was shorter—like it had just been buzzcut again as punishment for something. She had fire.

Nico didn't have words for how terrible he felt that it had taken so long, or how incredibly glad he was to finally be there.

She got up, staring at Nico's regular black clothes, at his neck—and how there was no zap-you necklace on it.

The lights on her cell door turned green, and she looked from them to him for an explanation.

Nico took off his backpack and wrenched it open, revealing a dozen fourteen-inch bolt cutters and as many rolls of fat electrical tape. He allowed himself just the faintest smile. "Ready to get out of here?"

"Yes." Bec grabbed some tape and a bolt cutter. "A million times, yes!"

0246

"You can't do this!" Living the Dream Guy yelled from inside the cafeteria guardroom. "I'll shock them all!"

Nico ignored him as he dragged a fourth cafeteria table to the guardroom window to tilt on its end like the others and block the guard's view completely.

"You think I'm bluffing?" Living the Dream Guy yelled through the glass.

Nico didn't even respond. It was enough that he knew the camera was recording. That Gold Wheels Preacher would see it was him. He got the table into place and dropped it back, just as he saw Living the Dream Guy jab his finger one by one down every button on his screen.

On the floor of sixty-eight cells, sixty-eight electroshock collars, wrapped in black electrical tape and snipped in half, just lay there.

In the locked guardroom by the stairs, Sports Radio Guy was just coming to. He put a hand to his neck, feeling the collar there. "Aww, shit."

In the cafeteria guardroom, Living the Dream Guy angrily hit the final button, for number sixty-nine.

Sports Radio Guy's body spasmed as he was shocked by Bec's collar.

Nico wished the other guard who had kidnapped him had been there for his comeuppance too.

Back on plan, Sam led the escapees in a single-file line, sprinting out the cafeteria door to the two-foot-wide opening in the fence he'd completed earlier. Everyone wore the hotel slippers Sam had been carrying in his backpack.

Nico hung back to make sure everyone got out safely.

Squirrel Boy and Bec stayed by him as the last twenty teens sprinted one by one out the cafeteria door.

"I don't know your name." Nico admitted to Squirrel Boy just before it was his turn. "I'm Nico."

"Peter," Squirrel Boy said, and then launched himself out the doorway.

As they ran across the courtyard, Nico couldn't shake the idea that somehow this was the universe's way of telling him that he was saving himself too.

Sam led the line south around the new building foundation to avoid the downed electrical wire.

"I'm sorry about snitching that one time," Peter told Nico, breathing hard. "I... I didn't do it again. Pizza's not worth it." He glanced at Bec, who gave him a supportive nod.

"It's okay," Nico told him. And it was. He did forgive him.

"You're really getting us out of here?" Peter slowed down as they approached the open chain-link barrier to the alley.

"Yes," Nico said.

Peter clawed at his bare neck. Nico knew just how he felt.

Bec put out a hand. Peter took it.

Nico extended his hand to Peter too. And together they crossed to the outside world.

Peter didn't let go, and neither did Bec or Nico. The three of them followed the others north and then west, everyone racing down the hill as fast as they could in the cotton hotel slippers with thin rubber soles.

The electric charter bus Sam had gotten them sat on the far side of the road, silent and dark.

Nico was the last to board.

Sam gave the tally as Nico quick-climbed the stairs. "Sixty-nine, plus you and me—seventy-one."

"That's everyone," Nico told Linda Sue in the driver's seat. "Hit it!"

Instantly she closed the door and the bus was moving down the street, soundless and building speed.

Nico unbuckled his tool belt and dropped into the front seat next to Sam. Every part of his body was heavy with exhaustion. He slumped there, too tired to move. Too tired to think. He'd only ever gotten *this far* in imagining things. And now that he'd done it, now that they were all free, he felt... unmoored.

Everyone else was quiet too, as block after block, they left the Institute behind.

"Where are we going?" Bec broke the silence from the seat across from them.

"Does it matter?" Peter asked.

Sam stood, grabbed the tour guide hand mic, and faced the group. "Everyone, I'm Sam. This is Nico."

Nico raised his arm and turned to the bus full of teens who were so like him it hurt. What could he even say to them? He was glad Sam was talking.

"We're heading to a private airstrip," Sam told them, "where we have a plane waiting. It will take you all to New York, where this kind of conversion shit is illegal."

"It's supposed to be illegal in California too," Bec pointed out.

"We'll get some lawyers on that," Sam said. "But first we're going to get you all to a safe space. No more prison cells, for any of you."

A cheer went up.

"And there's bags of regular clothes in the back. Help yourself. Help each other."

Another cheer, and then, conversation. They were talking. Introducing themselves to each other, going through all the clothes Linda Sue had picked up from the Goodwill her sister-in-law worked at. She must have cleared out the store.

They were all *finally* talking.

Sam sat back next to him with a satisfied sigh, and Nico realized his own job wasn't done yet. "Where are we going to put sixty-nine teenagers? Your apartment isn't big enough."

"It's all taken care of," Sam told him. "My grandmother's got a hotel on Staten Island. Technically, it was my grandfather's and he left it to me, but she's in charge until I'm no longer a minor."

Nico slumped back. It seemed like Sam had it all figured out.

"Guys…" Peter came up the aisle to them, pulling a rust-colored Harvard sweatshirt over a green T-shirt, but still wearing the orange jumpsuit pants. "Do you think I can get a camera and an internet connection once we're on the plane? A lot of us want to tell our stories. Take Dr. H and the rest of them down. Flood social media."

"Absolutely," Sam told him.

Peter nodded and went back to the others.

Nico could see it. Gold Wheels Preacher and his Institute drowned with the truth. He turned in his seat to watch them transform from a group of prisoners into regular teens in regular clothes ready for regular lives.

He really was done.

Which meant…

"Bond had it all wrong," Sam said.

Nico looked at him in surprise. Bond was his hero.

"Turns out," Sam traced his finger along the toolbelts between them. "Caring about others… makes you stronger. Braver." He glanced up at Nico. "It's what made you a hero tonight."

"Me?" Nico asked. He couldn't be talking about him. "How about you, Mr. Blackout?"

"Yeah," Sam chuckled. "That was cool."

"You *are* cool." Nico gave him a half smile.

Sam locked eyes with him and leaned in, until his lips were just a breath from Nico's.

Nico pulled back. His voice was a gravelly whisper. "I don't know what I do next. I'm not one of them." He tilted his head to the busload of rescued teens. "Godeane and Byron are going to go back to their lives. And you're going to go back to yours…" He turned to the window, letting his eyes lose focus on the freeway speeding by. After the private plane flight to New York, Sam would take everyone to the hotel *that he owned*, and Nico's job would be done. He didn't belong anywhere. He was so afraid to say it out loud that his voice cracked as the words came out. "I can't be all alone again."

"Hey." Sam took Nico's hand in his own. Entwined their fingers. "You're not alone. I'm right here."

Nico turned to him, wanting to believe that.

"The whole future thing?" Sam shrugged, a light in his eyes. "We'll figure it out. Together."

Nico shook his head, fighting back tears. "I don't deserve—"

"Hey." Sam put a gentle hand to Nico's face, cradling his cheek and jaw. "You. Deserve. Everything. Good."

And then Sam kissed him, deep and tender, and the walls fell from around Nico's heart. Maybe, just maybe, he did deserve some good. Some people who cared about him. Some… Sam.

26

SAM

Hergenreder was sitting by an empty fireplace in the law firm office, staring at a chess board on the side table next to him. There were only a few pieces on it, like the game was nearing its end. He glanced up as Sam and Nico entered. "I asked the lawyers to give me and Peter here a minute."

"His name is *Nico*. And I'm staying." Sam crossed his arms. "How come you're not in jail? They found the gun, your prints all over it."

"I have a license." Like he was bored listening to Sam, Hergenreder turned back to the chess board.

"From another state! You broke into my home and threatened me—"

"Your words. My words..." Hergenreder pantomimed scales of justice and lowered one hand to his lap, raising the other in fisted triumph. "I'm an adult, and a doctor, so mine count more."

"You have a mail-order PhD from an unaccredited for-profit university that's under investigation for student loan fraud," Sam shot back. Ari wasn't the only one who could do research.

Hergenreder narrowed his eyes. "I don't even know why you're here. It's Peter I have business with."

283

Sam pulled on Nico's arm. "You don't have to listen to him. Let's get out of here."

"He can't," Hergenreder said.

"What do you mean?" Nico's voice was tight with fear.

It made Sam desperate to protect him. But he couldn't physically attack Hergenreder, throw him out the plate glass window to the Lexington Avenue death he deserved. Sam wasn't strong like that. Like Bond. And even if he were physically strong enough, he was too fucking sensitive. Which left him only one option: he'd have to outthink him.

"You may have swayed public opinion against me, all those videos, but I still have one last move." Hergenreder glanced at the chess board.

This wasn't a game, this was their lives. Sam hated him. "You don't have anything. No institute. No money. No credibility."

"I did have money, before the accounts were frozen." Hergenreder steepled his fingers. "Quite a lot of it, actually, as you were so generous to share my finances with the world."

"Come on. He's bluffing," Sam said, but it was like Nico couldn't move.

Hergenreder's eyes locked on Nico's, pinning him to the spot. "You know the best thing about judges being elected? It's that they need to get elected. And that, in today's world, is a very expensive proposition."

Nico's voice shook. "What did you do?"

"I made a deal with the court. They've agreed to unfreeze my accounts and won't press charges against you for..." Heregenreder started counting on his fingers. "... assault, battery, stowing away, robbery, identity theft, fraud, destruction of property, trespassing, breaking and entering, grand theft auto, and... I'm out of fingers. All that, in exchange for my simply taking legal guardianship of one Peter Josefs."

Hergenreder moved the white queen on the board. "You're mine. Until you're eighteen, and by then, I'll prove you're mentally incompetent. Then the law will give me another seven years to break you, so you can be rebuilt in God's image. 'And the vessel that he made of clay was marred in the hand of the potter: so he made it again another vessel, as seemed good to the potter to make it.' Jeremiah 18:4." He gave Nico this smug expression. "I do believe they call that *checkmate*."

Sam's heart was pounding. *Clay! His blind spot!* "This isn't about Nico." Sam made his voice as strong as he could. "It's about Vanessa."

Hergenreder seemed surprised.

"Yeah. Your daughter and I, we had a good talk." Sam tried to get the upper hand. "You traded your whole life, your wife, your *kid*, all for this idea of being some savior, when all along it was just your hubris that you knew who she was better than she did!"

"I am the potter!" Hergenreder's voice boomed against all the hard surfaces in the room. "I have remade vessels in God's image!"

Sam barked a laugh. "Nelson? That vessel wanted to kiss me. Wanted to do a lot more, actually."

Nico gave Sam a *you didn't tell me that* look. He'd explain later. Right now he had to deal with Hergenreder.

"You and... Nelson?" Hergenreder seemed momentarily unsure.

"You're not 'curing' anyone," Sam said. "You're just scaring them back into the closet!"

"Lies." Hergenreder waved away everything Sam had just said. "I was too soft to save Vanessa. But..." He picked up the black king from the board, squeezing it in his fist. "I have Peter right where I want him." Hegenreder bared his teeth viciously. "And he knows it. Look, he hasn't said a word."

Nico did seem pale. Freaked out. He was completely still—his leg wasn't even bouncing. Like he was living one of his nightmares. But Sam couldn't snuggle him back to sleep this time.

Sam's mind raced. For Hergenreder, this was revenge for everything he'd lost. How did Vanessa get out of her father's grip? All Sam could figure was that she'd turned eighteen. Once she was no longer a minor, her dad didn't legally control her... Nico was a minor until September 18, just seven days after Sam's own birthday. Eight more months! With the court awarding Hergenreder legal guardianship, Nico was trapped...

Suddenly, Sam knew what he could do. He turned to Nico.

"Marry me!"

"What?" Nico said.

Hergenreder stood up in alarm. "You'd need to be eighteen, or get court permission. I certainly won't allow it!"

"I did a little research," Sam said. "Turns out you only have to be sixteen to get married in Andorra. They have Gay marriage, it's a tax haven, and it's where my parents' yacht is registered."

The panic was clear on Hergenreder's face.

Sam turned to look into Nico's eyes, past those rings of gray, green, and brown to who he was inside. "Marry me! A legal Andorran wedding—the US has to recognize it. And the second we're married, we're not minors anymore!"

Nico stammered. "But, but then you're stuck with me..."

"That's the point!" Sam put his hand on Nico's chest. "I love you. Whether you go by Nico, Peter, Jacques, Warren, I don't care. A rose by any other name... I love *you*."

Nico kissed him, fiercely.

Sam pulled back, just enough to ask. "Is that a yes?"

Nico's smile filled every corner of his face. "Yes!"

Sam turned to see Hergenreder picking up the white queen and staring at the two chess pieces in his hands, confused.

"You know the best way to beat a checkmate?" Sam kicked the board with the toe of his Church Ryder III dark brown suede boot with rubber sole, all Craig-Bond in *Quantum of Solace*, and pieces scattered to the floor. "You dump the game and go do something else." He bumped Nico's shoulder with his own. "Let's go get married."

1012

"Where's Andorra again?" Nico asked as they crossed the prewar building's lobby, all marble and bronze.

"Between Spain and France," Sam said. "But we don't need to go there—just to my parent's yacht."

Nico wrapped his arm around Sam. "You're my James Bond superhero."

"Nah," Sam said. "I'm just a guy, in love with his fiancé."

"We just skipped *boyfriend*, didn't we?"

Sam slipped his own arm around Nico's waist as they pushed out the building door into the sunshine. "Get ready for *husband*."

WED 23 JAN
2017
ALBA ANDORRANA: INTERNATIONAL WATERS
15 MILES NE GALÁPAGOS MARINE RESERVE
ECUADOR

Nico looked amazing in the white slim-fit silk-blend Tom Ford tuxedo with black Tom Ford O'Connor evening pants, giving Craig-Bond vibes from *Spectre*. His broad shoulders rocked the wide lapels. Sam was also Craig-Bond dapper, with *No Time to Die* provenance, sporting a Tom Ford black wool Atticus shawl-collar cocktail jacket with quilted satin lapel and cuffs, and Atticus evening trousers.

They sat side-by-side on the bed, watching the TV news report from outside the New York Public Library's main building. Bec was being interviewed, with a crowd of three hundred people on the steps behind her. They saw Peter with her, and other faces they recognized from the teens freed from the Institute. A couple of them had straddled one of the stone lions, proudly waving a rainbow Gay pride flag and the blue, white, and pink Trans pride flag.

"The loophole they've been using is religious freedom," Bec was saying, "but we don't allow human sacrifice in the name of religion. So why have we been letting them get away with this?"

The reporter spoke directly to the camera. "We're on day thirteen of the social media blitz against so-called conversion therapy—with a new first-person account of a young LGBTQIA2+ person being imprisoned in Dr. Eugene Hergenreder's Institute going viral every day."

The reporter spoke over images of police tape blocking off the empty Institute courtyard. Cafeteria. Prison cells. "Keeping children as young as eleven locked up for simply being themselves."

Nico's leg was doing the vibrating up and down thing, and Sam put his hand in Nico's. Squeezed. Nico squeezed back. He took a deep breath, and his leg stilled.

The reporter continued: "The Institute is in California, a state that has had SB 1172, a law banning therapy to change a minor's sexual orientation, on the books since 2012. Yet they got away with it for *years*. The stories these young people tell are harrowing, and now they have to rebuild their lives. The question is, will the changing tide of public opinion pressure the federal government to step in and stop this kind of inhumanity to our fellow humans once and for all?"

Sam's dad stuck his head through the stateroom doorway. "Ready to do something Michelangelo never had the balls to do?"

Sam used the remote to turn off the TV, not able to stop the nervous smile on his face.

His mom leaned in behind his dad. "You two really aren't supposed to see each other before the ceremony, but I don't know where else we could have put you to keep it all a surprise."

Nico stood up. "I feel silly in this."

Sam joined him. "Nah. You look…" Sam tweaked his bowtie, more to touch him than anything else. "Perfect. Even in board shorts, you're perfect."

"I'm not—"

"Hey. You calling me a liar on my wedding day?"

Nico put his hand on the back on Sam's neck. "It's *our* wedding day, isn't it?"

Sam grinned. "Hell, yeah."

2020

Up on deck, white twinkle lights wrapped the mast, the boom, the railings. The sails were down, sea calm, and the sun was just dipping into the horizon, making the few clouds glow with sherbet pinks and purples.

The moment they appeared from below, an instrumental ukulele song started, and Sam knew instantly it was Jake Shimabukuro—playing "True Colors," the song Cyndi Lauper made famous. It was a version he hadn't heard before. Deceptively simple, with these intricate flourishes, and so beautiful. They passed an open laptop and there was Jake, playing live via satellite link—Jake looked up and nodded to them! Sam felt starstruck.

Nico's hand was in his, and they walked the polished wood deck slowly, soaking it all in. Two bottles of Bollinger La Grande Année 2003 were chilling in a bucket of ice, for a champagne toast. Sam smiled—so cool his parents remembered that it was Bond's champagne and Sam had wanted to have a taste of it forever. Another perk of getting married on an Andorran yacht in international waters was there was no one to stop a bunch of seventeen- and eighteen-year-olds from drinking. Conveniently, Andorra didn't have a minimum age for drinking in private...

Ari was there, a white satin tiny hat perched on their head, and they gave Sam a slight nod. Next to them, with a gentle hand on their arm, was Frida, in fancy toile overalls, grinning at Sam.

And Sam's parents, standing right next to each other, like the time away *had* brought them closer... but Yolanda and Jesse were right there too, flanking them. He wished they weren't. That his parents had some perfect *happily ever after* that was a path for him and Nico. But whatever his flaws, Bond, James Bond, faced the facts.

And so did Solomon, Sam Solomon.

Sam almost laughed out loud. Because for the first time, that sounded pretty good.

And he had to admit, the view from the outside was that his parents weren't a couple so much as a couple of couples. Were they some sort of polyamorous foursome? He'd have to figure out how he felt about that later.

They kept walking, and his Savta was next. She beamed at Sam, face crinkling with so much joy.

Nico's people were there too. Byron, using a remote to fly the hummingbird drone in circles around them, dipping in for close-ups and then up high for arcing panorama shots as their "official" wedding photographer. Beatriz, Nico's old boss from Club Azul. And Godeane, standing at the bow of the yacht, a notebook in her hands. Their officiant.

They'd flown from all over the world because this wedding couldn't wait. Sam didn't want to wait, not even one more second.

2037

"Darlings, I have always wanted to say this, and thanks to the lovely people of Andorra, and the internet..." Godeane had a beatific expression on her lined face. "I now pronounce you husband and husband. That's your cue, boys. Time to kiss."

Laughter surrounded them. Loving laughter.

Sam and Nico's lips met, and it was official. They were safe, and together.

Cheers went up. Ari and Byron nodded to each other, each pressing a button on a digital screen in their hands—sending two fireworks whistling into the sky from the top of the mast.

Sam and Nico looked up to watch the orange lines arc into the deep blue sky... *BOOM! BOOM!* Fireworks exploded above the yacht in a blossom of silver and purple and another of turquoise and orange.

Sam leaned in to kiss Nico again.

Nico kissed him back.

The guy he loved. The guy who loved him.

2124

After all the congratulations, Sam and Nico were hanging with Frida and Ari at the back of the yacht. Ari popped the Bollinger and filled their champagne flutes. Frida toasted: "To my best friend Sam, I'm so glad you found the love you were looking for. And to your new husband, Nico: welcome to the family."

Sam saw Nico was blushing, and nuzzled into his neck, making Nico chuckle just as he said "Thanks."

They clinked glasses in all the combinations.

Sam took a gulp. It was bubbly, and bitter, and then more tart, and he couldn't help make a face as the tang of it made the hinges of his jaw ache. His tongue tasted like he'd licked a hazelnut shell, or maybe the bark of an oak tree. "Is it just me, or does this taste like ass?"

Laughter all around.

Nico tossed the rest of his champagne into the sea. "Let's call it an offering."

"I don't understand how Bond can drink this," Sam said. "It's his favorite champagne, in all the movies."

"Wait till you try a vodka martini," Ari deadpanned, and Sam had no doubt Ari knew how all the drinks tasted.

Nico leaned into Sam's ear. "You don't need to be Bond, you know?"

Sam thought about it. Maybe finally, he *did* know that.

"Just be you," Nico told him with a teasing smile. "That's who I fell in love with."

"Deal, husband." Sam closed the space between their lips. "That's a deal."

One Good Thing

Nico. Me.

We're an <u>us</u>!

Maybe everything can be right with the world after all. If we work at it hard enough. Together.

Gotta go. It's my wedding night!

DETERMINATION: Recruit Subject 1, Nicolas Hall. Field request.

DETERMINATION: Recruit Subject 2, Samuel Jonas Solomon. Intel request.

NOTE TO DIRECTOR:

Their individual recruitments should be done in such a way as to keep Subject 1 and Subject 2 in the dark about the other's recruitment. Secrecy will be key to maximizing their contributions.

Despite their marriage, for the purpose of international law, both subjects remain minors until they reach the age of eighteen. This is an eight-month advantage the agency should leverage ASAP.

AUTHOR'S NOTE

Once I had it, I couldn't let go of the idea to create a page-turning Gay teen action-adventure romance, where I'd get to celebrate and deconstruct the spy movies I love so much. With a Gay love story. Where they have to save the world. It didn't feel serious, but it sure sounded fun.

What I discovered as I wrote and revised (and revised some more) is that this *is* serious. Seeing our Queer selves having adventures, being the stars of the story, supported by a group of Queer and allied friends, saving the world (or at least part of it), and getting the guy in a romantic sense—that's not just serious, it's revolutionary.

A Different Kind of Brave is a book I would have loved as a teen. A book that would have changed my life. And while I don't have a time machine to send it back to teenage me, it's here for you, now.

And I'm so grateful to share it.

If you enjoyed, please help spread the word. Online reviews and word of mouth can make a huge difference. Thanks!

The light in me recognizes and acknowledges the light in you,
Lee
Los Angeles, CA

ACKNOWLEDGMENTS

Books can seem like solitary endeavors, but they're not.

It takes the energy and support of many people who lift the writer up, crowd-surfing style, to become an author. *My idea to my book.*

It takes the expertise and passion of a team to take the author's manuscript and shape and polish it into a published novel. *My book to our book.*

It takes a single reader to make this novel your own. *Our book to your book.*

My thanks to everyone who has helped on this adventure, especially:

My husband, Mark, whose love gives me wings.

Dad—our watching Bond movies together when I was a kid is one of my best memories of sharing something we both loved.

My agent, Marietta Zacker, for always being real and supportive and believing in me as an author.

Annie Harper, from the original Interlude/Duet team, for great notes on the manuscript.

The new Interlude/Duet/Chicago Review Press team, with special shout-outs to Jerome Pohlen (acquiring editor), Kristin Pape (developmental editor), Devon Freeny (managing editor) and the whole editorial team, CB Messer (designer of our amazing cover), Jonathan Hahn (interior designer), and Candysse Miller and everyone else on the publicity and marketing teams.

And for early feedback and encouragement, Gavi Wind, Johnny Wind, Greg Pincus, Lori Snyder, Kelly Peterson, Kendra Levin, Kim Turrisi and my SCBWI peeps, and the inspiring Queer KidLit Creators community.

All the supportive librarians, teachers, and other adult allies of Queer youth, for everything you do.

And you, readers. Nico and Sam's adventure wouldn't be happening without you!